THE HARMONIOUS BLACKSMITH

SUSANNA M. NEWSTEAD

HERESY PUBLISHING

First Published in 2021
by HERESY PUBLISHING
Newbury RG14 5JG
www.heresypublishing.co.uk

Cover design by Charlie Farrow

A CIP catalogue record for this book is available from the British Library.

ISBN ISBN 978-1-909237-14-8

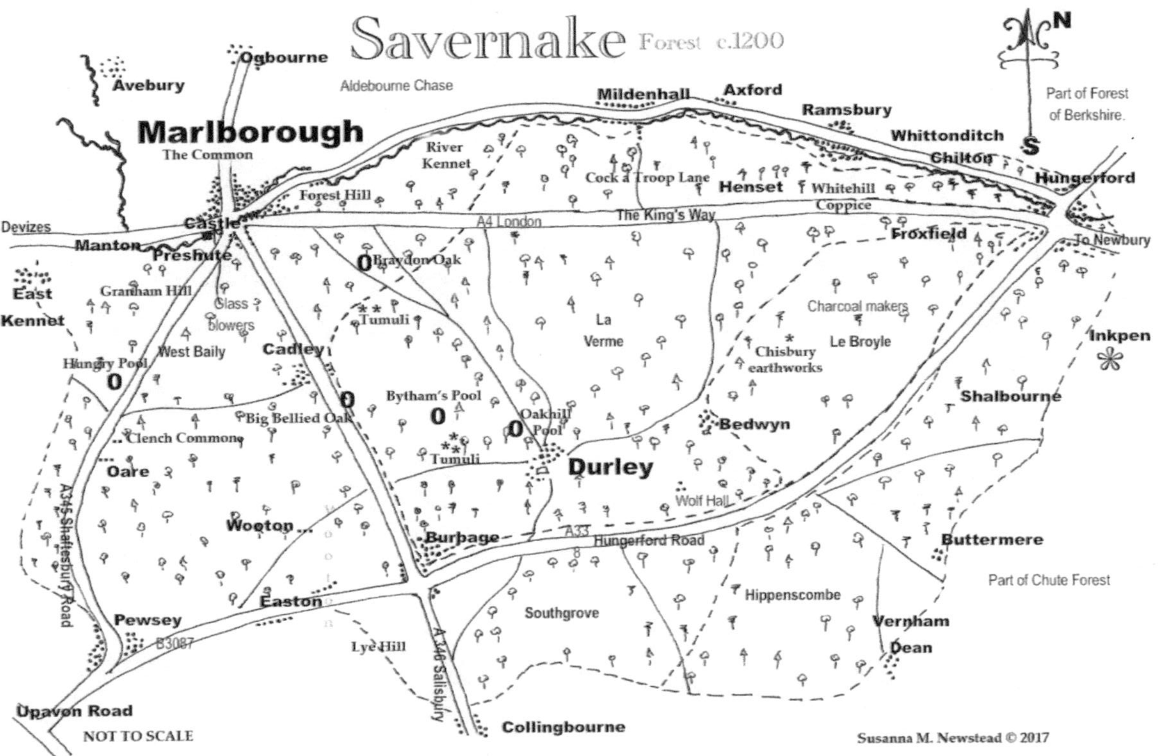

Savernake Forest c.1200
N
S
Part of Forest of Berkshire.
Avebury
Ogbourne
Aldebourne Chase
Mildenhall
Axford
Ramsbury
Whittonditch
Chilton
Hungerford
Marlborough
The Common
River Kennet
Cock a Troop Lane
Henset
Whitehill
Forest Hill
Coppice
To Devizes
A4 London
The King's Way
Froxfield
Manton
To Newbury
Preshute
Braydon Oak
East
Granham Hill
Glass blowers
Tumuli
La Verme
Charcoal makers
Kennet
Chisbury earthworks
Le Broyle
Inkpen
West Baily
Cadley
Hungry Pool
Bytham's Pool
Shalbourne
Big Bellied Oak
Oakhill Pool
Bedwyn
Clench Commone
Tumuli
Durley
Oare
Wolf Hall
Wooton
Burbage
A33
Hungerford Road
Buttermere
A345 Shaftesbury Road
Easton
Part of Chute Forest
Pewsey
Hippenscombe
B3087
Southgrove
Vernham
Lye Hill
A346 Salisbury
Dean
Upavon Road
NOT TO SCALE
Collingbourne
Susanna M. Newstead © 2017

CHAPTER ONE ~ THE SONG
VILLAGE OF EAST KENNETT
WILTSHIRE c.1200

Guy Ferrier was determined that he would marry.

He had reached an age when he thought that it was prudent for a young man to seek a wife.

He was a freeman. He had achieved stability in his business; he had a good house, enough money to run it as he liked and sufficient to be able to keep a wife and, should it transpire, children, in comfort.

But, he admitted to himself, he had not the first idea how he was to go about it.

*****

He mentioned his intention to his friend, Thomas of Kennett, a builder, one rainy October evening in front of his fire.

"Well yes, I see no reason why you shouldn't be married," was the answer. "You're a good looking, healthy, well-built fellow. You've a good standing in the area from East Kennett to Marlborough and are well respected. There'll be many a girl queuing up to take you in hand, I'm sure."

Guy chuckled. "I'm not sure I need taking in hand, Tom."

His friend returned the chuckle, "You know what I mean."

"I've managed on my own since I came out of my smithying

apprenticeship, what—nine years ago, after my father died—and frankly, although I am single and *you* might think I'm a good catch, no decent girl round here has ever expressed the slightest interest in me."

"That can't be true."

"There aren't that many unattached girls hereabouts," said Guy sadly. "Not of marriageable age anyway."

"What about Parnell?"

"What *about* Parnell?"

"*She's* not married."

"She doesn't want to marry."

Tom gave his friend a disbelieving look, "All girls want to marry... eventually."

"Well this one doesn't. And besides, I've known Nell since she was a baby in breech clouts. I held her in my arms when I was about... oooh... eight. She's more like a cousin."

"Oh, alright." Tom leaned back on his stool and stared at the rafters.

"Agnes. Agnes, the dairymaid?"

"Good Lord, no. Not with her sharp tongue. I'd end up on the end of a noose in no time."

"Tildy. Matilda Poulter. Think of all those lovely fresh eggs."

Guy just gave his friend a disparaging look.

"Thingy... you know... Thingy... oh, what's her name?" He ruffled his hair as if the answer lay in it and he could shake it out. Eventually it *was* shaken out. "Masters. Emma Masters. What about her?"

Guy nearly choked on his ale. Emma had been making a play for Guy for some time but he wasn't inclined to take any notice. "I want to be able to *like* the woman I marry, Tom. Besides, her father wouldn't consider me."

"Aw yes. Mistress Hoity-Toity."

"He's got his eye on a town marriage for her."

"Well good luck with that!" said Tom. "Bosom like an empty water flask and a face like a plucked chicken."

"Now, now."

"Well it's true." Tom went on laughing well after the joke had expired.

"You were lucky with your Alys," said Guy. "She's a looker and she's a lovely person."

"She is as dim as a halfpenny candle, that is why she's lovely, Guy! But I must say, I love her greatly."

"There you are then." Guy filled up their ale cups. "I want to be able to say the same."

"What? That she'll be as dim as a halfpenny candle?"

"Ah no. I don't think I could stand that. You have a large family with which to surround yourself—plenty of diversion—this would be just me, and the wife."

"So you want a wise and clever wife?"

"Well..."

"Then what about my sister, Isabel?"

"You know full well that Isabel is head over heels in love with Adam Partridge."

"Ah, yes..." Tom scratched his bristly chin. "Sometimes I wish I had never introduced them."

Guy laughed aloud. "'And Isabel, here is my good friend and fellow builder, Adam,' you said. I remember it distinctly."

"Pah!"

"Never before have I ever seen two people *actually* fall in love—been there at the *actual* moment—have one look at each other and it *was* love. I swear I saw Cupid's darts flash from their eyes—both of them."

"So, not Isabel, then," said Tom.

They sat in silence and listened to the rain dripping from the thatch.

"I have it. You must go to town."

"To town?"

"You need to... to put yourself in the way of a few nice young ladies."

"And how am I to do that?"

"Go to church. Walk about the market. Engage people in talk."

"About what?"

"Well... the weather, that's always a good thing."

"Rain...Tom. It rains in October."

"Well, talk about the rain then!"

"Oh I'm *sure* I will make a young lady fall in love with me by talking about the rain. 'Wet again isn't it? It must be awful for you ladies who must wear a kirtle... to always have to wear pattens and be wet about the hem...'"

"Ah no... Guy... that's not how it's done."

"I am not a natural, be honest."

Tom sighed, "I *will* be truthful, you are a man's man. Strong armed, blunt of speech, firm of foot and..."

"And...?"

"Quiet."

"Hmm," Guy looked away.

"Well yes. Quiet. You have a lot to say to me for example but to the fairer sex..."

"I never have any idea what to say... I once had three sisters, as you know."

"Yes, I know," said Tom with a grimace.

"And all were taken. One by one. First Joan. Then Ava and then little Dorcas. And she took our mother with her. I have no idea about women, Tom. I never learned. I grew up in an all-male household."

"Well, I don't know. You'll just have to try."

Guy fidgeted on his stool. "Alright. I'll do my best."

He got up, pulled down his cotte and adjusted his belt as if he would walk to town at that very moment.

"Sunday, I will go to St. Mary's."

*****

St. Mary's Marlborough was packed that Sunday in October.

At the very back of the church, almost hidden by a pillar of the side aisle, could be seen a young man, tall and dark haired with forbidding eyebrows drawn into a frown. His shoulders, under his best blue woollen cotte, were broad and muscled. His waist was narrow and cinched with a good tan leather belt which dangled down to his knees. Upon the belt, besides a very serviceable knife, was hanging a leather purse which, if we had had access to the inside, would show that there was a whole five pence residing there. Even though one *could not* tell it was full and heavy, thinking upon it, one might guess the man was well off. One might imagine there was more where that came from. Over the blue cotte, the man wore a dark green supertunic which was pearled with water droplets. As he'd stepped down from his cart that morning, the persistent rain had begun and before he'd entered the church, he'd been wet about the shoulders. His face was usually open and smiling, though there was a little worry line between the dark eyebrows. This did not disfigure an otherwise noble face. He stuck his thumbs into his belt; thumbs which were calloused, broad and flattened and ingrained with black. No, his hands were not his finest attribute. His hands were his livelihood. They were used to gripping a blacksmith's hammer, piling up charcoal upon his forge fire and holding fast to the tools of his trade. Or to the horses he was shoeing.

For Guy Ferrier was a blacksmith. But he was also a farrier—a man who shod and knew horses. He kept the horses of the locality on the roads, in the fields and in good health. He was an important man, a man of relative wealth and one to whom the area around looked up, for there was magic in metal and the working of it.

He looked around the church for someone he might know.

At his own church in the village of East Kennett, everyone knew him. Here he was a relative stranger.

And folk looked at him as if he was a stranger. And some even openly glared.

Guy looked down at his boots. Oh dear. He could not be seen to be staring about, looking at all the young ladies. That would never do.

He found a friendly face, one he knew at last and vowed that after the service, he would speak with him.

"Master Cowper? How is it with you?"

"God's blessings on you, Ferrier. You are a long way from home."

"It's true. Five miles, all told."

"And a perfectly good church to attend in your own village, of a Sunday, I think?"

"Yes indeed. But…" Guy thought quickly, "I am a little bored with the homilies of the good Father Francis. He can be quite repetitive."

"So you come to see how our Father Torold does it, eh?"

"That's right and…"

"And…?"

"And to have a look at this fine church of St. Mary."

"Ah yes. Much of it newly rebuilt. We shall have glass in the windows soon, I'm told."

"Glass?"

"Expensive. We have a glass maker here in the town you know. He will execute the work."

"Marlborough is truly a town of wonders," said Guy, smiling.

"May I introduce you to my wife, to my son, Joscelin, and my daughter."

Guy noticed the man did not give the female Cowpers a name.

"It's very pleasant to meet you all," said Guy charmingly. Under his eyelashes he perused the features of the young lady Cowper.

Fair of hair, her face was shining and her skin clear. Her eyes were the blue which songsters were wont to liken to the sky or to a cornflower. She was a charming little creature of about nine years of age.

Could he wait for the girl to reach a marriageable age? Ah no. He thought not.

"I see that we are to have another church at the far end of the marketplace, Master Cowper."

"Yes indeed. The castle garrison has outgrown its chapel within the castle walls and so we are to have a second church. St. Peter's, I believe."

"There's a thing. Will there be a rivalry do you think?"

"I don't know. It will be interesting to see who from this congregation will go to St. Peter's and stand amongst the rough soldiers."

"We shall be staying here," said Mistress Cowper firmly, taking her husband by the arm.

They bade each other a good day. Guy hovered in the nave whilst folk passed him; the men openly scrutinising his face and dress, the married ladies peering around their veils at his manly figure.

He counted five young single ladies of marriageable age in the church that day, with their families. He had no idea who they were.

"Guy!"

The blacksmith turned. "My Lord Lillebon." He bowed genteelly.

"What are you doing here?" said the small man with a foxy face and a dainty triangular beard to match. He beamed at the blacksmith. "Forsaken our church at Kennett, have you?"

"Ah, no. I was just... visiting friends and thought to come to church here, sir."

The jovial man nodded. "Fine church. I must think about updating our own at Kennett."

"Yes, my Lord Lillebon."

"Perhaps I could prevail upon you to execute some work... of some... metal... kind?"

Guy smiled sweetly. "It would be an honour." He had heard this speech before. He'd been asked countless times. The Lord was always saying that he was going to spend money on the church. He never did.

The party shifted to allow an elderly matron, on her stick, to walk around them. Into Guy's view came a vision of loveliness in a pale blue kirtle and a dark blue cloak.

The girl smiled at him under her fair eyelashes.

"This is the Blacksmith of Kennett, my dears," said the Lord Lillebon.

"Oh is he the one...?" began the lovely young lady whom Guy knew to be called Adela, though he had never before met her. He'd shod her horse though, often enough. Lillebon's daughter.

"The very same one."

"Oh, I would love to..." went on the girl.

"Come Adela," said her mother, the Lady Lillebon. "We take dinner at the castle soon."

"Oh Father, one day, can we go to the forge and...?"

"Yes my dear, one day."

"Walter..." said Lady Lillebon in an admonishing tone.

"Sybil?"

"A forge is no place for a noble young lady."

"But I do so want to hear him sing. They say he's magical," said Adela.

Poor Guy blushed as red as an autumn sunset.

"Oh please... I... I..." He was very tongue tied.

"A forge is a good place if she has a horse which wants shoeing," said the lord firmly. There's nothing wrong with that. And Guy here is a fine farrier."

"And wonderful singer we are told," said Adela, with a pert expression.

"Oh I don't... know... I..." stammered Guy.

"Yes. He is. I have heard him." Lord Lillebon tapped Guy upon the breast with his gloves. "They say you can extemporise upon most subjects, young man. Is this true?"

"Well... I... if you give me..."

"Then you must come one day at dinner and entertain us. Mustn't he, Sybil?"

The Lady Sybil was not so sure. She saw how her daughter was looking at the handsome young farrier beaming down at her.

"Before Christmas. Then we can talk about you coming at

Christmas itself to sing for my guests."

"Yes my lord."

"There we are then." Lillebon collected his family and servants. "Off we go, into the rain."

Guy was left looking after them, at the bright hole which was now the open doorway. Lord Lillebon was wrong. The sun had come out.

"I am in love," said Guy to himself dreamily.

*****

All the way home to Kennett he hummed a tune. A new one of his own making.

"Da da da dah, da dada da da,

Da dada da da, da da dah."

Then he began to form words to the tune.

"Eyes of sky blue,

Skin as a ripe peach,

Hair as the golden rays of sun."

He happily called out to people on the road as he drove. His pony knew the way home, he could give all his thought to the making of a song.

As he neared Kennett he began to sing it at the top of his considerable bass voice. There was no doubt his voice was beautiful, as smooth as a water-washed pebble, as rich as a Christmas pastry and as low as a rumble of thunder.

"Lips as cherries,

Cheeks as a sunset,

A brow as white as a..." Hmmm, he'd have to think about that line.

"I would love her, always would love her.

Love her as the cob swan loves his pen.

Ever and ever.

Love her forever,

Never forsaking till the day I'm done."

Yes that would do.

Then he sang it at the top of his voice when he reached the last hill before the road to his forge—all of it—with his missing line, *"A brow as white as the upland hare."*

He sang it again as the wheels of his cart trundled over the small bridge over the river Kennett which gave the village its name.

He reached the forge with its house behind, set away from the other houses of the village against the threat of fire. He was still humming his new tune when, as he bent to undo the traces of his pony, Hurryup, he saw a pair of feet draw up by the cart.

"Good day to you, Nell."

"Good day, Guy. Where have you been? We missed you at church this morning."

He straightened. "Ah yes. I went into town for a change."

"And what does Marlborough town have that we do not... on a Sunday?"

Guy pursed his lips. "I have no idea. But it was a… nice experience."

"Nice? It's been raining most of the day."

"Well then let's go into the forge and get out of the wet."

He took the girl by the arm which was encased in lavender wool and steered her into the forge building.

"Mind the soot. I wouldn't have you dirty your fine Sunday kirtle in my awful place of work."

"It's not awful. It's a decent man's place of work. God's good work and a boon to the community."

Guy chuckled. "If you say so, Nell."

He hung the cart harness onto a peg in the forge and looked up into the rafters, listening to the heavy rain.

"You'll be soaked if you go home now. Stay a while and take some ale with me."

"I promised Father I wouldn't be too long."

"And you won't. He won't mind you staying with me."

She looked at him earnestly then. Her head lifted to his face for she was small like a sparrow and he, as tall as a heron.

He saw a girl of one and twenty, with straw blonde hair and eyes the colour of the river in spate. Her hair was tied up into a piece of linen and perched in ringlets on her head, escaping down the sides of her face. Her figure was willowy under her lavender kirtle and her movements were easy and graceful as if all her joints were made of liquid.

She ducked under his pony's chin and patted him on the cheek. "Good old Hurryup. You need a rub down and a manger of..."

"Oh, alright. You make me feel guilty."

"He's just taken you all the way into Marlborough and back, in the rain. The least you could do..."

"Oh, Nell, do be quiet. Once again you make me feel guilty."

She smiled with lips which were pale peach in colour. Not like the ruby lips of the wonderful Lady Adela. "I like to keep you on the straight and narrow."

Guy fetched Hurryup further into the building and they both began to rub the pony dry.

Once in the house, Guy poured ale from a jug into two pottery beakers.

"Your continued good health."

"Your health too... which will not continue fine, if you ride about to Marlborough in your cart in the rain ."

"You think I will catch my death?"

"Someone has to tell you."

Guy laughed. "And I would let no one but *you* do so."

"So, what were you doing?"

"I am not going to speak of it, for you would laugh and make fun of it and before I know it, it will be all over the village."

"Oooh, a secret?"

"Perhaps."

Parnell sat down on a stool and leaned her elbows on the trestle. "It's a woman. You have a woman in Marlborough." She dipped her finger in her ale and drew a heart with the wetness of it, onto the table top.

"No. There you are wrong."

"She is somewhere from here to there?"

"Wrong again."

Nell frowned. "Hmm. I cannot imagine. You went to church to… ask God…"

Guy laughed again.

"No, to ask the priory… to take you in… as a postulant!"

Now Guy really laughed and folded his arms over his chest. "The Priory of St. Margaret of Antioch? A postulant? I think before that happens, Hurryup will live up to his name!"

"I will keep thinking. I will get to the bottom of it."

"You may try."

Guy uncovered the fire and blew on the flames. "Hmmm, chilly now isn't it?"

Parnell did not answer but looked at the wall.

"So, did you want something in particular?"

The young woman swivelled her eyes towards him but not her head. "Father does."

"Oh?"

"He sent me to invite you to dinner on Tuesday."

"Ah. Dinner? What have I done to warrant this honour? The Lord's bailiff, freeman of this parish and all round influential man. He wants me to come to dinner?"

"He can ask you, can't he? He's known you all your life. He's fond of you."

"The old devil only wants my company when I can do something for him."

"Really?"

"Hmmm, really."

Parnell pouted prettily.

"So what does he want?" asked Guy, prodding the fire with a poker of his own making.

"I have no idea."

"Aw, c'mon. There isn't a breath your father takes without you know what he says with it."

Nell grew a little coy. "I have a feeling that he wants you to do something for him... true."

"What?"

"I cannot possibly say."

"Yes you can." Guy lurched towards her and took her by the arm and tickled her mercilessly at her waist. "Tell me now!"

"I yield!" she cried, laughing uncontrollably, her hair tumbling down from its linen band.

She hurriedly wound it back up again and wiped her eyes of laughter-filled tears. "I think he wants you to find me a husband. But you are not going to, are you, as I am not going to get married?"

"Well, no. I know that."

"I cannot. I have to look after my father."

Guy sat down on a stool. "You are sure that he wants me to find you a husband?"

"That's what he said. And I told him he'd never manage it. And neither will you."

"I'd never find a man who'd have you!" said Guy cheekily.

"And there's not a man I'd have."

"Well there we are then. As our lord and master is so fond of saying."

"Lord Lillebon?"

"Why does your father suddenly want you married? He's never been bothered before. In fact, he was positively happy that you weren't interested in marriage so he could have you at home to do his bidding."

Once again Nell sat and faced him over the table. "I think it all began with his visit to the doctor."

"Doctor Johannes of Salerno in Marlborough?"

"Yes. After that Father went to the astrologer."

"Yes... Erm... Master Celest?"

"Yes. And, well it seems that Father is ill."

"Oh no. Ill... how?"

"I will admit that he has been having difficulty swallowing of late and he feels very nauseous."

"He's not that old. Is he?"

"He tells me he is fifty nine."

"Oh."

"And so he wants someone to care for me should..." Suddenly Nell's composure shrank and her lip began to quiver.

"He thinks he's going to die."

"Aw c'mon Nell. He may be ill but it doesn't mean he's going to die... does it?"

Parnell of Kennett wiped her eyes with a shaking hand. "The astrologer told Father that he was to put his affairs in order."

"Oh, Jesus... love us and save us."

"And I am... one of those affairs."

"And he wants you to have a husband... before...?"

Parnell nodded. "And I told him that I won't marry. Even if he's gone."

"Oh Lord!"

CHAPTER TWO ~ THE CURSE

Tuesday came in with a blustery beginning and continued gusty until dinner time.

Guy laid down his tools at the fifth hour of the day and washed himself in the large stone trough he kept in the forge. He donned a clean shirt, his best cotte and ran the few paces around the corner to the house near the manor, where the bailiff lived.

Smoothing down his wayward hair, he called out. "Master Truman. It's Guy Ferrier."

A voice answered and bade him enter.

The cottage was spacious, well fitted out and very warm, for a raging fire burned on its stone platform in the middle of the large room.

"Are you cold today, Master Truman?" said Guy, as the wall of heat hit him. "It's mild out."

"Cold? Aye, I'm cold."

"Oh. That's not good." Guy took his courage in both hands. Did he really want to know the answer to the question he was about to ask?

"Um... are you feeling unwell, perhaps?"

"Unwell? Unwell! I'll tell you, young man. Unwell is not a big enough word for it."

"Oh... um..."

Parnell now came into the room, carrying a bowl in rag wrapped hands, of what looked and smelled like a delicious stew. The aroma wafted up and made Guy's mouth water.

"He's not too unwell to take some of my rabbit stew though."

Guy noticed that Master Truman seemed to sit up straighter in his chair and his eye looked a little more engaged—like a blackbird that had seen a juicy worm.

"Well... I suppose I could have a few mouthfuls."

"Sit, Guy," said Nell. "You're like a column in a ruin, standing all alone."

"What seems to be the trouble, sir?" asked Guy, finding himself a place to sit and taking out his spoon from his purse.

"Oh... it's hard to say..."

"Do try, Father," said Nell. "You know that you said you'd tell Guy everything."

The elderly man tutted and shook his wispy-haired, not so grey head.

"This sort of illness is... is difficult to explain."

Guy and Nell exchanged glances. "Why's that?" asked Guy.

"Well for a start... it's not a *real* illness."

"What do you mean, sir?"

Nell ladled out some stew into a bowl.

"What Father means is... his body is..."

"I can tell him, you forward girl—it's my body."

A smile escaped Nell's lips. "As you wish, Father. But don't leave it too long in the telling, for your stew will cool."

Master Truman came straight to the point. "I have been cursed. There! See? Cursed. And that's an end to it."

Guy nearly choked on his broth. He put down his spoon and gave his attention to the bailiff of Kennett. "Cursed? And what makes you believe you have been cursed?"

John Truman fixed a beady eye on Guy. "My body is a fine example of God's work, young man and I know that it would not let me down. I haven't had a day's illness in my whole life, why should it start behaving badly now?"

Nell made a disparaging noise like a sneeze which ended in a disguising cough.

"Well, sir," said Guy gently, "You are no longer a young man... perhaps..."

"Nonsense."

"You are closer to God's span of man's life at three score years and ten than you are to..."

"Nonsense. I am merely getting into my stride."

"Oh, Father please..." said Nell with a scoff. "Fifty nine is a good age. Admit that you are only eleven years from God's declaration of our span. You are closer to the gates of Heaven than you are to..."

"Don't argue with me, girl."

Guy intervened. He knew what their arguments were like. "Sir, you feel that you have been cursed? If this is so, who do you think is responsible?"

"If I knew *that* for certain, Master Ferrier, I would have it out with them. Without a doubt." He gave a little cough as he spooned more liquid into his mouth. "See, even this stew, which is very fine I must say, is hard to get down."

"What did the doctor say to you sir, if you would allow me to be so bold as to ask?"

"Rubbish. Absolute rubbish."

"Now Father, that isn't quite true... is it?"

The manor bailiff huffed and puffed. "He told me that I was getting on in years and that as we get older, the gut doesn't work as well as it should."

"That, like our bones, there is some difficulty moving and so food gets stuck. That's why you are having difficulty swallowing," said Nell. "And that's why I have been making you dishes which are easy to take."

"Pah... mashed up food. Like babies! Soup. Pah!"

"Oh, I see," said Guy.

"And Father wasn't very pleased with the doctor, were you Father?"

"No indeed. Especially when he said I was to drink less ale. So I went to the astrologer." The bailiff's face cleared and his expression was one of smugness. "And, as I thought, *he* told me the truth."

"That you had been cursed?"

"Now, Father..."

"He told me that... that..."

"That you were a curmudgeonly old man who imagines himself ill and..."

"Parnell Truman!"

Parnell giggled.

"He told me that I was unpopular because of something I had done. And that it was that action which has led to my insides being upset."

"There you are then... all in your mind," said Nell.

"How do you...?" began Guy.

Bailiff Truman glared at him. Guy had been going to ask how he'd got from 'all in the mind' to 'being cursed'.

The blacksmith wriggled on his seat. "Do you have any knowledge of the thing which might be causing the... upset?"

Truman spooned more broth into his mouth and swallowed noisily.

"The Widow Berefield, perhaps?" said Nell loudly.

"Nonsense," said her father again.

"Ah... the old lady who lives in the cottage by the hill path?"

"Lived in the cottage," said Nell with a mischievous grin. "She's not there now. *Now* she has to live with her son and his family at Fyfield."

"Why?"

Master Truman seemed to shrink in his seat. "I threw her out."

"What? Why?"

"My lord and master told me to make way for a new building. The only way we could do that was to demolish her hovel. And she'd not paid her rent last Michaelmas."

"Wait!" said Guy, "The Lord Lillebon wants to build something there?"

"Aye, a barn."

"But, forgive me Master Truman, the lord speaks about his plans to build, over and over and it never ever comes to anything. I ought to know... he's asked me so many times to..."

"I work for the lord and I do as I'm told."

"Father didn't want to do it, but..." said Nell

"So you believe this woman has cursed you?"

"Not completely... maybe not her... but maybe someone... else."

"Good Lord, sir, are you so unpopular that you have more than one person willing to curse you?"

"Bailiffs are rarely well liked, young man. We have to do things for the good of our lords which people don't appreciate."

Once again Guy exchanged a look with Nell. "And so you think that this curse..."

"A rhyme no doubt pronounced at the dead of night, which has stiffened my gut and which does not allow me food. I will waste away."

"Ah no... I don't think..." said Guy. "I don't think you should let it get the better of you."

He saw Nell wink at him.

"Better of me?" bellowed the man. "There's no fighting a curse, Master Ferrier."

"The astrologer told you that you had to put your affairs in order, did he?"

Master Truman gave his daughter an evil look. "Well, not in so many words, but he said I needed to sort things. And *that* is what he meant."

"And Nell tells me that this includes plans for her if you should... not be able to fight off this curse."

"Can't leave the woman alone in the world."

"I will be perfectly alright and you are not going to die, Father," said Nell.

"No. No. I'll not have it. Ferrier... she needs a husband. Find her one."

"But…"

"I beg you. I am too ill."

"No… I can't. It's not really anything to do with me."

"I am making it something to do with you. If I go then Parnell will be out on her ear… I know it. This house belongs to the lord and there is no way she will be allowed to stay. It will pass to the next bailiff."

"Master Truman…"

"No, I am not listening." He pulled off a piece of bread and then chewed and swallowed. This brought on a coughing fit.

"See… see?" spluttered the bailiff. "This is how it will end. I shall choke to death."

Nell gave her father a cup of ale. "Drink this slowly and it will help."

"Master Truman. I cannot help you to, as you say, put your affairs in order. However…"

"Yes?"

"I might be able to help you…" Guy gave a quick look at Parnell. "Help you to… dispel this curse."

"Dispel… the curse?" said the old man.

Parnell sat down heavily on a stool, her mouth open. "How dispel the curse?" she said.

"Well you know that it's always better to stay on the right side of a blacksmith." He grinned.

Master Truman grew puzzled. "Huh?"

"Oh yes."

"No one has come to you to… curse Father, have they?" asked Parnell with horror.

"Ah no. I wouldn't allow it." Guy was firm in his denial. "Although you're right to think that I *might* have done it."

"Oh Guy…"

"I didn't because I don't do that sort of thing, though I know that blacksmiths all over the land *will* pronounce a curse, if paid enough."

"I know that you have helped folk with their warts," said Nell.

"And cured them, yes."

"By allowing them to put their hands into your water trough."

"That's right. The trough I use for quenching my work." Guy smiled widely. "The blacksmith is a magical fellow, there's no doubt."

Now Parnell pursed her lips in disbelief. But one look at her father's face and she could see that he was indeed being drawn into Guy's tale.

"So, you might be willing to help Father rid himself of this curse."

"I might... yes." Guy went on sipping the soup from his spoon.

Parnell sighed. "Oh don't be so... annoying and tell us how it can be done then."

Guy laughed and put down the horn spoon. "A new moon is required for this spell to be broken. A new moon and my anvil."

"The anvil in the forge?"

"The very same."

"What do you do?"

"Ah no... the words and actions of the counter charm cannot be discussed beforehand with... ordinary people." Guy winked at her.

Now Master Truman cleared his throat. "And what would you be wanting in return, Master Ferrier?"

"Nothing much. A simple coin. Laid on my anvil at the onset of night."

"Coin? Just one coin? That seems very... cheap."

"Well Master Truman, it is merely an exchange. The cost is immaterial. You want something—you exchange a coin for the lifting of the curse. It's a balance, see?"

The bailiff gave a determined look at his daughter. "If you lift the curse, I will not die?"

Guy smiled at Truman, "You will not die of the curse. I cannot say that you will never die. We must all die."

Parnell jumped up eager to be about the business. "Then let's go."

"Ah no... a new moon... We shan't have that until... Let me think...

October 13th, I think. In Libra I believe, which will be perfect for that is the sign of the scales."

"Huh?" said Truman.

"The scales—a weighing scale. One action equalling another and achieving equilibrium and dispelling the curse for good."

"Oh Guy, I had no idea you knew so much about this sort of thing," said Nell.

"What happens in my forge on that night must never be spoken about to a living soul. Or the curse will return."

"Oh no... no," said the bailiff, looking decidedly perky and full of health.

"In fact, all that is required of you, is that you place the coin on the anvil and watch as the anvil is turned."

"Turned?"

"Turned away from evil."

"Yes. Yes. I... I... I... see."

Guy wiped his spoon and put it away. "Very fine stew Mistress Truman," he said.

"I have some honey bread if you will stay a little longer?"

"Oh, your famous honey bread—naturally I will."

"And will you sing for your supper, Blacksmith?" asked Truman. "I would so love to hear the tale of Wayland the Smith again."

"Of course," said Guy, winking once more at Nell. She threw her eyes to Heaven and went to the pot board to take up the sweet bread and honey.

His eyes lingered on her a little too long.

She knew what that signified.

Master Blacksmith had made the whole thing up, in order to convince her father he was not dying. But she had no doubt that it was going to work.

As she turned back and Guy began his song of the mythical blacksmith and his nocturnal shoeing, she mouthed the words, "Thank you."

*****

Dinner over, Parnell accompanied Guy to the house door. She drew it close behind her so that her father might not overhear and whispered, "That was very kind, Guy. If it helps him recover, then your little white lie will be worth it."

Guy chuckled. "Who said it was a little white lie?"

"What?"

"Blacksmiths *are* magical creatures and my anvil does *indeed* have the power to make or break a curse."

"But..."

"I'll expect you after sundown, when fully dark on the 13th then, at the forge. Bring a penny." And he was off into the night.

*****

The night of the 13th was dark and a cold mist had crept up from the little river opposite the forge. Guy could no longer see the dark shadow of Sanctuary Hill which loomed up in front of his home—sky and land blended together. Ah well. No matter if we cannot see the new moon, we know it's there and that's all that's required for the turning to work.

Guy went into his forge and lit the lamp. He gazed around. He was a tidy fellow; everything had a place and everything was in its place. His work in progress lay across his anvil; a pitchfork for Master Jekyll, the pig keeper. He removed it and tossed it into a straw-filled box which lay in the corner.

He gathered up several horseshoes, old ones which he'd taken from beasts in the past week, and arranged them around the floor, circling the anvil, all of them pointing with the open ends facing it.

No harm in making a bit of a show.

He heard the voices approaching as he placed his last horseshoe and leaned to open the door. "Come in. God's blessing on you. It's a foul night."

"I don't usually like to go out on such a night," said the bailiff looking right and left.

"Have no worry, Master Truman, I have banished all devils from the place."

Parnell, closing the door, gave Guy an exasperated look. "Devils indeed," she said under her breath.

"Right," said Guy rubbing his hands together with a sandy rasping sound. "Let's begin."

Master Truman wrapped his brown cloak more firmly around his body.

"Now, you will see that at the moment, the anvil is facing with its horn towards the east."

"Towards the river, yes," said Nell.

"This indicates that the curse is active."

John Truman jutted his jaw. "How do you know that?"

"I... just do..."

"Father, please."

"And so I will now take the anvil and turn it to the west."

Master Truman scoffed. "One man cannot lift that great thing alone."

Guy flexed his muscles and grinned. "All that is required is for you to watch carefully. You may feel a little lightheaded but it will pass as I put the anvil back onto its tree trunk."

He reached out and put his hands to the heavy iron anvil. Gritting his teeth he lifted it a few inches from the cut surface of the tree trunk upon which it rested.

A siffling wind came in from the east and the door rattled.

Nell shuddered.

Guy turned the two ends of the anvil. The pointed horn end was now facing west, the blunt or heel end, east.

"And now," said Guy as Master Truman prayed under his breath, his eyes closed, "All that is needed is for you sir, to place a coin upon the anvil."

The bailiff opened his fist and showed the coin already lying in his palm. His hand shook as he laid it on the cold metal.

Once again a breeze seemed to blow on them from an unseen place.

"Now you must go. I have words to speak to complete the breaking of the curse and they must be uttered in private."

Nell looked back once as she left the forge to see Guy staring at her, his hands on his hips. Master Truman walked out, head held high.

Once they'd gone, Guy let out a long breath. "All right Johnny. You can come out now."

From behind Guy's long leather apron which had been hung on a wooden peg driven into the wall by the door, came a young lad of about seven. Guy picked up the coin and held it out. "The bellows please?"

They exchanged bellows for coin.

"Come... I promised you buttermilk. Let's go into my house."

"Did I do alright, Master Ferrier?"

"Perfectly, young Johnny. Perfectly. Not a word to anyone, mind."

*****

From that day, Master Truman began to grow in strength. His gut still bothered him but he learned to take water with everything he ate and although he did feel that there was a lump in his throat sometimes, it began to bother him less.

Nell came up to the forge three weeks later. The day was dull but there was no wind or rain. Guy had the doors open and the noise of his hammering carried along the lane. The sound of his singing also threaded its way down the road.

"Lips as cherries, brow as white as the..."

It stopped as Nell came into view through the double doors.

"Good day Master Blacksmith."

"Good day, Mistress Truman."

"I came to thank you for what you did for my father, it was very kind. He is already feeling much better."

Guy put down his tools and wiped his brow on his forearm. "I couldn't see him suffering as he was."

"He was suffering but in more than just body."

"Oh…?"

"He was very concerned for the Widow Berefield. My father isn't a bad man. Sometimes he hates having to do the things the lord requires him to do. It tears him apart."

"Is the woman in distress?"

"Not any longer, it seems."

"How so?"

"She has remarried." Nell chuckled, "It seems that Master Miller from Clatford was looking for a wife and Mistress Berefield fitted his requirements perfectly."

"Ned Miller? Looking for a wife?"

"His second."

"Ah, yes. Margaret died last year didn't she? And so the widow is now mistress of the mill?"

"It seems things have worked out for the best."

"It seems so."

They looked at each other with their own thoughts locked in their heads. Then Guy said, "Is it so easy to find a wife… or a husband, in this part of Wiltshire then?"

Nell looked up quickly, "Well, I wouldn't know."

"No more nonsense about your father requiring *you* to be married then?"

"Not a further word has been said," she answered.

Guy took hold of his bellows' handle and gave the flames a puff. "Good."

Parnell wandered around the forge. "Shall we see you at church on Sunday or will you be going to Marlborough... again?"

Every Sunday in the past few weeks, Guy had been going to St. Mary's in the hope of meeting the Lady Adela again, but she had not been there and he had been very disappointed.

"I think I shall attend Kennett's Christ Church once more this Sunday. Poor old Hurryup is too tired and elderly to keep making the journey there and back to town every week," he said, trying to be convincing.

"Hmmm. Father Francis will be pleased to see you. He has noted your absence."

Guy tried not to look guilty.

"Why was the town so interesting, Master Ferrier? You never did tell me."

Guy turned the spade blade which he had been fashioning and leaned on the anvil balancing his work between his hands.

"I went to..."

"To...?"

"Never a word to anyone, Nell."

"Upon my sainted mother's grave," she said with a cheeky grin, totally at odds with the seriousness of her words.

"I went to meet people."

"People? Can you not meet people here?"

Guy laid his spade down on the wooden bench. "I know everyone here and for several miles around and they know me. In the town... it's all new. I wanted to meet some new people."

Parnell gave his face a penetrating look. "Meaning you wanted to meet some young ladies?"

"How else am I to find a wife?"

Nell took in a quick breath. "A wife?"

"There is no one hereabouts and if I am not to spend the rest of my life alone, I must widen my search. The Clatford miller is not the only one looking for a partner."

Nell's mouth fell open.

"I am thirty one in December. It's time I gave some thought to my future."

"Yes... yes... I see," said Nell.

There was an uncomfortable silence.

"I will see you at church on Sunday, then?" Nell turned to go.

"Not a word Nell."

"Never. My lips are sealed."

*****

East Kennett church was a small building which housed the whole village comfortably. It was an old Norman church, and was a fine example of local building techniques, being built with the chalk blocks known as clunch interspersed with the local flints which turned up at every ploughing of the land. The inside was a riot of colour.

Over the chancel arch, a beautifully painted Garden of Eden, with Adam and Eve either side of a tree with pink blossoms and red apples, loomed up into the darkness of the rafters. The north and south walls were painted with Biblical Kings, Saul, Solomon and David, with their fashionable clothes and gorgeous crowns. Here and there were painted interesting patterns of spots and wavy lines dotted with the faces of little coloured devils. Someone in Kennett had been a consummate artist many years ago.

Young Simon Plimmon tolled the bell for the first service of the day and folk hurried through the gloom of the morning, to find their accustomed places, nodding at and acknowledging neighbours.

Father Francis inclined his head to Simon by way of thanks. He was getting a little long in the tooth to pull on the bell rope now. Best he leave it to a younger man. He must admit, he wasn't feeling all that wonderful that day.

Dressed in his best robes, for today was the feast of the Evangelist Luke, Father Francis began the service of Terce, the third hour of daylight. After a while he said in Latin, "O glorious Evangelist, who, on account of thy purity, was so beloved of God, as to deserve to lay thy head upon His divine breast. In faithfully detailing the humanity of Jesus, you also showed us the divinity of Jesus and His genuine compassion for all human beings." Father Francis gave a little cough and an odd sigh. But he carried on.

Parnell leaned sideways to look at the priest through the chancel arch. Not everyone could see him. He was carrying on with his Latin quietly but he had his hand upon his breast. After a while the Latin became more stuttering.

Once again Nell peered through the chancel arch.

Father Francis coughed again, this time he clutched his arm and grimaced.

Gingerly, he turned, stepped down from the altar step and walked slowly forward almost through the arch.

"My good friends. It seems that I am unwell... I am sorry..."

A ripple of unrest went through the congregation.

"I will be unable to..." Father Francis grimaced again, baring his teeth and began to breathe in huge gasps until at last the man pitched forward, his arms outstretched and hit the flagstones of the nave with a thud.

At first no one moved. Then there was a susurrating whisper which echoed around the box-like building as folk peered through the arch.

After a while Lady Lillebon, who was standing at the front, motioned to her two maidservants to kneel and see what was wrong with the priest who had not moved.

Before they could approach the man, Nell had leapt over to Father Francis and called his name. "Father Francis. Speak to me. It's Nell. What ails you?"

Capable hands now reached out and took hold of the priest's vestments. They turned him. Nell looked up. Guy was bending over the priest of Christ Church.

A few other people now came up and peered over one another's shoulders.

"Room... give us room," shouted Guy in his bass voice.

Elbowing people out of the way, he bent forward and lifted Father Francis as if he had been a dry leaf. "I shall take him to his house. Make way there."

"What's wrong with him?" he heard one woman say.

"My lord?" said Guy quizzically.

"Yes Ferrier, you have permission to remove him to his house," said the surprised lord of the manor coming through the press of people. "The service is at an end. Make way there!"

"It had hardly begun," said Nell, following Guy and opening the door for him.

By the time they reached the priest's house only a hundred feet away, they had outdistanced the pursuing throng.

"What is it?"

"What's happened?"

"Is he hurt?"

"Has the devil taken him?"

"Oh shut up Maudie," said one authoritative voice. "You and yer ruddy devils."

"Well it... could be..." Voices drifted over to them.

Guy pushed the door of the priest's house and went inside, Nell trailing him. Lord Lillebon followed and after a short while, the steward came after him. No one else dared to enter without permission from their lord and they all milled around in the garden. Father Francis, a beatific smile on his face, was laid gently on his bed.

"He was to tell the tale of the martyrdom of Luke, and of his wicked murder by the mob," said the lord sadly. "I asked him for it specially in honour of this day."

"He will be telling us no further tales, my lord," said Guy.

Nell lifted a tearful face to her lord. "I'm sorry my lord, but Father

Francis is dead."

All present crossed themselves.

CHAPTER THREE ~ THE NEW PRIEST

Poor Father Francis was hardly settled in his grave before the Lord Lillebon had proposed another priest for East Kennett village.

As was his right, he had the privilege of appointing the incumbent to his own church.

Father Fabian had been a member of St. Oswald's Priory, a minor Augustinian foundation in Gloucester, a place where the Lord Lillebon owned lands, and this was to be his very first church.

Naturally upon the premier day of his service at East Kennett, the church was packed to the roof for no one had yet seen this enigmatic and, it was said, *young* man and everyone wanted to know what he was like. Would he be as boring a preacher as Father Francis had been, or would he turn out to be someone a little more interesting? Would he be as kind and considerate as Father Francis or cold and detached?

Guy donned his best cotte, brushed his hair and attempted to get some of the black from his hands, by scrubbing and rubbing with soap. As a consequence he was a little late and so had to squeeze in at the very back.

He noticed that there were people there that day who had never worshipped in this church; some who rarely attended this service and many from the villages and lands about. Guy nodded to a few people he knew well, then he bowed his head and gave his mind to the Latin of the service, the words of which he knew by heart but did not understand. He really couldn't see very well in the packed church, but he was taller than most folk and by standing on tiptoes and craning his neck he could catch a glimpse of the officiating priest's back.

At last the man turned and Guy had his first good view of his face.

The blacksmith gasped inwardly in admiration. The man was simply the most handsome male creature he'd seen for a while.

A slight tan, (or was it an olive-tinged skin ?) deep dark brown eyes, fringed by long, curled girlish lashes. His hair was as dark as Guy's own but wavy and lustrous - hair a young girl might envy. His lips were as plump and red as a holly berry. It was hard to gauge his figure, encased as he was in the stiffly decorated ecclesiastical robes of a celebrant priest but he was tall, not as tall as Guy, but taller than many men here and there was no doubt his shoulders were broad under his dalmatic. There was an air of nobility about him; the way he held himself in his embroidered robes. There was no doubt the man knew he was good to look upon.

Firstly, Guy searched for Mistress Truman to see if he could catch her eye but her own eyes were firmly fixed to the front of the church and he could only get a glimpse of the back of her head. Then he looked around for the Lillebons. As usual they were up at the front and the Lady Adela seemed as transfixed by the new priest as was the rest of the congregation.

But Guy had noticed a flutter of some kind of unease. The men did not seem as happy as the women. Some of them were whispering to each other. Others smoothed their hair or scratched their ears, a sure sign of perturbation. One or two rubbed their chins. Another sign that all was not well. A couple grabbed hold of their wives' arms, proprietorially.

Guy thought that he could understand the reason. As long as he could remember, the priest of Kennett had been a man of mature years. This new man was not more than five and twenty—and dashingly good looking. The men felt threatened.

He tried to quiz the faces of the women present. Their faces and body language too, were readable. To a woman, they looked on with admiration at this fine specimen of manhood. They were almost transfixed.

By walking to the side of the throng, close to the wall, excusing himself and squeezing between the ploughman John Plimmon, Simon's father and Master Fulke, one of the lord's cowmen, he could see the face of the woman Guy had convinced himself he loved. He saw the same expression upon her face as, no doubt, had been upon his own when he had first seen Lady Adela. Adulation.

He leaned round the body of his neighbour. There was Parnell. *Her* face was quizzical. He watched her eyes range over the figure of the new priest and to his surprise, he saw her shake her head very slightly. He doubted anyone else had seen it.

Suddenly she seemed to know that someone was looking at her and quickly she turned her head towards the wall upon which he leaned. She saw him.

Her eyes rapidly raised to Heaven and in that moment, Guy knew exactly what Mistress Truman thought of the new priest.

*****

Father Fabian, standing in the church door and acknowledging everyone, as they left, looked down his straight and perfect nose. "And who have we here, sir?"

Bailiff Truman took his daughter by the arm. "May I present my daughter, Parnell, Sir Priest."

"Your only daughter, Bailiff Truman?"

"Yes, Father."

"Perhaps that is a good thing. It's a good job; I cannot imagine a whole load of daughters as handsome as this one, springing from your seed, my good man. That would be more than any man could bear."

Bailiff Truman blinked in surprise. Too many uses of the word good, thought Guy.

"She is the image of her mother, alas dead these few years," Truman almost stuttered.

The new priest of Kennett smiled and everyone noticed how perfect were his very white teeth. "And unmarried, I see?"

"I have no desire to marry," said Parnell curtly.

"Beautiful and spirited, also," said Father Fabian.

"Another feature, I am told, I have from my late mother," said Nell, backing away.

She trod on Guy's toe and immediately swivelled to face him and looked up with, "Oh, sorry, Guy."

"She is my help and housekeeper and looks after my health which I must say is not good," said her father, looking sad.

"Then you are very fortunate to have such a beautiful nursemaid," the priest positively grinned and passed on to speak to others.

"Oh, dear." Guy heard Nell whispering under her breath.

"You do not approve of our new priest, Mistress Truman?"

They began to walk towards the large yew trees which lined the path to the church, her father following.

"I will not make a judgement until..."

"Aw, c'mon, I saw your face when first you saw him. Whilst everyone else was struck by his handsome visage and noble bearing, you were shaking your head in disbelief."

"He is far too fond of himself," said Nell.

"Ah... the new raiment... it seems Father Francis' ecclesiastical robes were not good enough for the great Father Fabian. He has to have new..."

"New and ostentatious. What was wrong with the plain and serviceable robes which the church already possessed?"

"Not grand enough for our Fabian," chuckled Guy.

"This isn't a grand church. He may have come from the Priory in

Gloucester but here we are simple and have no need of show and... pomp."

"So our first impression of him is?"

"Vain and too full of himself, as I said."

"Hmmm." Guy turned to walk backwards down the path so he could see her face. "Let us see how he fares in the weeks to come. I should hate to prejudge him."

"Would you like to engage in a wager, Master Blacksmith?"

"Mistress Truman, a wager, conducted in the churchyard? God's acre?"

"Then let us step outside the gate and I will wager you a horseshoe to a batch of my honey cakes, that the man doesn't last until Christmas."

"That long?"

Nell chortled with glee. "You saw how the men viewed him."

"And I also saw how the women behaved when first they saw him," said Guy.

"And what was that greeting for me all about? He is a priest, a man of God. He's supposed to be celibate. That was not the sort of thing a man of the cloth should be saying upon the first time of meeting one of his female parishioners!"

Guy inclined his head. "I think you are not the only one who is getting that sort of greeting."

The priest was bending and bowing over the back of Adela Lillebon's hand, his eyes stretched up to her face under those very fine eyelashes. Guy's heart tightened.

"Pah! I am not fooled," said Nell. "Like some."

"There are some clerical men who believe that marriage is *not* incompatible with their calling. That indeed, it enhances their role in the community," said Guy, "and prevents sin."

He fell in with Nell at last and strode by her side away from the church.

"I thought that the church was growing ever more displeased with those who remain married. Were there not unhappy murmurs when wives are allowed to reside with clerical husbands? It was forbidden a long time ago," said Nell.

"Who knows? Many a housekeeper is really a tacit wife. It is very hard to prove... unless there are children of the union."

"No... don't tell me!"

Guy chuckled like a broody hen. "What? That the new priest of Kennett is looking for a wife?"

"No! He can't be. Surely, besides being a priest he is a monk who has taken a vow of chastity?"

"Apparently."

"So he is not free to marry!"

Guy looked back up the church path. Now the priest was fawning over the very pretty daughter of the baker who, as Guy's friend Tom had said, was as 'dim as a halfpenny candle.'

"No. But if he can find himself a lover...?"

Master Truman caught up with them.

"Or several," said Parnell.

"Dinner at our house, Guy?" said the bailiff.

Guy winked at Mistress Truman. "I would be delighted," he said.

*****

Strangely, that day they did not speak much further about the new priest of Kennett, except to comment upon his looks and bearing.

"And he has a good voice," said Master Truman after dinner. "He can be heard at the back of the church which is a good thing."

"I must admit, he delivered everything in a very clear voice," added Parnell. "He was... interesting."

"Better than Father Francis, in this respect," said Guy.

"But the man was old and we could not expect..." began Master Truman, trailing off, as they remembered the kindly old priest of Kennett. And that was the last they spoke of Father Fabian that day.

Guy sat back on his stool, "Has the Lord decided yet what he wishes to do with the land at the bottom of the hill, by the bridge? Where the cott of Mistress Berefield is located?"

"A barn, he told me. But he is so often away from Kennett at his other properties that I cannot see anything being done this season. He has not spent above five weeks this year at Kennett."

"I wonder if he is the same in all the places he owns?"

"You mean so undecided about what he's to do?" asked Nell.

The bailiff tutted. "He is a mild man. Dare I say it, ruled by his wife. A man who cannot seem to make up his mind about anything. I can get no firm instructions from him about anything unless I push."

"So far this last summer, he has spoken to *me* about new hinges for the door to the church, nail studs for the manor gate, bars to secure a chest and bracing for the bell tower. With none of them have I had any firm instruction," said Guy.

"And so you do nothing?" said Nell.

"How can I?"

"But you have made new frames for the Lillebon carriage."

"The ladies' carriage, yes. That *had* to be done or they'd be spilled out onto the stones when next they travelled the roads."

"And we cannot have the Lady Adela flung from her carriage into the mud as a wheel falls from her conveyance, now can we?" said Nell with a snide look.

"The potholes are appalling at the moment," said the bailiff, oblivious to the undercurrents in the conversation going on between Nell and Guy.

"The rain Father, it's all the rain."

Guy gave Nell a piercing look. "I do what I am asked. Like your father."

"Except mend the gate, the door and the church tower…"

"Humph. What are you implying?"

"It has been particularly rainy this year. And windy. Don't you think?" said the bailiff.

"Implying? Why nothing. Just that you jumped to do the Lord's bidding when it came to the carriage. Anyone might think that you were fond of the Lillebon ladies."

"I don't think I have seen the river so full for a long time."

"1198, Father. You remember the floods?"

"Why can I not be fond of them... in a respectful way?"

"Oh yes, indeed. The river burst its banks."

"You followed Lady Adela's movements very closely at church today. Indeed followed her out. I am surprised you didn't stand on her hem."

"I followed *you* out, Nell, as well you know. It was you who trod on Lady Adela's heel."

Nell's look was confrontational but at last her father said, "Whose heel, my dear?"

"No one, Father. No one."

More ale was poured into cups.

"Tom and Alys are to be parents, did you know?" said Guy at last changing the subject.

"Yes," said Nell curtly.

"I have been asked to be Godfather. What do you think of that?"

Nell rose to clear away the food from the table. "Are you sure you want to be a Godfather?"

"Why should I not?"

The bailiff was paying attention again. "Oh yes, you'll make a capital Godfather, as long as the child is a boy. Yes, I'm sure of it."

"If I have your endorsement sir, then I shall say yes." Guy opened his eyes wide and stared pointedly at Nell.

"It will be good practice for when you have children of your own," said Parnell cheekily.

"Children... children? Are you getting married, young Guy?"

Guy screwed up his mouth and glared at Nell.

"No, sir. No. Not yet."

"You should. You are not young, you know."

"I am but thirty..."

"Yes, not young. I was twenty two when I fathered Nell's brother. Only twenty two. And then twenty eight... when he died."

"Yes, sir. That was tragic."

"And then I had to wait until I was thirty five for my Nell there."

"And then shortly after, you lost your wife. Yes I know," said Guy with a sad expression.

"No more children. None... only left with Nell."

"And you would not remarry?"

There was no answer but a wistful stare.

Guy and Nell looked at each other. They had heard this information many times before.

"So my advice is, don't wait, my lad. You will regret it."

But this was a new development from the lips of the bailiff; that Guy should get himself a wife and have children. Guy began to wonder if, contrary to his instruction, Parnell had told her father that Guy was considering matrimony. He cocked his head at her in a question and she, in answer, shrugged.

"I will think upon what you say, sir."

Outside the door as Guy left, he rounded on Nell. "You have told him!"

"I most certainly have not."

"Then what was all that about?"

"He has guessed that's all."

"How can he guess?"

"Oh, your general demeanour, the spring in your step, the look in your eye. I suppose he too has seen the way you look at the Lady Adela."

"I do not look at her in any... special way," said Guy assertively.

Nell smoothed her voice, "Guy, you know that you cannot marry her. You know she is too far above you?"

"I would be a fool were I *not* to know it."

Nell sighed.

"And I am not a fool," he added.

"Guy..." Parnell took hold of his sleeve as he turned to leave. "I would hate to see you hurt."

"That is kind of you." His tone was not convincing.

"You are very dear to me," said Parnell. "I do not want to have to attend to you whilst you recover from a broken heart."

Guy opened his mouth to speak; nothing came out but, "Good afternoon Mistress Truman."

"Good afternoon Master Ferrier."

*****

It was a bright November morning and Guy was in good voice.
"Here's a health to the pretty girl, the one he loves best;
She kindles a fire all in his own breast,
Which makes his bright hammer to rise and to fall,
Says the Old Clem to the Young Clem and the Old Clem of all," sang Guy as his own hammer rose and fell. The Clem to whom he referred was St. Clement, the patron saint of blacksmiths, (or one of them) whose day it was.

He began to form the next stanza of his song when he became aware of horses approaching the forge. He was sure they were going to pass by, but no, they stopped outside.

He heard voices, clear in the cold air and further pushed open the door of the forge to see who were his visitors.

A lady, muffled up warm against the chill, sat upon a palfrey and several men milled about her, both on foot and horse. The sun was behind her and it was difficult to pick her out.

"My good farrier," said a voice, "Might you look at our lady's mount? It has cast a shoe."

"Gladly, sir."

The lady was then handed down from the horse.

"Come into the warmth, my lady," said Guy. "The fire is lit and it's burning nicely. It will drive away the chill of the morning."

The woman shivered under her furred cape and nodded, following

Guy in. He cleared her a space to sit.

"Now let's have a look at your beast."

Two or three men stayed outside with the other horses and three came in with their mistress on foot. Guy led the palfrey into the forge.

"I heard you singing as we came up the lane, Master Blacksmith," said the woman. "You have a very fine voice."

"That's most kind, my lady." *Her* voice was familiar to him.

She peeled her cloak from her shoulders and gave it to one of her men and turned to speak to them. "You may all wait outside."

One man argued with her. "But Lady, your father said..."

"I do not care what my father said. You will wait outside."

They bowed and disappeared.

Adela Lillebon rubbed her gloved hands together and looked around the forge. "So tell me... what were you singing?"

Guy's heart was pounding but once he began to deal with the gentle grey palfrey, the agitation in his breast calmed as he gave himself over to his work.

"Oh. It was just a little ditty which I was making up as I went along, my lady. Today is the feast of St. Clement and he's important to us blacksmiths. It was in his honour."

"It's true then, that you can make up songs and tunes in your head upon any subject matter?"

Guy tried not to look at her, he knew that if he did, his face would grow as red as a robin's breast.

"I seem to be able to put a tune to words and hold it in my head." Guy lifted the palfrey's legs to look at the hooves. "And recall it at leisure."

He discovered the problem with the horse. "Ah see here, the trouble with your mount. We shall have this done in no time."

"But I do not wish it to be done in no time, Master Ferrier. I wish to spend some time here listening to you sing. And making up songs."

"My lady, I have work to do..."

"You can work and sing. I know you can." She had now found

herself an old tree trunk to sit upon closer to the fire, and was arranging her red kirtle around her. "So… I will give you a title and you will make up a song."

"I… can… but…"

"There will be no buts, Master Blacksmith."

He looked up from his scrutiny of the palfrey's hoof.

That morning her skin was indeed pale, as pale as his song about her had made it; today her cheeks were a becoming peach colour, a reaction to the cold through which she had ridden that morning. That line too in his song had been correct.

He looked away. "I must just…"

"A cat… and the moon…"

"I beg your pardon…?"

"The song I wish you to sing will be about a cat and the moon. Oh yes and if you can do it… a cow. And… a spoon. "

"Oh…"

"You may begin whenever you have it."

Guy's brain was blank.

"I *have* given you a rhyme, Master Ferrier."

"Erm…"

"Is there a difficulty?"

Guy began to clean up the horse's hoof prior to re-shoeing it. Frantically he cudgelled his brain for a song that he had already composed which might do, with a little changing about of words. He decided on one of his nonsense songs.

"I once knew a cat who played on the fiddle,

With a hey and a ho and a hole in the middle.

That caused the cow Brantle, to fly to the moon,

And … um."

Adela laughed. A sharp disbelieving chuckle.

"And the milk from her udder ran out from a spoon."

Adela chuckled again and this time clapped her hands. "Brantle… how very clever, Master Farrier. A dance tune. Very good. But it doesn't really make sense."

"Well, if you will allow me to say it, the words you gave me were hardly... connected?"

"Ah, I see. I shall have to be more careful in my choices. Right." She looked at him cheekily. "Shall we try... something like, a valley, a broken heart, a violet and perhaps...?"

Again Guy was frantically trying to make a connection with the words as they tumbled from her mouth.

"A willow tree?"

"Hmmm...?"

Guy worked on the horse and, as he thought, the tune came to him first. He hummed it before he added the words.

"Oh, that is a sad tune..." said Adela.

"I think that it will be a sad song."

"Violet, valley, willow, broken heart."

"Down in the valley, where I chanced to wander,

I heard a sweet voice singing sadly and low.

'Oh where have you gone, my sweet heartsease, my violet?'

'Oh where I have gone to, you never shall know.'

Said a voice from the willows which leaned o'er the water.

'For I lie in the earth with a heart that is broken...'"

"Oh no, Master Ferrier, that is too sad," said Adela, interrupting. "Let us try another set of words."

"As you wish."

"Let us use... blacksmith, ladylove, forbidden and... heartache."

He looked up quickly. She stared at him unabashed, with her bright blue eyes. "What can you do with that?"

He cleared his throat.

"A blacksmith he courted me, twelve months or longer,

My heart it was won by his hammer in hand.

With his hammer in hand oh he looked mighty clever,

And I was his ladylove, my heart his forever." He stopped.

Adela's eyebrow went up. "You have not used all the words..."

"I haven't finished," said Guy.

"Forgive me."

"Our love was forbidden, our union unwitnessed.
He said he would marry but alas he's untrue.
Oh, witness have I none save our Lord Almighty
And may he reward him for loving another.
I once loved a blacksmith and he proved deceitful.
My heartache will kill me, I know not what to do."

Adela was silent, then, "I am sure you would not be so... untrue, Master Blacksmith," she said.

He gave a little bow, "It is but a song, mistress."

She took in a breath to give him more words but he turned his back with, "I must now make a lot of noise. You will not hear what I sing."

He began to fashion a horseshoe for the little grey palfrey and as he hammered, he sang a song he had made up over a year ago.

"Oh, the blacksmith's a fine and a tall, sturdy fellow!
Hard is his hand, but his heart's soft and mellow.
See him stand there, his huge bellows a-blowing,
With his strong brawny arms all muscled and bare.
See the fire in the furnace a-glowing with embers;
Bright is its sparkle and yellow its glare!"

The door to the forge opened a chink and a figure passed through letting in the cold air. Guy caught the movement in the corner of his eye. "Father Fabian? This is a surprise. Is there something I can do for you?"

Father Fabian's eye travelled from the figure of Guy working over his anvil, to the lady seated in the glow of the fire. "I wondered who had all the retainers outside. My Lady, forgive me..." He bowed low. "I did not realise it was you resting here."

"No matter, Father. The good farrier here was tending to my horse and as he works he has been singing for me. It has been most... illuminating."

"Ah... yes. I had heard he could sing. Songs of his own making. That's right, isn't it Farrier?"

"Ferrier."

"He is very adept," said Adela proudly.

"I have to say he is not the only one in the village who can compose poems... I..."

"You too can sing, Father Fabian? Oh not just the mass but..."

"Ah no. Alas I am not a composer of *songs*, merely poems." He bowed again, his hand on his heart, "Meaningless little things, I'm sure. But I have been known to trot them out, when the fancy takes me."

"Oh, do let us hear one now," said the Lady Adela, "I am in need of diversion today."

"Oh no... I could not possibly..." Father Fabian suddenly became bashful.

"Perhaps we could put the two of you together and have a competition..."

"Oh no!" said Guy, straightening from his work. "That must never be."

"Why not?" said Adela with a tinge of impudence. "It could be most amusing. I will adjudicate."

"Of course," said the priest, "I have the... erm... advantage of being able to write down my verses. I have no need to keep them all in my head." He looked very pleased with himself and flung Guy a supercilious look. "Perhaps my lady would like to read some?"

Adela's face suddenly became stony and hard. "Sir Priest, as you should know, that would not be possible. I should be unable to comprehend them," she said.

"Oh and why is that, my lovely lady?" He gave another slight bow.

"I cannot read, sir," she said with a suppressed irritation in her voice. "As I'm sure you know."

And suddenly Father Fabian knew he'd made a grave mistake.

CHAPTER FOUR ~ THE DOOR

Adela stared with unsuppressed annoyance at the priest. Guy looked from one to the other before bending once more to his work and, after a short pause for thought, Father Fabian cleared his throat. "Then my dear lady, I will read them *to* you. Let me know when I might call upon you... to..."

"I will think about it."

"What did you want to see me about, Father?" said Guy at last, to break the uncomfortable silence.

"See you?"

"I thought you might be needing my..."

"Oh yes. The hinge on the church south door."

"Ah. My Lord Lillebon tells me it has been a problem for a while."

"It can no longer hold the door. I fear it will fall off. It must be mended... and soon or there will be an accident."

"I will come and look at it this very forenoon, Father. It's true it's a very old door."

"Good." The priest shifted from foot to foot.

"Is there anything further?" said Adela Lillebon coldly.

"No... er... no..."

"Then we bid you good morning, Father."

Guy averted his eyes, for if he had looked at either of them, he would have laughed out loud. He continued his making of the horseshoe.

The priest disappeared, to be quickly followed by one of the attending men from the Lillebon estate, who squeezed through the door.

"Mistress... are we...?"

"No, we are not."

He fled.

Guy moved to the palfrey and began to gentle its nose in preparation for the shoeing.

"Are you finished with your singing, master blacksmith?" said Adela, all harshness gone from her voice. "Will you begin again?"

"For the moment, I think not," said Guy. "I never sing when I shoe a beast."

"Oh." Adela jumped down from her tree trunk. "Why is that?"

"It is *most* unlucky."

Her large blue eyes became rounder. "Oh, why?"

"If a farrier does not have his mind upon the horse he is shoeing and speaking softly to it—and of course, if he is singing he cannot— then the Devil may creep into the forge and frighten the beast."

"Oh..."

"Many's the smith who has been surprised by the Devil and kicked by the panicked horse he is tending. And we don't want that, now do we?"

"In broad daylight, Master Ferrier? The Devil?"

"Oh Lady Adela... you have no idea." His face was perfectly straight and serious. "The Devil is all around us... always. Does not the church tell us this?"

Lady Adela was unsure. She scrutinised his face for the smallest inkling of a jest and then said, "I will wait outside then."

Guy bowed and turned back to the palfrey.

"Well my lass..." said Guy. "We shall have you rideworthy in the blink of an eye."

"I beg your pardon?"

"Ah... er... No mistress, my lady, the horse."

"Ah yes." Adela looked around the forge as if she was searching for the Devil. "Thank you for your songs, Master Ferrier."

"It was my pleasure."

The door closed and Guy chuckled.

"St Dunstan, as the story goes,

Once pull'd the devil by the nose,

With red-hot tongs, which made him roar,

That he was heard three miles or more", he sang.

This song was delivered at a whisper and with another chuckle to finish.

Adela walked about the roadway outside, kicking up pebbles. Her retainers watched closely and the boldest of them offered her his cloak to sit upon. She waved him away with her hand. Another gave her own cloak to her and she allowed him to wrap it around her shoulders.

She walked to the river fifty paces away and stared into the depths.

How dare the priest make a fool of her before the blacksmith. The new priest might be a good looking fellow but the blacksmith was just as handsome and more... well... genial. And the priest was, just that—a priest—holy.

She looked back at the forge building. Oh for someone... amiable in my life. Fun and outspoken. Someone who will not hang upon my every word and do my tiniest bidding or fawn upon me. Oh for someone with whom I can converse and laugh.

Guy came out of the forge door leading her horse and she picked her way through the riverside grass towards him.

"We are ready, mistress," said her father's groom. "We can be on our way."

"Thank you Master Blacksmith," she said. "Perhaps we can converse again soon. Send your reckoning to my father."

But she knew that unless she could contrive to come to the forge, it was not going to be possible to see him again. Everywhere she went she was accompanied. Everywhere, she was watched. If it were not the fact that her maidservant had a head cold that day and was unwell, she would have accompanied her. Adela sighed, then perked up. Ah... did she not just hear the priest say that the church door was in need of work? And that the blacksmith was to be there later? Could she slip out of the manor and across the road to the church?

"I have changed my mind, John. I will not ride out. It's too cold. We shall return home."

There were a few groans from the rest of the retainers who, no doubt, had been looking forward to riding the horses out across the downs that morning.

"You must go to the church as you promised, Master Guy," she said, "to make good the hinges."

"I will. I always keep my promises, my lady," said Guy.

She nodded, mounted her horse and rode back the way she had come.

*****

Guy watched her go with a heavy heart. He had somehow picked up the feeling of her own sadness. She seemed lonely and listless. He knew what loneliness felt like.

Parnell's words came back to him. "You know that you cannot marry her. You know she is too far above you."

He knew this to be an immutable truth—and yet—his heart pounded when he saw her. His mouth became dry, his usual calm confidence deserted him when she spoke to him. Why had she spoken to *him*? She'd no need to converse with him whilst she waited. She could easily have walked back to the manor and waited there.

Ah... of course, she had wanted him to sing for her. Many people, it seemed, were in awe of his ability to sing and to compose songs on the hoof, so to speak. She was just the same. To Adela he was merely a curiosity. There was nothing in it. It was nothing.

He mentally shrugged and went back into his forge to finish the pitchfork for Master Brewer.

Not long after this, he covered his fire, shut his forge gates and, tossing his bag of tools over his back, he strode along the lane to the church of Christ.

The sun had at last warmed the air and the slight frost had turned to dewy droplets on the grass. His feet crunched on the gravel path. Nodding respectfully to the plot where lay his father, mother, and three sisters, and crossing his breast, Guy entered the ancient building's newly built porch and stopped to inspect the outside face of the inner door.

His calloused hands grasped the edge of the wood and he pushed it open more fully, for it had not been latched. The sunlight caught the blackened metal decoration of the door hinges which made the most awful, long drawn out squeal as it moved.

This was an ancient door. Upon it in metalwork were patterns, some of them hardly decipherable now, of people and animals. Guy thought he could make out a pig and a sheep. Some said that the door had once borne images of the Bible story of the flood of Noah, though it was hard to work out now. Many pieces had rusted and fallen off. Guy worked the decorations with his fingernails just to see which pieces were secure. He bent to look at the bottom hinge. The part known as the knuckle where the pin entered was rusted.

Suddenly there was the sound of a rush of soft cloth. Guy jumped up in alarm.

"Master Ferrier. You startled me."

"And you, me, mistress... my lady."

She carried on quickly, "I came to the church to pray and..." She gestured to the dark interior.

"Ah yes. You are not riding today."

"No. I... I... changed my mind. It's too cold."

"Erm and I..."

"Have come to look at the door hinges as you promised?" She smiled sweetly.

Guy took hold of the door once more and gave it a slight wriggle. "Ah ... Father Fabian is correct. The rusting of the hinge has made the door unsafe."

"What must you do with it?"

"Take it off and make a new piece here..." He bent to look more carefully. "In fact there is little point in making a new piece and joining it to old, for the whole thing is rusted and will soon become useless."

"And you can tell by looking at it..."

"Even you, mistress, would be able to tell that the hinges are past their useful lives."

"Show me."

He rummaged in his leather bag for a sharp file and attempted to release the hinges from the wood. That part was easy for they almost crumbled to dust. He scrabbled in his bag for a piece of metal.

"What are you looking for?" Adela leaned over him, too close for Guy's comfort.

"A fulcrum..."

"A what?"

"Something with which I can lever the bottom of the door."

He supposed something like this was far beyond the knowledge of a lady as much as the intricacies of embroidery would be beyond him.

Lifting the door slightly he forced the metal piece under the door edge. Then he rolled up his sleeves to his armpits and spitting on his hands he took the door in both, winding his brawny arms around the wood.

"I may not accomplish this alone. I may need help, for the door is solid oak and very heavy."

"Oh, surely..."

Suddenly Guy felt a little embarrassed. Why did he begin this? It was not going to work. Surely he would be embarrassed by failure—too late now.

He leaned back and put his foot to the metal bar under the door rim. Taking a deep breath, he pushed down on the lever and lifted at the same time, gritting his teeth and grimacing as he set his cheek to the door. The muscles of his upper arms argued with him, 'We can't do this. It's too heavy.'

'You will,' he said to himself. 'You cannot fail before your lord's daughter.'

The door suddenly shifted and Guy shifted with it. "Stand back," he growled and staggered with the effort of holding it. Teetering under the weight he lifted the door from its hinges and quickly set it down on edge on the flagstones. Then he walked it, edge to edge to the wall of the church's south side. The sweat stood out on his brow and his arms would have ached with the effort were he not a brawny fellow.

One of the three hinges broke completely and landed on the flagstones of the porch with a tinny jingle. A second was so loosened that it came away with the door. The middle hinge was all that had been keeping the door upright. Without its pin, it had come loose easily. Now, it too was broken.

Guy bent double to regain his breath, for his lungs had been at full capacity bracing his broad chest, helping his arms to lift.

"Oh Master Ferrier, that was…"

"Foolish, I think," said Guy quickly, "for had the door toppled, it would have crushed you, or me, like a… like a… as flat as a…"

"Flat cake," said Adela, laughing.

"Aye… a flat cake," Guy joined her laughter.

They watched each other's amusement for a moment.

"Oh master blacksmith, you must compose a song about a door which was so heavy that it flattened a lover and his lass."

Guy turned quickly so that she could not see his face. "Well, it looks as if we shall need three new hinges here."

"And you must go to your forge to make them?"

"I must."

Guy was mentally measuring the size of the hinges in order to copy them. He bent and stretched out his hand to pick up the broken one which had landed on the flagstones. Adela too had reached for it and their fingers met on the cold stone floor.

Lady Lillebon's small fingers were uppermost and did not allow Guy's large blackened digits to pull away at once. After a heartbeat his fingers closed over the rusted metal and he stood.

"Mind the door. Don't come near. It may fall. I must go and make good the metal work." He reached for his leather tool bag.

"Master Ferrier…" Adela took in a sharp breath. She was desperate to keep him at the church door. "Tell me… what do you think is on the door… the decoration? I cannot make it out."

"Please do not get too close."

"I promise." She pointed, "Here for example."

Guy screwed up his eyes the better to see the patterns. "I think that looks to me like some kind of bird."

"Oh yes, a bird. Indeed." Adela pointed again, "And here, I think this looks like a tree with apples."

"With more birds in it."

"And here, is this Noah and his wife?"

"Yes, I think it might be."

There was a little silence as two pairs of eyes raked the patterns on the door for further recognisable images.

"And here see, here is a place where there has been some metal decoration, but it has gone.

"Ah yes."

"It looks as if the door has lost a four legged beast. How odd that I have never before looked at this door in detail. It's amazing," said Adela in wonder.

"It is amazing," said Guy, looking directly at Adela Lillebon.

"Oh, Master Ferrier, do you think you could make the missing pieces?"

"The… missing…?"

"The metal decorations which have fallen off. Someone in the village might remember what was on the door."

"If I had the time, I suppose I might."

"I will see if I can find out anything," said Adela, "and I can let you know."

Her heart said, 'Anything... anything to be in your company again.'

And Guy's heart sang, 'Anything, mistress, to spend more time with you.'

But they said not a word to each other.

*****

Emma of Milton was the raven haired daughter of the steward to the Lord Lillebon. The Lord owned many manors up and down the south of England and she usually stayed at the main manor of Milton a few miles away but now and again she accompanied the Lord Walter and his steward to the village. The poor girl was as thin as a reed and as flat chested as a page and not particularly attractive, suffering, sadly, from poor skin, but she made up for it by being quick-witted and some might say amusing—to others she appeared simply scornful—and to some, downright mean tongued.

One such was Parnell Truman. "What is she doing here?"

"She has come with her father on manor business," said Guy repeating the gossip he'd heard around the village.

"He doesn't need her here for 'manor business', does he?" said Nell.

"He can't arrange a marriage for her if she is not with him, now can he?"

Nell put a jug of milk onto Guy's table. "Your milk."

"Thank you."

"Marriage? Of course he can. It will have nothing to do with the girl and everything to do with her parents and those of her espoused."

"And do you happen to know who her espoused is?"

Nell gave Guy an 'I am completely innocent, I know nothing' look.

"Come on. I know you know."

"Master Blacksmith, you weren't thinking of offering for the girl yourself, were you?"

"Certainly not."

"She comes with a pretty parcel of land and a good dowry."

"That's all that is pretty about her."

"Hah! The girl cannot help her looks."

'That's rich coming from you,' thought Guy silently. 'You who have disparaged her many times for her face.'

"No, but she can certainly help her nature."

Nell slowly walked round the table in Guy's small cottage. "Ah. You too have fallen foul of her spiteful tongue eh?"

"No, not me. I don't think she'd dare, but…"

"But?"

"I have heard what she's said about you." He turned away and began to wipe his wooden breakfast bowl, until it shone.

"Me?"

"But of course, I don't agree with a word of it."

"What did she say?"

"Oh no, I couldn't possibly tell you. And now, if you will allow, I must be off to work."

"Guy!"

The blacksmith put down his dish, grinned and exited the cottage.

Parnell Truman followed. "What is she saying about *me*?"

As Guy entered the forge, he said, "I do believe the words, maid… and… old… were mentioned… and now what was it…? Ah yes." Guy reached for his leather apron and tied it around his waist.

"All girls of eighteen think a woman of twenty one is old."

"Halfwit… and I do believe the words, 'too pretty to be real', came out of her mouth."

Nell half closed her eyes. "Why was she speaking to you…about me?"

"Oh, goodness me, no. She wouldn't speak to the likes of me. I am far too lowly." Guy didn't tell Nell that the girl had often made a play for him and he'd ignored her. "As you know I have been working on the church door and I caught the tail end of a conversation in the church."

"To whom was she speaking?"

"I believe it was the Lady Adela."

"Oh!"

"Now I have a pot to fabricate... so if you'll give me some room?"

Nell didn't move but stared into space.

"Mind the sparks..." Guy gave a puff on his bellows as he rekindled his forge fire.

"Ooh!" Nell jumped.

Guy chuckled.

She walked a few paces away. "So do you want to know who she is to be married to, or don't you?"

"The last I heard, Steward Masters was in talks with someone in town."

"Devizes... or Marlborough?"

"Marlborough."

"Then you have heard correctly."

Guy began a new song. And Parnell, vowing to save the news until he'd finished, listened to his tune.

"In the winter's cold, in the summer heat,

You may hear the constant, ringing beat,

With which he swings his hammer;

He thumps when the iron's hot, all day;

He finishes work and he's off to play;

He thinks that thing he cannot say.

Then hey ! and ho ! for the cheery clamour,

Of the busy blacksmith's mighty hammer."

"A new one?" asked Nell.

"This morning's offering."

"Can you sing of nothing but blacksmithing? It gets rather tedious," said Nell quietly with rising eyebrows.

Guy pulsed his bellows again. "Alright." He fed the fire with a few twigs and as they crackled and spat, he began to sing.

"There was a girl lived in the town.
She dressed herself in a silken gown.
With a bow and a knife all by her side,
To her lover's house, where he did bide,
To her true love's house she did ride."

"Ah..." said Nell, "That sounds much more interesting. Is it one of those where the girl gets to... erm... kill the ungrateful lover? I do hope so."

"You will not know. Until you tell me the name of the man Emma Masters will marry, I'll not sing the next verse."

Nell chuckled. "Poor man... it's..." But before she could utter the man's name, there was a commotion at the door.

Tom Kennett came bowling into the forge, stumbling and almost falling, his face a picture of horror. "Guy! Guy! Quickly, I need your help... it's Alys... she's had an accident!"

*****

Nell and Guy flew from the forge and being Guy's nearest neighbours they ran the short distance to the cottage where Tom and his wife lived.

Alys was sitting on a stool, cradling her arm and alternately screaming and moaning, rocking back and forth.

Tom grabbed her by the shoulder as he almost fell through the door and she screamed louder.

"What?" yelled Guy, throwing his hands out beside him in a gesture of bewilderment.

"Her arm... her arm, she has burned it badly," screamed Tom.

Without further ado, Guy picked Alys up; she was as pliant as if she were unconscious, and ran back with her to the forge.

Nell trailed him shouting, "What do you mean to do? What's happening? How can I help?"

Guy burst through the forge doors and immediately took Alys' arm and plunged it into his stone water trough. He held her close to him, until she stopped moaning.

Then she started to tremble.

"My cloak Nell! Quickly."

Nell almost ripped the cloak from its peg and wrapped it around the stricken girl.

"Now in my house... look and you will find a small wooden pot. I think I left it by my bed. Bring it here. Swiftly."

Without a word, Parnell ran through the back door.

Although Alys had ceased to shiver and moan, she was on the point of fainting.

"No, no Alys. You must stay awake," said Guy in an authoritarian tone. "And we must keep your arm in the cold water for a while yet."

Tom took over and supported his wife on a stool, holding her arm in the cold water. Tears had stained his face and he too was trembling.

"It's alright. We have acted quickly. I promise things will be alright," said Guy with authority.

He leaned over the water trough and peered into the depths. He could see Alys' lower arm lifeless and floating in the water, a pale shadow with a long red streak. The sleeve of her cotte was in tatters.

A pot was put into his hand.

"Thank you Nell. Now if you will, I have some rags in a basket on a shelf by the door. Can you bring them? Oh and some honey... I have the honey you left me the other day; it's by my milk jug, in the blue pot."

Parnell nodded and ran to do his bidding.

Both Alys and Tom were breathing quickly and Guy did his best to reassure them.

"We all need to take deep breaths... it's the shock you see. Deep breaths. One, breathe in, two, breathe out..."

Alys had now begun to cry silently.

Tom folded his arms more securely around his wife's body. "Now, now. Guy will know what to do... he has had more burns than..."

"Aye I have. I've got the scars to prove it and nothing has killed me off yet!"

Guy was dipping his hands into the trough, stirring up the water over Alys' arm. "Whatever happened?"

Tom wiped his nose on his sleeve. "Alys has been feeling bad this week. Nauseous and weak. Then yesterday she had a fainting fit. It was the same today, only today... she did not fall onto the floor..."

"She fell into the fire?"

"I heard her screaming. Thank God and all his saints that I was out the back and not working today."

"My sleeve... it caught fire and I could not put it out," said Alys in a stuttering voice.

Guy caught hold of her other hand to find that there were burns there also, where she had tried to pat out the flames. That too he thrust into the water.

Tom crooned sweet words to his wife and began to rock her back and forth in his arms.

At last Nell returned.

"Can you wet some cloths, Nell?"

"Surely."

"Do not wring them out. They need to be very wet and cold."

Guy took the blue honey pot from her hand and mixing the clear liquid of the unguent with the honey, he smothered it over the remaining dry cloth.

"Right, now we shall lift your hand and I will take a look."

Alys nodded, sniffing.

Slowly Guy lifted Alys' arm from the water trough. The skin was red and blistered and some of the wound was black where the cloth of the girl's sleeve had stuck to the injury.

"Keep bathing it with the wet cloth. Keep it moist and cold."

Parnell plunged her hand into the water and a strange metallic smell rose from the trough.

Guy held the trembling woman's hand still and Parnell continued to press the cloth to the wound. "How does it feel now?"

"It hurts... oh it hurts," snuffled the injured woman, "But... but it is feeling a little better,"

"I told you it was wise to go for Guy," smiled his friend.

"Tell me when it hurts much less," said Guy, hovering over them with his mixture of unguent and honey. "This is the best remedy I know for a burn. The special unguent is good at saving the skin and the honey keeps all the impurities away."

He pulled up his own sleeve. "See here, this was a wound much worse... ten times worse than yours, Alys, and now look. Six months ago this looked as if I would lose my hand." The scar was a puckered white mark about four inches long.

He winked at Parnell, who smiled back.

A little while later Alys sat up straight and said that she felt much better and stronger.

"Now is the time for a little ale, I think," said Guy and Nell found his flask and a horn cup to pour it into for Alys.

"I will gently push this onto your wound, Alys, and it must stay there for a while."

She took her lips in her teeth and nodded.

Gently Guy took the cloth with the honey and carefully laid it over the six inch burn on Alys' forearm. "Now let me look at the hand."

Alys stretched out her other arm.

"Ah this is much less serious. I can smear the unguent directly onto the burn. It's naught but a blister or two."

Alys smiled for the first time, "Thank you Master Ferrier."

"The water in my trough is very special. It has marvellous healing properties."

"Ah yes, I know that you cured Alain's warts with it not long ago," said Tom. Alain was his young brother-in-law.

"I did."

Alys' breathing had now settled and she was looking much better.

"You must be careful Alys," said Nell. "Faintness is not good. You must go and see Goodwoman Little. She will make sure you are alright. I have no doubt it is something very simple which will pass but you should make sure all is well."

Alys whispered something but no one could quite hear what she said.

Tom lifted her from her seat.

"Let's go home now."

"Take the pot Tom, keep the wound cool and put this on every so often. It will save her skin."

"Should she cover it?" asked Parnell.

"No, it's best left to the air. But it must be kept clean."

Between them Tom and Nell got the young woman out of the forge door and into her home.

"Wait for me," said Nell, looking back as she left.

*****

Guy did not wait for Nell. He had work to do; he was never short of work, for he was the only blacksmith for miles and idle hands would mean a backlog of jobs.

Once more he took up the new pot which he had been crafting for the Widow Poulter and began to fashion the sides.

A little while later Nell appeared in his vision. He had not heard her come in.

"How is Alys?" he asked.

"Singing your praises."

"Why did she not know to put her hand immediately into water? I would have thought… it's common sense."

"You know Alys… she is…"

Guy stopped tapping, "… as a barrel short of a few apples…?"

"And that's not being cruel."

"Her own husband calls her as dim as a halfpenny candle."

Nell laughed through her nose. "That was very well done, Guy. Thank you."

"I only did what I would do... and have done... for myself."

"Will it scar, do you think?"

"Undoubtedly. But I wasn't going to tell her that."

Nell put her palm on the back of his hand, "You are the kindest of men. And the cleverest."

"That is something coming from you. You who are usually scolding me."

Nell looked offended.

"For what it's worth, I think the same of you. Kind and clever," he said.

"Aw... no... I would have panicked. But you... you took control and none of us felt that the situation was beyond your direction."

Guy smiled and went back to tapping his pot. Nell, as was her habit, wandered around the forge.

"What's this?" She held up a piece of metal about seven inches long. "If I didn't know better, I'd say it was a dog."

"It is a dog. Or it will be."

She looked perplexed.

"It's for the church door. The metal work..."

"I thought you'd mended it. The hinges."

"I have but..."

"Oh, I see... the decorations which splay out from the... whatever it's called...'"

"The knuckle. The round piece where goes the pintle. Then there's the leaf."

"The flat part which goes onto the face of the door?"

"Yes."

"So why are you making a dog?"

"It's a very ancient door and you know that there are several animals decorating the outer face? Quite a few are missing and I am replacing them."

"Oh... have you the time for such foolish things?"

"In my spare time."

"Has Father Fabian asked you to make them?"

"No." Guy tittered. "I doubt the man even knows the door represents the story of Noah."

"Then why are you doing it?"

"Can I not do something... frivolous, if I wish? Do you not make things because you want to?"

"So you are doing it for the glory of God?"

Guy felt himself blushing as he said, "I suppose so."

Nell watched him carefully. "Ah no... there's more to this... than meets the..."

"So, you were about to tell me who Mistress Masters is to marry."

"Don't change the subject." Nell gloated. "I know who has asked you to do this. It's Lady Lillebon...Adela."

"It might have been."

Guy began to make up the second verse of the song he had begun that morning.

"I once loved a lad and I loved him so grand,

Broad was his back and strong was his hand.

But faithless his heart as so it did prove,

And now he's rewarded me well for my love,

He's gone to be wed to another..."

"Guy, you do not have to..."

Guy sang louder.

"I watched as my love did to the church go

And I followed him on with a heart full of woe..."

"Guy... I hate to see you torment yourself over her."

The blacksmith put down his hammer. "Nell... it's none of your business, I'm sure. I am a free man and you are not my wife to lecture me so."

Parnell's eyes filled with tears. "No. No. But I cannot see you be hurt."

"I will not. Now, you must have work to do?"

She left dry eyed and angry.

CHAPTER FIVE ~ SIR GUISCARD

Almost as soon as the words left his lips, he knew he should not have spoken so, and a heartbeat later he was out of his forge door looking for Nell, but she had disappeared in the small stand of trees between the forge and Tom's house.

He went back to his workshop and took out his frustration on the Widow Poulter's pot.

The morning was not quite over when he had yet another visitor. The doors were open and a slight figure rounded the doorpost as if it was trying not to be seen. It squirmed along the wall and stood before him.

"Mistress Marjorie?"

"Master Ferrier."

The girl shifted from foot to foot and periodically gave a nervous glance out of the door at the roadway. "I have come from my mistress," she said at a whisper.

"Ah." Ferrier tried not to flush but all the same his face grew hot. He turned back to his work so she might not see. "What can I do for her?"

"Lady Adela says she has found some drawings of the door and wants you to meet her after vespers at the church, so she can..." The girl looked down quickly, "...show you what she's got." She sniffed.

"Ah…" he said again.

"So that you can better make the little metal figures. Does this make sense to you? Because it doesn't make any sense to me. And when I asked her she said it was nothing to do with me… and I was to mind my own business."

Guy went to his bellows and pulled down the wooden handle which worked it. This noise and action, he hoped would cover his embarrassed confusion.

"Yes… it does… make sense. Tell her I will be there. After vespers."

He watched her go, as she walked towards the manor house and her mistress who waited at their gate. Guy leaned out of the door and could just make out the figure of Adela in a blue kirtle, clap her hands once and look in the direction of the forge. He ducked in quickly. He wasn't going to allow her to see him.

All afternoon he could think of nothing but the church door and its decorations and the designs which Adela must have somehow retrieved. He found himself staring into space, imagining what might happen in the church porch after vespers.

Late afternoon he was still periodically staring at nothing through the forge door when another figure came forward out of the sunlight and into his vision.

"Master Blacksmith?"

"Hmmm."

Guy's eyes focussed on a well-dressed young man, who was leading a horse by the rein.

"Tell me, is this the village of Kennett? East Kennett. We seem to have lost our way."

"It is sir. This is East Kennett. Mine is the first building in the village."

"Ah. I've walked a long way; this horse is lame and I have no idea what is wrong with him."

"Bring him in and I will have a look at him."

Guy wandered into the afternoon sunshine to find a further four, horsed and wealthy young men milling about in the wake of this obviously well to do one with the lame gelding.

"The manor is over there isn't it?" asked one of them, staring down his nose at Guy.

"Just past that stand of trees, on the left, sir."

"Guiscard, shall we go on ahead? Let them know we are here?" asked the first man.

"No, you stay here with Charlemagne and I will go on with the lads. Come when he's mended."

The men rode off in the direction of the manor house gate and Guy was left with what seemed to him to be the friend or trusted servant of the man called Guiscard.

"A long way, you say?"

"We have come from the other side of Newbury. From a place called Thatcham. I... we... are in the mesnie of Sir Guiscard Courtenay."

"His horse?"

"I walked with it, he rode mine. It began to limp a few miles back."

Guy began to look over the horse. It tossed its head a few times and showed displeasure when it was touched upon the right gaskin.

"You have ridden hard today?"

"All day. We set off at dawn wanting to make Kennett by dusk." The distance was almost thirty miles.

"And you have done it by riding an injured horse into further injury," said Guy baldly; he knew he did not dare be too reproachful. These people were far above him in status.

"That's Guiscard all over!"

"Hmmm."

The man came closer. "Henri Courtenay. Guiscard's cousin."

Guy gave a bow. "Guy Ferrier, blacksmith."

The young man smiled.

"There is nothing I can do for the beast and I have no stabling here. He has a muscular problem here. It has nothing to do with his hooves or shoes. Best you get him to the stables at the manor. The grooms will look to him."

"Aye, no doubt they'll know what to do."

The man turned the limping horse in a circle meaning to go out into the air. But the horse was fretful.

Guy put a calming hand on the horse's nose and spoke under his breath in his ear.

"We heard, though, in the town, that you are a veritable magician with horses," said Henri with a sardonic smile.

"They exaggerate. Because I'm a farrier, they seem to think I know everything there is to know about horses."

"Ah..."

"And when I am shoeing, well, yes... I do... but otherwise..."

The man chuckled. "But you ran your hand along his leg and knew immediately what was wrong. That's not knowing?"

"I was lucky. Best you take him to Kennett Manor."

"Well it's there we are headed anyway."

Suddenly Guy heard the bell ringing for vespers.

"Excuse me, sir. I am called to church."

Guy plunged his hands into the trough of water and ran them through his hair. He had time to roll down his sleeves before the man had accomplished the horse's turn.

He pulled off his apron, tidied his clothes and shut the door of the forge behind him. Then he made off in the direction of the church.

His pace was swift and he caught up with the young man who was leading Charlemagne.

"Have you never been to this part of the country before, sir?"

"No. None of us have. Except Guiscard. We are simply visiting."

"Are the Lillebons family to your lord?"

"Ah, no. But if all is well, they soon will be."

Guy had reached the end of the lane where stood the church lychgate, Master Truman's house and the gate to the manor of East Kennett.

"Your way lies there, sir," he said. "Good afternoon."

The man was still speaking and his words rode over Guy's parting farewell, "Our lord is to marry the Lady Adela Lillebon."

Guy's heart plummeted to his boots.

"Marry?"

"Aye, if the reckonings can be achieved and agreements over dowry and such like organised, they will be married by the spring."

Guy's mouth was suddenly dry. "Does the Lady Adela know that her father has espoused her to Sir... ?"

"But of course, they have been betrothed since they were young."

"Does she know that he is coming to Kennett today?"

"Ah, no. That was to be a bit of a surprise," said Henri with a suggestive grin. "We all know how the ladies love a surprise." And he walked the horse through the manor gates.

"Perhaps not this one," said Guy to himself.

*****

All through the service, Guy's mind was fixed upon the young man who had looked down his nose at him from his horse, Guiscard Courtenay. He'd only had a very brief glimpse of him but what he remembered he had to say to himself, he did not like.

A short man with short cropped blond hair and a short beard—everything about him was ungenerous—sharp angular bones, not particularly regular nor fine featured but imperious and arrogant; narrow eyes, which reminded Guy of the little reptiles to be found in the pond behind his house. He began to see the man as a quick-legged lizard, scuttling to hide under rocks. That made him chuckle under his breath and his neighbour, standing in the nave of the church, looked at him with puzzlement.

Guy gazed around. The man Courtenay and his cronies were not in the church and neither was his lord, Walter Lillebon, but Adela was at the front with her maidservant and household. She fidgeted with something in her hand and Guy noticed it was a rolled piece of parchment. No doubt the drawings he should look at after the service. He closed his eyes; the end of the Latin could not come quickly enough.

At last the priest gave them the blessing and it was all over. Folk began to shuffle out, following Father Fabian to the outer door. As was his custom, Fabian turned at the porch and spoke with every member of his congregation as they left, particularly the younger women.

Adela smiled but was cold. Parnell gave him barely a thank you. Alys simpered. The Widow Poulter, who was but six and twenty, walked away with him down the gravel path and engaged him in talk about her eldest child.

When would they all leave? It was growing darker.

Adela doubled back into the church and with a nod to Master Truman, Guy walked purposefully round the building and disappeared. He leaned against the flinty wall, waited and sighed, his eyes closed for a moment.

When he opened them they'd unwittingly fixed themselves upon the plot in the graveyard where lay his family. A vision of his father and mother came into his head. What would they think of him? His three younger sisters? How would they see his actions?

Peering around the edge of the wall, Guy saw that the priest had gone and he scuttled for the porch.

Adela was there alone. "I did not think you were coming."

"I said I would. I keep my promises, my lady."

Adela looked past him. "We are alone now?"

"I... I think so..." he looked around for the maidservant.

"No, no Marjorie has gone home. I dismissed her. She is still a little unwell."

"Then yes, we are alone. The priest may be in the church but..."

"No, I watched him go to his home with a woman."

"Ah."

Adela pressed the parchment up against his chest. "I have some drawings of the pieces which are missing from the door."

Guy's brow furrowed. "How can you..."

"My father has a chest full of documents and when I was a child I used to look through them. I noticed that one of them was a page full of little drawings of animals. It wasn't until today that I realised that they were the drawings of the church door made by someone many years ago, perhaps when the door was fitted."

"Over two hundred years ago?"

"My father keeps all sorts of strange things in that chest. Things to do with the estate and village."

"Ah." He took the parchment from her.

Stretching it out, he compared the drawings, made in faded ink, with the ironwork of the door. The parchment showed the complete complex pattern of the decorations and Guy realised just how many parts were missing.

"Ah this will be really useful."

"I must put it back... soon."

"Let me commit the pattern to memory and then you may have it."

Guy sat on the porch coffin seat. "Curlicues here..." he mused.

"What are those?" asked Adela.

"Curls. See here." Guy stretched out his hand and traced a pattern on the church door. "And in this one is... or was, a boar." He pointed to the parchment.

"And there," Adela sat beside him. "Is a goose," she said with a quietly suppressed laugh. "And this, is it a badger?"

"Aye."

"What's this?"

"Erm... a strange animal. With a long nose?" Guy shifted the parchment this way and that. "Or two tails, I don't know."

"That's definitely a cat."

"And that's a sheep. That one is still there."

"Without a doubt," she laughed.

Their thighs were touching, their shoulders were close together. Guy jumped up.

"Here, my lady, I think I have it in my head now. The pattern.

Return it to your father's chest."

She reached out and grasped the parchment and their fingers met. And stayed there.

"Master Ferrier."

"Yes, Lady Adela?"

Her face came close to his. "You will need to come down here periodically to fix the animals to the door, won't you?" Her face came nearer.

"I will... certainly, yes."

"It will take some time to complete, will it not?"

"Yes. I have no doubt... it will take months to..."

Their noses were almost touching.

"I will come to see how things are progressing..." Her voice slowed to nothing.

"What is progressing, my little angel?" said a sharp voice.

Guy and Adela guiltily sprang apart.

Guiscard Courtenay stood with his hands to his hips and looked from one to the other. "What is progressing?"

Guy bowed.

Guiscard ignored him and reached for the parchment. "What's this then?"

"The blacksmith is attempting to replace the patterns on the door of the church, Guiscard," said Adela adroitly removing herself from close proximity to them both.

"Is he now?"

"The ironwork has perished. And he has been drawing the pieces that are missing."

Guiscard took the parchment in his hands, stretched it out and scrutinised it.

"How very clever."

"He *is* very clever," said Adela and at the very moment the words were out of her mouth, she desperately wished she'd not said them.

Guiscard gave the parchment back to Guy.

"Well, he had better get on with it then." The man did not smile.

Adela lowered her eyes.

Guy bowed again and left. As he walked away, the parchment clutched in his hands, he heard Guiscard Courtenay say, "And why must you help him in his task, my little angel? Are you suddenly become a blacksmith?"

Adela took hold of her betrothed's arm and steered him away. "Oh it's just that he was unsure about the animals which were once on the door. I was the one who noticed they were missing so… we were trying to identify them."

"A case of two heads being better than one, eh?"

Adela gave a good impression of innocence, Guy realised. "We were just working out which were which."

"Hmmm."

Guy looked back. He didn't think Sir Guiscard was convinced at all. Not at all.

*****

What was he to do? He had to get the parchment back to Adela's father's chest. If he was found with it, he was sure he would be accused of stealing it. He searched the forge for somewhere to hide it and decided the best place was underneath his anvil. No one was going to move that. He folded the parchment in two, lifted the edge of his anvil and slid it underneath the flat end. Then with a mind which was troubled and thoughts which were fragmented, he went back to the Widow Poulter's pot, in the semi-darkness.

At last it was finished and he blew out his lamps, covered his fire and went home.

His house was but a few paces from his forge, a one roomed affair with a steep thatch, cruck walls and a bottom plate of sarsen stone.

He ducked under the door and was immediately struck upon the back of the head.

Woozy, Guy fell to his knees and someone pushed him, fully onto the floor and stayed him there with a booted foot.

"Well, Master Blacksmith Ferrier. I believe your name is Guy. How are we this evening?"

Guy realised that there were others present in his house and although his vision was a little distorted, he managed to see a man in a blue cotte, standing a little way away from him.

The man above him was wearing red.

"Cousin, that's enough, surely. There's no need to brain the man." This was Henri's voice. The voice of reason, Guy decided.

Guy was a strong man, well able to take care of himself, but he often found it wise to feign fear and weakness. He pushed himself onto his knees. His attacker stepped back.

"What can I do for you, Sir Guiscard?"

"It's more a matter of what you must not do, farrier. For me."

"And what is that, sir?"

The man walked around him and slowly Guy rose from his knees, unfolding his bulk and height with deliberateness.

Guiscard Courtenay was a little rattled but looked around his compatriots for backing. They moved in closer to him.

"The little maidservant…"

"Marjorie?"

"Says that you and my affianced, the Lady Adela, have become quite friendly lately…" He shook his head and tutted.

"That is because, as she told you, we have been trying to restore the church door."

Guiscard's fist bunched as if he would strike but thought better of it. He judged Guy's midriff too hard for his admonishment. He picked up the fire poker.

"Did I ask you to speak, Farrier?"

He struck. Guy side stepped and cannoned into one of the other men who fell to the floor. Quickly Guy reached the cottage wall and set his back there. Now they were all in front of him.

"You will leave her alone. You will never meet her again, do you understand?"

Again the poker came swishing for his ribs but Guy was too quick and he caught it in his large hand and held it.

Guiscard was now furious and was forced to let go. Guy held onto the poker.

"Hold him!" yelled Guiscard. Only two out of the three men moved. Henri Courtenay stepped up to Guy and turned to face his cousin putting himself in between them.

"Leave him, Guiscard. He's had his warning."

"I want to leave him with a warning he will not forget in a hurry."

Guy stood up straight and fended off the two knights who were a little the worse for drink.

"Come Guiscard. We are missing valuable drinking time." Henri, who was the most sober of them all, threw a sidelong look at Guy, "I'm bored with this."

Guiscard was as tight as a boiled owl!

Guy, towering above them, gave Henri a nod and turned to the main man.

"I am sorry if I have offended you, sir. I really didn't mean to be so... annoying." He smiled a feral smile, "I will do nothing further to irritate you. I promise." He put down the poker.

"Come on Gus... we are all a bit drunk," said another of the men. "He isn't worth it."

He was busily sizing up the muscles on Guy's upper arms and deciding that it wasn't worth a pummelling.

Guiscard Courtenay wiped his mouth and grinned.

"Watch your step, blacksmith!"

"I always do, sir."

Guy's opponent growled again. "Mend your blessed door yourself and leave my Adela alone."

Guy bowed.

Sir Guiscard Courtenay spat at him.

It took all Guy's willpower not to retaliate as the gobbet of spit ran down his cheek. He merely turned his back to open the outer door for them to exit. It was not a wise move. Before Guy knew it, Guiscard had retrieved the poker and swiped hard for Guy's ribs.

There was a dull cracking sound inside Guy's chest; his breath was driven from him, he stumbled.

Then he watched helplessly as three out of the five men ransacked his home, breaking, destroying and disordering. There was no steadying influence now; Henri had left.

Parnell found Guy at the hour of compline, staring into space, huddled into a corner of his house.

"I thought something was wrong. There was no light in your house when I passed."

"Why were you passing?"

"You always have light in the house in the evening."

She took in the disarray.

"Oh Guy... what have you done?"

CHAPTER SIX ~ THE HARE

Parnell raised Guy from the floor and found a stool which still had all its legs. Sitting him down, she looked round for a beaker which had escaped the breakages. Guy thankfully sipped water from it.

"I suppose this is Courtenay's work?"

"Guiscard Courtenay and his cronies. All but one."

"He's a foul man. I have no idea why our lord has chosen him to marry Lady Adela. He's usually more caring about this sort of thing."

"Money, I suspect."

Guy tried to take in a deep breath but failed.

"You're hurt?"

"I think I've broken a rib."

He tried to raise his left arm and rotate his shoulder but again, it pained him.

"Ah well. I still have my right arm. I can still work."

"You will find it difficult."

"I'll manage."

"Guy, what have you done to the man? I heard him earlier saying something about the church door."

"As you know I am trying to replace the figured metal decoration on the old door. The Lady Adela found some drawings which would help me decide which animals of the ark went where.”

“And Courtenay objected?”

“He objects to the Lady and I being in the church porch together, no matter how innocent the meeting.”

“Well, he will be in the church porch with her soon enough, my father tells me; they’re to marry after Christmas.”

Guy swallowed. “Christmas? So soon.”

Nell hunkered down in front of him. “Guy, you will have to let go. If you don’t... if you don’t stop seeing Lady Adela, Guiscard Courtenay may kill you.”

But Guy said nothing.

“Come, I’ll help you tidy the place. We need to have light, it’s got so dark now.”

“I think they have trodden on every candle I own. They are all in pieces and all my lamps are smashed.”

“I’ll go home for some rushlights. That should suffice. Wait for me.”

Without a backward glance, Nell exited the cottage.

Guy struggled up and followed her out into the night. He had lamps and candles in the forge and his fire was damped down; he could light them from there.

He’d been in his forge for only a short while when he was aware of a presence behind him. Slowly he turned.

“Lady Adela?”

She came out of the shadows. “I shouldn’t be here.”

“No, that’s right, so perhaps it’s best you go home,” said Guy in a harsh tone—harsh for him.

“Did he hurt you? I have seen the mess they’ve made of your home. I am so sorry,” she said.

“No, it’s nothing. Nothing that can’t be replaced or mended.”

Guy took a lantern from a shelf and lit it from the forge fire. He lifted it high so that he could see her in the shadows.

"This must be the last time…" he said.

"No… please… No don't say that."

"My lady…"

"I have come to ask you something."

Guy lowered his lantern; his ribs were beginning to hurt. "Ahh," he whispered, giving voice to his discomfort.

"You are injured!"

"It's very little, really. And before you ask, there is nothing which can be done about it."

"It?"

"My broken…"

"Broken?"

"Rib."

"Oh." Adela took a step forward. "No one knows that I am here."

"And it should stay that way."

"But I have come to beg you to do something for me."

"I should do nothing…"

She was lighting a candle from the flame in the lantern which Guy had set on the bench and steadying it on the anvil in a pool of wax.

"Master Ferrier… Guy… I know how clever you are. I know that you are a gifted blacksmith. I know that you have cured many folk of their ailments."

"In truth… most people cure themselves. If they believe that something will work, then it often will…" said Guy with a sheepish grin.

"But you have helped many people. Please. Help me now," said Adela, coming one step nearer.

"I must not help you. I must not be seen with you."

"Guiscard Courtenay."

"What about him?"

"He's a pig."

"Then do not marry him."

"Believe me when I say, I don't want to marry him. I have never wanted to marry him." She moistened her lips. "I want to…"

"I can do nothing."

"Oh, but you can. I want him gone."

"Believe me, mistress, so do I."

She smiled softly. "And if he was gone, what would you do?"

Guy turned away and lit another candle. "What could I do?"

"You could take me away from here."

"That is impossible."

"You are a free man. You may go where you wish. You have a talent which can be used anywhere."

"My Lady Adela… I cannot leave here. This is where I belong. You cannot leave. Your father would come after you."

"Take me away from here. Please."

"Adela, I cannot. The life of a blacksmith's wife would not suit you. You are used to finer things. I cannot give you what you want."

A great fat tear rolled down Adela's cheek. "You would leave me to that monster, Guiscard?"

"Speak to your father."

"You think I haven't?"

There was silence then, as neither of them quite knew what to say next.

Eventually Guy sighed. "This is foolish. It cannot end well."

"Guy please… help me." She reached out and took his hand and held it. He didn't pull away though he wanted to.

"I want you to…"

"Please, Lady Adela…"

"I want you to… curse Guiscard."

"What?"

Very quickly, she said, "I want you to do something which will make him change his mind about me, or go away for good or…"

"Curse him?"

"Make him an imbecile... lose his wits, fall from his horse, something... anything so that he cannot or does not wish to marry me. I'm sure that is not beyond your capabilities."

He pulled his hand away. "No! I cannot do that!"

"You are a blacksmith. I know that blacksmiths are special men with otherworldly talents."

"This one does not pronounce curses. Ever."

"I know that you lifted a curse recently for Master Truman."

"That was supposed to be a secret."

Adela simpered a little..."Well, it was a secret. Until Marjorie got it out of little Johnny Harvester."

"That was..."

"He did not lie then?"

"I lifted a curse for Master Truman... so that he would not believe himself ill. There is no truth in the magic. It was a ruse."

Adela leaned forward, "I don't believe you. Master Truman *is* recovered." Her eyes blazed. "If you can lift a curse, you can pronounce one. "

Guy stared at her for a heartbeat. Was this the sweet Adela he thought he knew?

Should he do it, simply to please her? He did not believe in the magic which he sometimes performed, knowing that it was the power of suggestion which had, more often than not, produced results. Certainly he had cured some minor ailments but he put that down to the ingredients present in his quenching trough. He was sure that it acted as a medicine of sorts. He didn't understand it but he had never questioned that it was perfectly... normal.

"I cannot do it."

"Not even for me? Not even for money?"

"Never for money."

Adela's face turned hard. "Where is the drawing... the church door drawing? I must take it back."

"It's here... and safe."

"They haven't destroyed it or taken it then?"

"No. I hid it safely before they came."

He made for the centre of the forge. "It's under my anvil. I will lift it and you must pull it out. My ribs will not allow me to lift it for long."

She nodded briefly and Guy, gritting his teeth, took the end of his anvil once more in two hands. Taking in the deep breath which was required to help him lift the great weight, pained him and he groaned.

Adela quickly retrieved the parchment, folded it into four and pushed it into the roundness of her crespinette which held back her curls that day.

A breathless voice said, "I wondered where you'd gone. I have found some... oh..." Parnell returned and entered the forge by the back door.

She gave a quick curtsey, "Lady Adela."

Adela's face was hard and her voice cold and devoid of any emotion. "I came to retrieve something which the blacksmith borrowed from me."

"Ah..."

"Our business is now concluded. Good evening." She pushed past Nell.

"God keep you, Lady," said Parnell.

She looked at Guy with a fierce expression. "Business?"

"Come into the house and I will explain."

"I am agog with anticipation, Guy," said Nell.

*****

Parnell was aghast when she was told what Adela had asked.

"She wants you to curse him?"

"She has no wish to marry him and wants me to make him 'disappear'. Either by illness or accident."

"Oh Guy, you would not do it...?"

"What do you think?"

"Your immortal soul would be in such peril if you…"

"I would never do it. Not even for her."

"She is a selfish, spoiled, exploiter of others."

Guy turned away from her. He loved Adela; he could not hear her spoken of in this way. But he had to admit that there might be some truth in Nell's words.

"Has she told you that she loves you, Guy?"

"She asked me to take her away from here…"

"But she has not declared her love?"

"No. And I have said nothing to her either. Except that she would make a very poor blacksmith's wife."

Nell nodded. "At last, you are coming to your senses."

Guy felt like crying but he would not be so unmanly in front of Nell. "It's late, we should retire."

Nell didn't move. "You must forget her, Guy. Let her sort her own life."

"She will get nothing from me."

"Good."

Guy picked up a rushlight. "Here, to light you back home. And thank you for your help tonight... in the house."

"I will come tomorrow to see what you need. Meanwhile, I think your bed is whole and unscathed. Go and lie down on it until dawn."

"Goodnight, Mistress Truman."

"Goodnight, Master Ferrier."

*****

Much of the night, Guy lay upon his bed staring up at the rafters of his one storey house. The owls who inhabited the riverside trees hooted with gleeful regularity and he wondered what they found to speak about so late in the season.

He folded his arms behind his head and his rib pulled unmercifully. It would be six weeks before the rib would be fully mended; he'd had a broken rib before so he knew how it felt. He would try hard to keep working.

And to keep singing though he didn't feel like it.

He fell asleep trying to make up a new song and, for a change, not one about love or loss. Or blacksmithing. One about a hare running free on the downs.

He woke with a start sometime after dawn, to an insistent banging on his door. Throwing on a shirt, he staggered to unlock it.

Adela was hopping from foot to foot.

"Oh Guy... thank you... thank you!" She threw her arms around his neck.

He was very aware that he was unwashed and sleep tousled and that he was wearing nothing but yesterday's shirt.

"Lady Adela... what?"

"You did it... I am so grateful. You did it!"

"I did what?"

"You said you wouldn't but... Oh you are so clever, for it happened this very morning and..."

"WHAT happened?"

"You must know... for you made it happen and so quickly!"

"Go home, mistress, for you are deranged."

"No, Guy. You must know. It's Guiscard..."

"Oh!"

"He went out to hunt very early this morning and his mount threw him. A large hare ran between the hooves of his horse, they say... Oh, what is his silly beast's name...?"

"Charlemagne?"

"Oh no, it wasn't that horse, was it? He was riding another. And he was thrown off, over a hedge."

"Is he..?"

"It was you wasn't it...? They say that sorcerers can change their appearance and become whatever they want, but that hares are most often seen."

"Me?"

"It was you. You changed yourself into a hare, didn't you and…?"

She stopped and took a step back looking a little surprised at his befuddled expression.

"You woke me with your banging on the door. I have not been out this morning. I have slept late." He rubbed his sore side. "It wasn't me."

"Then you must have done it in your sleep. Dreamt about it."

"If I had dreamt it, I am sure I would have remembered," said Guy irritably.

"Well however you did it… thank you."

"Lady Adela, please believe me, I did nothing."

"You did. You must have done, for how else can we explain it? I asked you to make him fall from his horse and the very next day, he fell from his horse." She giggled like a small child.

"Is he…?"

"Dead?" Guy crossed himself.

"No, but he's as like the dead as he can be. Father Fabian thinks that he will not recover for he sustained a huge bang on the side of his head and folk rarely recover from such wounds."

"Oh so, Father Fabian is become a doctor now is he?"

"Are you not happy Guy… happy for me?"

"Happy? I am concerned for the man Guiscard Courtenay. He lies injured, likely to be mortally wounded. How can I be happy?"

"But you must be happy for me, for if he dies then he cannot marry me and take me away." Adela pouted. "I thought you'd be really pleased."

"I wish no man ill, Adela. No man."

"But he beat you yesterday?" she said, looking totally perplexed.

"The man was drunk and had misunderstood the situation. I have no quarrel with him."

"Even if he wounded you?"

"Even if he wounded me."

"But…"

"I admit, at the time I was very tempted to plant my fist upon his smug chin but upon thinking about it, what would it serve?"

"Oh, you are so much the good Christian, turning the other cheek!" said Adela sarcastically.

"I suppose I am," answered Guy. "Is this not what we are asked to do by Our Lord.?"

"Well… I will believe that you did it, even if you say you didn't."

She turned around in a happy dancing circle. "I'm free of him!" she sang.

"Adela… please, tell no one what you think. If you speak, my life may be in danger."

"What do you mean?"

"If people believe that I cursed a man to death, then, they will decide that it is murder and I will be arrested." An uncomfortable feeling began in the region of his midriff. He knew it. Fear.

"You have told no one… have you?"

"No. No one."

"Then it must be kept a secret."

They stared at each other for a moment.

"I must go and dress. I have work to do."

"I can be at the church later. I will go and pray for Guiscard… but of course I won't really," she said with glee.

"I am busy today. I will not be at the church."

"Oh…" She was very disappointed and shuffled her feet.

"Another day then?"

"Perhaps."

"Good morning, Master Blacksmith."

Guy bowed and a sharp pain flashed across his ribcage. And his heart.

"Good Morning my Lady."

*****

Parnell met the Lady Adela running down the lane from the forge house. She dipped a curtsey as she passed but the girl did not seem to see her, though the road was empty.

Nell reached the house just as Guy was drawing on his cotte. With his back to her and grumbling in pain, he adjusted his belt and swore.

"Master Ferrier! SO early in the morning?"

"Nell... I'm sorry. It's damned painful this morning."

"Movement should ease it, but be careful. I will bring you some willow bark remedy later. That will help."

"Thank you."

"What was she doing here? Does she not realise what harm she has done?"

Guy sighed and sat down heavily on the only stool with four good legs.

"She came to tell me that... Guiscard Courtenay lies mortally wounded at the manor."

Nell's fingers went to her lips. "No!"

"He was out early this morning, probably not even at that time quite sober and apparently his horse was startled and he was tossed over a hedge."

Nell sat on the edge of the table in the middle of the room. "No! Is he likely to die?"

"They tell us so."

Nell immediately saw the connection and the danger. "Guy... you did not...?"

"No, I most certainly did not. Lady Adela believes I did but... but I didn't."

"Then it is an amazing coincidence, isn't it?"

"Don't tell me that *you* don't believe me?"

"Lady Adela, with whom you are in love without a doubt, asks you to rid herself of her suitor and she even asks you to make him fall from his horse and..."

"No, I didn't do it."

"The next day, the man is thrown from his horse."

"Men fall from horses all the time."

Nell jumped up. "Adela will be happy."

"Ecstatic."

Her face took on a worried look, "Guy, she will not tell anyone will she?"

"I have begged her to keep silent. If she thinks that I really did curse the man then I think she will keep the secret, as she sees it."

"She is a foolish woman... I'm sorry Guy but she is. She is what she is and has been made so by her parents. I hope she can keep her mouth closed."

"There is already a rumour going about... a story..."

"A story... about what?"

"That a hare darted between the horse's hooves and made him throw Courtenay."

Nell's face darkened. "No... a hare? The beast of magic and shapeshifting?"

"Many believe it's magical. As far as I'm concerned it's simply a beautiful fleet animal, good for stew," said Guy in a disbelieving tone and with the edge of a smile.

Parnell Truman wandered around the cottage for a moment. "Promise me, Guy, that you had nothing to do with this man's 'accident'."

"Do you wish me to swear upon the church Bible? We could go up there together now."

"No... no, that's not necessary."

"I will swear if it will make you happier."

"I would be most happy if the Lady Adela was to go back to the manor at Milton Lillebon and stay there."

Guy grinned.

"There she could cause no further harm. I was hoping that Sir Guiscard would take her away with him to Thatcham and that would be the end of it, but now…"

Guy cocked his head. "Mistress Truman, I do believe you are jealous."

"Nonsense!" said a rapidly flushing Parnell.

CHAPTER SEVEN ~ THE OLIPHANT

Guy found his work quite difficult that morning but he soldiered on. Luckily there were no horses to shoe that day; he thought that task might be beyond him at the moment and so he concentrated on finishing those items the villagers had asked him to make. Two thirds of the way through the working day, he began to fashion a new piece for the church door.

He took a stick and drew from memory, in the raked out ashes of his fire, the odd creature he'd seen on the parchment Adela had found, and stared at his drawing. Whatever was it? Not that it mattered.

He turned the strange shape this way and that. The animal had been there originally so it must go back onto the door. He struggled with it for a while and then set it to cool on the bench.

As the light was fading and he was thinking about giving up for the day, a figure appeared in the doorway.

"Steward Masters, with what can I help you?"

The man came into the light of the forge. No matter how he tried, Guy could not like the steward, the lord's manager of his manor. He found him haughty and self-important.

That was what happened when the lord was absent for much of the year and his man, set to run the manor without him, was left to his own devices. He'd begun to feel the manor was his.

"Ah yes... Master Ferrier."

"I was just about to close up."

"I will be brief..."

There was another figure lurking in the semi darkness behind him and for an instant Guy's gut tightened as he remembered the contretemps of the previous day. But it was not one of the knights.

The steward's daughter, Emma came into the forge behind her father. "Good evening Master Ferrier."

Guy nodded his head deferentially, "Good evening, mistress."

The woman was wearing a gown of tawny with a supertunic of pink over it. Both of them were of the finest wool and showed her wealth, or rather that of her father.

"You know my daughter Emma, of course?"

"I do, sir," smiled Guy.

"The Lord would have you come and sing for him, Ferrier. Might you be able to do that tomorrow? Let us say at the fourth hour of the day when dinner has commenced?"

Guy bowed and his rib pulled. "I would be delighted sir, except..."

"Except...?" The man had already turned in order to leave but he swivelled back, an irritated expression on his round, rubicund face.

"Except? My dear man...? Do you have an objection?"

"I would have thought that such gaiety would not be... seemly... with one of his guests lying gravely injured at the manor? His future son-in-law, no less."

"It is not for me to say but the lord no doubt feels that some... diversion... is in order. He would not have misery prevail, Master Blacksmith, at such a time, at East Kennett Manor."

"Then, if the lord wishes it, I will attend."

"Good." Masters faded into the gloom with no farewell.

Emma did not immediately go with him.

Here was another spoiled girl. Another child given too much freedom. She wandered around the forge, picking up this and that.

"What's this?" she said eventually

"It is a piece for the church door. I am mending the little sculptures which appear on the surface there, mistress."

"Oh, I see. It is an oliphant."

"A what, mistress?"

"An oliphant. Huge beasts which are to be found in hot countries and which give us ivory for carving."

"Oh... thank you. I was unaware of its name though I know of the beast."

The woman preened herself.

"That's what happens when one has had an education, Master Blacksmith," she said haughtily. "One can read about other places far away and the animals which inhabit those places, and learn about things."

"I have no doubt."

Emma Masters was a girl upon whom her father had lavished money in order to get her an education. Guy knew this was so that Emma might marry well, rise up the ranks and take her family with her. However, even though the girl had had an education, she was not the brightest star shining in the little village of East Kennett and she was, as Guy had noticed before, quite plain with poor skin.

It was also clear that she did not see well at a distance, for she screwed up her eyes and that gave her a perpetually puzzled expression. Added to this, she had a habit of pursing her lips which made her look as if she had tasted something unpleasant.

"What other animals are there that you do not recognise, Master Blacksmith, on the church door?"

"Oh there are no others, Mistress Emma. My education is sufficient for pigs and sheep and geese. These are around me every day."

Emma laughed, though she did not realise that Guy was being facetious.

"But if I do find any other animal that I do not recognise, then surely, I will come to you to have you identify it for me."

"I would be glad to," she said looking coy.

A voice from a little way off shouted her name and she chasséd to the door with exaggerated movements of her hips and shoulders.

Guy chuckled to himself, 'Well, she couldn't use her bosom to impress, she didn't have one.'

"Good evening."

Guy ran his fingers through his hair.

"Oh please God. Save me. Now I know she has more than a hankering for me," he said out loud.

*****

The next morning whilst he worked, Guy spent a great deal of time, perfecting the songs he would sing for the Lord Lillebon and his guests at dinner. He had finished the song he called the Running Hare.

'The hare is running for his life.

The hunter is running for his dinner.

Run like the wind.

He hears the dogs baying.

He hears the men shouting.

Run for your life.

He is the friend of the Goddess moon

He lies still, still under her.

No cover but her rays.

All he has are his fleet feet and his brown skin.

He will outrun you. He will hide from you.

You will not catch him.'

And then he began a new one about a beast with two tails. Whereas the previous song had been haunting and sad, this one was a little more fantastical and jolly. 'Well,' said Guy to himself, 'a beast who looks so cannot have a serious song made for it.'

He sang to himself as he beat out a sheet of metal.

'I am grey but I am not a cloud,
I have two tails and I'm not a cat,
I have big ears but I'm not a hare.
I am huge, stand tall and proud,
I am grand but I am not fat,
Approach me if you dare.'

He had heard about oliphants from other poets and song makers but of course had never seen one. And now he recalled it, the shape of the creature was impressed in his memory somewhere from some source.

If they wished him to sing a new song, he would make another as he went along. He knew he could do that. He knew that he was a little nervous about singing for the Lord Lillebon and his guests and realised that it wasn't them he felt he had to impress. It was Adela.

Why did he feel he had to do that? It was foolish. There was no benefit to him at all in impressing the Lord's daughter.

He buried his misgivings in the making of another figure for the door. This time an easy one—the goose—a bird that was synonymous with silliness; with foolishness but also with bravery and steadfastness.

By the end of the day, he would have four new animals to attach to the church door. But first, the manor beckoned.

The hall was all bustle and noise, as Guy entered the door and sought out the figure of the steward who, grabbing him by the shoulder, took him up to the high table and presented him to Lord Walter Lillebon.

"Ah, Master Ferrier, you have arrived." Sir Walter clapped his hands and the place grew quieter. "Here at East Kennett, we are very lucky to have a songster of great merit, my friends. Guy, our blacksmith, is here to sing for us. Let us put down our knives and spoons for a moment and lend an ear."

Many folk went on chattering but, at Sir Walter's insistence, Master Steward banged a pot on the table and suddenly there was silence.

"What will you sing for us first, Master Ferrier?"

"A new song, my lord," said Guy, bowing to his master. "One which is inspired by the decorative figures which I am replacing on the door of our church."

"Ah yes, my daughter tells me you have taken that task to yourself." He leaned forward and sought out the face of his priest. "We have a very fine old door, Father, you may not realise its antiquity. I believe we are the only church for miles around to have such a perfect example of a bible story told in images upon a door."

"I must make a study of this, my lord. Indeed, I was not aware we had such a thing," said Father Fabian.

Guy's eyes caught Adela's flushed face, as she leaned forward to speak to the priest.

"It is the story of the flood of Noah, Sir Priest," she said confidently. "It is most beautiful... or it will be when it is completed again."

"Then sing, Guy," said the lord. "Sing and we shall all listen."

"It is called the oliphant, my lord. A strange beast with a tail at both ends of its body..."

People chuckled. A strange animal indeed.

Guy sang the first two verses he'd made and then when folk began to grow restless and chatter again, he sang the last verse at a higher volume.

'My roar is louder than the lion,
My feet are harder than the iron,
My horns are sharper than the sword,
I once was human, a mighty lord,
Strong and wise, but I changed my form,
As necromancers can perform.
Beware the oliphant's fearsome brawn
Lest he bring you down.'

Lord Lillebon clapped effusively and stamped his feet and others followed his lead.

"Let us hope we never meet this oliphant here, roaming around the downs," he chuckled.

Guy bowed once more. "That is unlikely, my lord, for I am told that it is a creature out of the heat of Africa and will not live here."

"Ah... is it indeed? So do you have a song about a creature that *does* live here?"

"Yes, my lord. I do." And Guy launched into The Running Hare. *"The hare is running for his life..."*

He was three lines into his song when one of the Courtenay party leapt up from the trestle and yelled, "Is this some kind of sick joke?"

"Sir Thomas, calm yourself..." said Sir Walter, rising slowly from his seat. "Master Ferrier does not mean any disrespect, I'm sure."

"My lord, cousin and friend lies mortally wounded and this imbecile sings about a hare!"

Guy had stuttered to a halt.

"No, no, Sir Thomas... Master Ferrier means nothing with his song. I am sure he does not even know that poor Sir Guiscard was injured today. Let alone that it was a hare which startled his horse, precipitating him from his saddle."

Guy bowed low though it hurt him. "I am deeply sorry if I have offended..."

Sir Thomas gritted his teeth. "Obtaining vengeance eh, Blacksmith?"

"I assure you sir..." said Guy, trying to keep the peace.

"Please, Sir Thomas," said the Lord Lillebon, himself a peaceable and mild fellow, "You cannot be more wrong..."

"The man had a quarrel with my lord Courtenay, sir. Yes, it was true that a hare startled his horse. Guiscard was not riding the beast to which he was accustomed today. The blacksmith knew this... he had refused to treat Charlemagne, Guiscard's mount, though he was asked. He knew that Guiscard would be at a disadvantage and I know it was a hare which caused the accident for I saw it happen. A hare... and it was *this* man... shapeshifted into a beast!"

A collective gasp rolled around the hall and then a babble of shocked conversation.

Sir Thomas raised his voice over the murmuring. "It is well known that blacksmiths are sorcerers and magicians. They are capable of evil magic. I would not be surprised if Guiscard has met his end in this way... by him!" He pointed an angry finger.

Sir Walter Lillebon stammered. "Sorcery? What sorcery?"

"This man achieved mastery over his rival by changing himself into a hare. He knew that the horse would bolt."

The crowd was quite silent now except for the hiss of whispers.

"And what quarrel could he possibly have with my blacksmith?"

The man Thomas Courtenay turned to Sir Walter. "It pains me to say it, my lord. He harbours an obsession for your daughter, Lady Adela. Guiscard merely told him to never see her alone again and..."

"See her again? When has he seen her alone?"

Now Adela leapt up from her seat. "I told you father, Master Ferrier and I have been repairing the church door. I have been... helping identify the animals which are missing. There is nothing sinister in it."

"Helping....?" said her shocked father.

"There is nothing in it, I tell you. For Heaven's sake, we have been in the church porch. Do you think that I would risk my reputation whilst standing in the house of God... with a mere blacksmith? Father, you know me better than that."

The Lord Lillebon's eyes searched for Marjorie, Adela's maid who was seated further down the table. "Girl! Have you been with your mistress as you should have been when she has been... helping the blacksmith?"

Marjorie gulped. Could she tell a lie; such a lie in front of all these people and worst of all, in front of the priest? She had already been paid by Courtenay to tell about the meetings of her mistress and the blacksmith and when she had been asked to turn a blind eye. She felt guilty.

Adela stared at Marjorie, her eyes beseeching her to lie.

The maid closed her eyes, crossed her fingers behind her back and spoke. "I have my lord. There has been nothing untoward. It is as my mistress has said."

"Sir Guiscard was mistaken, Father. I have done nothing wrong. It's all a silly misunderstanding. Ferrier is innocent."

The Lord Lillebon chuckled. "Well then... hear that Sir Thomas? My blacksmith could no sooner change himself into a hare than he could... oh... marry my wife! Now... let's go back to the singing. Have you a jolly song, Guy? One which doesn't feature hares or oliphants?"

Guy gave Sir Thomas a piercing look. "I do sir." And he began a song about a foolish miller and a beggarman.

Sir Thomas sat down but Guy heard him say, "You haven't heard the last of this, Blacksmith!" before the knight downed his cup of wine in one gulp.

*****

Later that day, Guy took his newly forged figures to the church porch and began to attach them to the wood of the door.

After a while he became aware of someone standing behind him, watching.

"A goose, an oliphant, a dog and... a rabbit...'" said Emma Masters.

"Hare," answered Guy without turning. "It's a hare. Its ears are too long to be a rabbit. And it is sitting like a hare."

"Oh yes, of course."

Tap, tap, tap. 'Keep your back turned and keep working, Guy,' he said to himself. 'She'll get bored and go away.'

Emma slid herself onto the coffin ledge beside the door and leaned back.

"A hare... do you like hares, Master Blacksmith?"

The blacksmith didn't reply.

"What was all that nonsense at dinner earlier about a hare and you becoming one to injure Sir Guiscard Courtenay?"

"Just as you say, Mistress Emma... nonsense."

Tap, tap, tap. The hare was now back in its place in the curled ironwork of the door.

"And then you make up a song about hares. You must like them."

"Emma. Go. Away."

"That is most unkind, Master Ferrier. I am really interested in your work. I think what you are doing is marvellous."

Guy picked up the next animal. He'd chosen to fix the figure of the dog onto the space between the hinge plates of the door next. He took some small nails in his lips and offered up the animal to the surface wood. Tap, tap, tap.

"You are so clever, Guy," she said. "You can do so many things."

Guy ignored her.

"You cured Alain's warts, and Johnny told me you lifted a curse from Master Truman."

"How have you learned about that?"

"Oh Johnny Harvester will talk about anything if you feed him," said Emma.

Guy tutted.

"And you saved Mistress Alys' arm, I'm told, when she burned it."

"I had the common sense to plunge it into cold water, that's all. Now excuse me..." He pushed between her knee and the edge of the door by the hinges.

"We have known each other many years, haven't we, Master Ferrier and in all that time, I did not realise that you were such a clever man."

"Emma, you are sixteen. I have known you all your life. Since you were a small girl running around without a breechclout!"

Emma did not like that. She didn't like it at all.

'Keep going Guy, she'll go away,' he said to himself.

He took the goose between his fingers and offered it up to the curlicue nearest to the hinges.

"Excuse me... I need to be closer to the door. Will you move?"

Emma stood angrily. He expected her to say something like, 'how dare you?' but instead she said, "Do you know what? I wouldn't be at all surprised if you did turn into a hare and try to kill Sir Guiscard Courtenay."

"Don't be foolish Emma. You know that is utter nonsense."

Guy fixed the goose to the door and stepped back to admire his handiwork. Emma's hand flicked out and grabbed him by the sleeve.

"In fact, do you know what? I think I actually saw you do it. What do you say to that?"

"That would be a lie and you know it."

"I saw you running up the road and next I looked out of my window and there was a hare leaping across the grass towards Sir Guiscard's horse. It can only have been you because suddenly you were nowhere to be seen."

"Your eyes deceived you. I was in bed till late this morning."

"He could not have run anywhere, you foolish girl," said a calm voice. "It would not have been possible for Master Ferrier to have run anywhere early this morning."

Parnell Truman came into the dimness of the church porch.

"Oooooh," said Emma. "Mistress Truwoman-tell-no-lies. And how might you know this... eh? Mistress Goody-goody."

"Because last night he sustained a broken rib when Sir Guiscard and his friends attacked him. He can barely lift his hammer to fix these nails, Mistress Storyteller."

"So it's true. They did have a quarrel?"

Guy intervened. "Sir Guiscard made a mistake which I do not hold against him. He accidentally broke my rib last night."

"So how do you know where he was, eh? Eh, little Miss Perfect?" asked Emma.

"I know because I was with him, that's why," said Nell suddenly. "Early this morning, I was with him. I had been there a while."

Emma's mouth opened so wide, they were sure she should swallow herself. "You... were... with him...?"

"I was. So no amount of tale telling, of fantastical stories or... anything is going to alter the fact that Master Ferrier could not have changed himself into a hare. It's sheer rubbish and you know it."

Emma flounced about the small porch. "Oh... wait till I tell my father. The bailiff's daughter and the blacksmith. Together all night. Oh, what a story!"

"Did you hear Nell say we were together all night?" said Guy sharply.

"Together... how delicious. Mistress Goody-goody isn't so good, after all."

She collected her fashionable supertunic over her arm to show the fine lining and strutted out of the porch. "Wait till I tell... oh... tell... everyone," she said and she chuckled all the way down the church path.

Guy put down his hammer and looked at Nell sidelong. "Oh Nell, now look at what you've done."

"I don't care. I'll not have her spreading such vicious gossip."

"And that's not what she's marching off to do now?" Guy stood, arms akimbo. "It will not do your reputation any good."

"Better than her lying about you becoming a hare. That's much more dangerous."

"Aye... well..."

"Oh Guy, don't be so prim. What's my reputation against... possibly your safety?"

Guy collected his tools. "Put like that, I suppose..."

"I don't care that people think that you and I were alone all night in your house."

'What about your father?"

Nell threw her hand in the air. "My father won't care."

"Oh Nell..."

"Well you could be grateful," she said.

"Grateful that you have just branded me a seducer!"

“And given you an alibi.”

Guy grimaced and Nell gurned back, poking her tongue out from her mouth.

CHAPTER EIGHT ~ DANGER!

The next morning as Guy was opening the forge doors, Master Truman came breathlessly hurrying up the lane, clutching his chest.

"Guy, Guy... a word with you?"

"Yes, Master Truman?" One look at his face and Guy knew what the visit was about. "I suppose you have heard the story about Nell and me?"

"I had it from Mistress Palfreyman, who in turn had it from Ada Whitman..." The bailiff panted like an old cart horse.

"Who had it no doubt from Emma Masters," said Guy.

"Ah... you know then?"

"I do, for I was there when Parnell made up the ridiculous tale."

Guy blew the forge fire into life and fed it with twigs.

"So are you going to offer for Parnell's hand?" said Master Truman, his body stiff and his face unreadable.

"Offer for her?"

"You have deflowered my daughter, sir."

"I have done no such thing."

Guy came round his bench and towered over the diminutive bailiff. "What has Nell said? Hasn't she told you she just made it up to get Emma to stop spreading the rumour that I turned myself into the hare which caused the accident to Sir Guiscard?"

The bailiff rolled his shoulders. "And did you?"

"Did I what?"

"Cause the man to…"

"Oh, Master Truman. Are you too taken in with such silly tales? I thought better of you."

Truman folded his arms across his chest.

Guy copied him with a twinge of his rib. "No I did not. I would not be able. It is impossible for me to change into an animal. I am a *man*."

"Are you going to marry Parnell?"

Guy turned his back on the village bailiff. "I could do worse I suppose but…"

"I would give my permission," said John Truman on a sigh. "You know I would."

"And risk your daughter marrying an evil sorcerer? Surely?" There was a hint of humour in his voice.

"No, no. I…"

"Oh! So now, you have changed your mind, sir?"

The bailiff shook his long locks, "I have known you a long time, Guy. I cannot think you would…"

"No, I would not."

He pulled on his bellows and the flames shot high with a roaring sound. "If you have not spoken to her, go and ask Nell what it was all about."

"I do know that Mistress Masters and my daughter do not… get on."

"They detest each other. Let's not mince words." Guy lowered his tense shoulders. "Speak to Nell. She will tell you what happened. Emma was miffed that I had rebuffed her advances. Not for the first time. I know that she likes me. She tries now and again to get close to me. And I resist."

"She is to make a good marriage in Marlborough town," said Truman in surprise.

"So I heard."

"To young Master Weaver."

"Poor man. I doubt that she'll stay faithful."

"The sooner she leaves the manor the better we will be."

"I will say Amen to that. Now if you'll forgive me, I have some work...?"

"Parnell? Why would she lie... for you ?"

"Ask Nell, herself."

"Well, come to dinner today and we shall both ask her."

*****

The weather deteriorated quite suddenly later that morning and an icy rain began to fall. Guy locked up the forge and ran around the corner to the bailiff's house, through a sudden shower of hailstones.

He burst into the cottage and apologised for the rudeness of his arrival. Parnell turned quickly and smiled.

"Set yourself down by the fire," she said. "Father won't be long."

Guy took out his knife and spoon and slid onto a bench. "Have you told him what happened in the church porch? With Emma Masters?"

"I have. He knows what the wretched girl is like. But it is difficult to get him to realise that you and I are not..."

"He'll come round to it."

Parnell turned back to her cooking. "He only thinks it because, deep down, he wishes it were true."

"Would it be such a terrible thing?"

Parnell did not reply but answered with another question. "Have you heard?"

"I have seen no one all day. Had no news. I've been alone in the forge after your father left."

"Late last night..." Nell became very still and held her wooden spoon over the pot. "Sir Guiscard's situation worsened and... he died, Guy."

There was a moment's silence.

Into Guy's mind came the vision of the drunken man in his cottage, slashing and smashing with the iron poker he'd previously used on Guy's ribs.

"Guiscard Courtenay is dead?"

"Dead of the head wound."

Guy crossed himself. "May God take him to his bosom. He was only a young man."

Nell turned, her face riddled with concern. "Now he's gone… they might…"

"They can try to blame me, but I doubt they will make the accusation firm."

"Why not?"

"Quite apart from the fact that I was elsewhere, when the hare made the horse stumble…"

"A fact I have tried to drum into a few heads this morning."

"They will need to take the body back to Thatcham, the place from which he hails. I do not think they will bury him here. They will need me to line the coffin for the journey. No one else will be able to fabricate it," smiled Guy. "There is no one for miles who can do it."

Nell stirred her pot once more, "And you will not agree to make it, if they carry on with their foolish tale?"

"In a nutshell, yes."

Master Truman stumbled through the door and gave an exaggerated shiver. "Brrrr. Oh what a terrible day." He shook off his wet cloak.

"Ah Guy, you are here already."

"Sit down Father, food is ready. And in this weather it will cool quickly," said Nell, ladling the thick stew into bowls.

Her father chuckled a rasping laugh. "Do you know Guy, she is always concerned that I will be eating cold food—as if that could ever hurt me?"

"You are not well. You have been out in the north pasture barn and it *is* cold. You need some goodness and warmth."

"See how she bullies me? She will bully you when you are married... you know she will."

Nell and Guy exchanged glances.

"Father, I have told you, Guy and I are not going to marry. I only said that we had been together because of that odious creature, Emma."

Master Truman turned his eyes, red with the cold, onto Guy and Guy noticed that his lips were blue. "And now that Sir Guiscard Courtenay is dead, it is even more important that everyone knows that you were nowhere near when the man fell from his horse."

"I was asleep in my bed. The Lady Adela came banging on my door early... she woke me," said Guy, a touch of exasperation in his voice.

"I saw her running back to the manor," said Parnell, "as I was coming to see you."

"The Lord's daughter?" said Truman.

"The Lady Adela... yes."

"Alone? What was she wanting with you, young man?" said Truman.

Guy licked his lips and sought Nell's eyes pleading with her to say nothing about the request which Adela had made of him. "I have no idea, for once she had woken me and seen that I had been asleep late, she left and the next thing I knew, Nell here was at the door."

"Hmm." The bailiff spooned the stew into his mouth. He coughed. "Pass me the meat and bread."

Nell reached over and took hold of the plate, sliding it towards him. "Father, Guy was just saying that they will need him to make the lining for the coffin to take the body back to Berkshire. The sooner he can make it, the sooner these men will be gone."

"They made Thatcham to East Kennett in one day on swift horses," said Guy. "To return it will take them three days with a lead-lined coffin on a cart."

"The longer they stay here with nothing to do but think ill-thoughts," said Nell, "the longer Guy is in danger."

Master Truman chewed carefully. "I do not like it. I do not like it at all."

Guy blew on his stew. "I don't know about you but I doubt this stew would cool in a snowstorm."

Nell realised he was trying to change the subject. Guy did not wish either of them to worry about him, she thought. She reached for some bread.

Suddenly the bailiff gave a loud belch and banged on his chest. "Oh forgive me my manners. I am still having difficulty swallowing. Something seems to have got stuck."

"Here Father, take some water."

"Water... water? Nah. I'll have some ale like the sensible man I am." He stood and reached for the ale jug.

Guy jumped up and poured for him.

"So that is the end of the lord's plans for his precious daughter," said Nell. "With the death of Sir Guiscard."

The bailiff swigged down his ale. "They have been promised for years. Not met above a half dozen times but promised since they were children. What will the lord do now?"

"He will have to find her another man." Nell blinked at Guy.

The blacksmith blinked back at her. "Another *wealthy* nobleman," he said.

"What will Lady Adela think about that?" said Nell.

"She can think nothing," said Truman. "She must do as she's told."

Both Guy and Nell wanted to say, 'And when has she ever done that?' But they stayed silent.

The meal over, Guy was taking his leave when Bailiff Truman, escorting him to the door, said, "And so when my time is come, I would die happy if I could be certain that you and Nell would be wed."

"Father, how many more times do I have to tell you? It was but a little lie to stop Emma Masters. We had no intention of..."

"Someone must look after you."

"Oh, not that again."

"Sir, I do not have to be married to Nell to look after her… look after her as a brother might," said Guy.

Master Truman shook his head.

"Ah well… as long as there is breath in my body, I shall keep trying. Now!" He shook his cloak. "I am back to the north pasture barn. I have work to do."

He left the cottage and disappeared into the freezing rain.

Nell and Guy stood looking at each other for a few heartbeats.

"He'll not give up," said Nell.

Guy shrugged and followed the bailiff out into the icy rain.

*****

Guy had the leisure later that day to finish the penultimate piece for the church door.

He conjured up from his memory, the drawing of the lion which was lodged in his brain and began to fashion it from metal.

The day grew darker and he lit a lamp or two in the forge, humming to himself.

The cold rain had given way and in its place a harsh wind had grown up. It battered the forge building and rattled the doors, like a demon trying to gain entry; but Guy worked on.

Upon the next day, he knew that he would have to travel to the town for supplies. He needed lead for Sir Guiscard's coffin and a few other items. Best he finish work soon and retire at a decent hour for he'd have to be up early. He covered his fire, put away his tools and laid the lion to the side for finishing later. Yawning, he locked the forge and travelled the few paces to his home.

He never locked the empty house door. No one in Kennett ever locked their doors. They had very little to steal anyway and the villagers were a close knit lot who would be unlikely to thieve from each other.

He unexpectedly entered a warm fug and the brightness of candles.

"Parnell!"

"I have been tidying and mending and have brought you food and candles. And rekindled the fire."

"That is very kind of you."

"I know that you'd be happy to live like a hermit but, before they destroyed everything, you had a nice comfortable home. I want you to have that again, Guy."

His eyes swept around the cottage. "Thank you very much. I can see that you have been busy."

"Come... come and eat. Father has secured some beef from Forceleap Farm. It's very fine."

"It will be if you have cooked it." The smell was making his stomach grumble. Even though he was a relatively wealthy man, he could not normally afford to eat such good beef.

He sat down wearily.

"I have to be off early tomorrow." He poured a cup of ale. "I must go into town."

"Oh... do you think I might come with you? I have some errands to run and I have no wish to go alone with the cart or ask one of the grooms if I can ride pillion."

"Certainly. I'll be taking the cart to fetch metal from Master Smith."

"Then I will leave you to your meal and ale and see you early tomorrow morning." She smiled sweetly. "Good night Guy."

She lingered by the door, until he said, "Good night Parnell."

Guy sat a long while thinking and listening to the fierce wind. It sounded like the moans of a deep voiced man in pain and the languid whistle of a shepherd after his sheep dog.

Then there came a different sound. Horses' hooves. They did not pass but stopped outside the door. Guy listened intently and then put down his cup.

"Blacksmith! Farrier! Come out here!"

The meal he had just eaten gave a lurch in his stomach and he felt ill.

He filled his lungs. "I am just about to retire. Whatever you want, can it not wait till tomorrow?"

The three voices laughed.

"It cannot wait. Come out here!"

Guy dithered. He did not, if truth were known, know what to do. He knew the voices. He knew the dangers. He was quite a distance from the nearest house, Tom's, and knew that it would be hard to call for help. He looked round for his quarterstaff. Miraculously it had escaped the ravages of the destruction of his house, because it had been lying against the house wall outside. He took it up and felt instantly better with its familiar weight in his hands.

He walked slowly to the door and opened it. However he did not go out into the darkness.

"What can I do for you, sirs?"

"The coffin," said one of them, "we hear that the Lord Walter has asked you to make the lining?"

"That is true. And he has paid for the metal himself. I shall go and fetch it tomorrow."

A second knight now spoke. "Make the lining, Blacksmith. The lord's joiner is making the wooden coffin."

"In fact he's making two coffins," said Sir Maurice Poulteney, the youngest man.

"One for dear Guiscard and one... for you."

"I'd take your time if I were you, over the making of it. For when it's done, Blacksmith... you're a dead man."

*****

Guy slammed the door shut and bolted it fast and stood behind it for a long while. He heard the horses turn about and ride down the road. Then as the sounds faded, the wind yet again buffeted his little house. And still he stood behind the door.

That was how he felt. Buffeted. Blown about. For the first time in his life, it seemed, he was unable to stand on his own two feet, for the world was blowing him hither and thither.

'Damn the stupid girl, Emma! Damn his infatuation with Adela Lillebon, for it was this stupidity which had led him to where he now stood. Damn Parnell Truman for her insight.'

He threw on his cotte, grasped his quarterstaff and opened the outer door once more. It was almost taken out of his hands by the fierce gale. Drawing it closed again, he marched up the road, past the small stand of trees, turning into the garth of the first house, that of his friend Tom.

He called above the gale. "Tom! Tom, let me in... It's Guy."

After a long while, the bolts went back and Tom, looking sleepy and dishevelled, stared up at him. "What the..."

"Can I come in?"

"It's late."

"I know... I'm sorry... I need to talk to someone."

Tom made way for him and shut the door on the wind which bore rain once more.

It took Guy quite a while to explain everything to Tom and Alys, for not only did they not grasp what he was saying upon the first telling, Guy was disordered in his thoughts which was not very like him.

"And so tonight, they came and threatened me. They are determined to kill me it seems, in revenge for the death of their lord. A death which was, there is no doubt, an accident."

Alys shoved her knuckles in her mouth. "Oh Guy, what will you do?"

"It should take me a day to get the lead and probably two days to fabricate the coffin and then, they will come for me, they say."

"We must tell the Lord Lillebon. He'll know what to do," said Tom.

"I would hope that the Lord Lillebon would have some influence but I am not so sure."

Tom shook his head. "Why are they so convinced of this silly tale that you killed their lord?"

"I will tell you Tom but you must promise to tell no one. No one."

Alys once more gasped and put her fingers to her lips.

"The Lady Adela and I have... become... friends... nothing more... simply keeping company over my task at making the decorations for the church door."

Tom and Alys looked at each other with suspicion in their eyes.

"The Lady really did not want to marry Sir Guiscard and she came to me the night before he was struck down asking me to...."

He paused and closed his eyes. "To curse him so that he might not be able to marry her. She wished me to make him change his mind or... sustain... damage in some way."

"Damage?"

"She asked me to make him fall from his horse."

"Oh Guy, Jesus' wounds... you...?"

"I did nothing, Tom. Nothing. I promise you. You know me. I am a mild man. I could no more pronounce a curse than I could fly to the moon!"

"You are a very clever man; nothing is beyond you. Building, thatching, making things, singing... but no, I do not think you could fly to the moon," smiled Tom.

"I could not curse him and I told her so."

"But then the very next day, the thing she has asked you to do... comes to pass and..."

"And she came to thank me. Of course I told her that it was impossible. I hadn't done it."

"But she didn't believe you?"

"I swore her not to tell," said Guy. "The next thing I know that stupid girl Emma Masters had made a play for me..."

"Again?" asked Alys.

"Again and I rebuffed her... again. This time she really took against me and vowed to tell everyone that she had actually seen me change myself into a hare and cause the accident to Sir Guiscard's horse."

"Oh Guy… she's an unkind woman, that Emma," said Alys who had felt the rough edge of the steward's daughter's tongue often.

"I think if she has told no one else, she has at least spun the tale to the companions of Sir Guiscard," said Guy.

"And that is why they believe it so vehemently?"

"I think so. I do hope it is not the Lady Adela who has told the tale."

"Emma will be easier to approach," said Tom. He turned to his wife. "Alys, have you heard anything? In your work at the manor, have you heard Emma saying anything?"

"No, Tom. I haven't."

"Not in the dairy?"

"I never see Emma… well, hardly ever. She considers herself far too important to talk to the likes of me."

"Yes, she would," smiled Guy.

"What shall we do?" asked Tom.

"I do not think I can be seen anywhere near the manor, nor can I speak to Emma. Can you catch her tomorrow and tell her just what danger she has put me in? She must retract her tale. She must own up."

"Aye… I can try it. Tomorrow. Where will you be?"

"In Marlborough buying the lead."

"Be careful Guy."

"I do not think they'll attempt anything until I have finished my task… indeed, they may just be bluffing."

"Their sort like to terrify our sort," said Tom seriously.

"But if they aren't bluffing, Guy," said Alys. "You must not be alone."

"Until they have gone with their heavy burden, you must stay amongst witnesses," said his friend.

"I will ask Master Bailiff tomorrow when I return, if I might stay with him. They are hardly likely to tackle the Lord's man, are they?"

"I will watch your back, Guy," said Tom. "Just ask."

Guy took Tom in an embrace, pecked Alys on the forehead and left the cottage.

By the time he reached his home, he was wet and shivering. And not just from the cold.

*****

Guy waited by his cart the next morning. He was jittery and wanted to be away from the village. For the first time in his life, East Kennett was not a place which felt safe for him.

At last, Parnell came jogging up the road, a blanket cloak clutched round her shoulders and a cloth bag in her hands. "Thank you for waiting. My father is being difficult this morning."

Guy handed her up next to the driver's seat. "Is he alright? I didn't think he looked very well yesterday."

Nell made herself comfortable and stowed away her bag. "He still has the swallowing problem but he will not listen to me about eating. He will eat things which give him pain in the gut. I am fighting a losing battle, Guy."

"I will have a word with him tonight. And I have a favour to ask him."

As they jogged along the road, Guy told Nell all about his problem.

"One day I will kill that girl," she said when he was done with his tale, "and while I'm at it I should give that Lady Adela a slap too."

Guy chuckled, "That I would like to see."

"Oh, so you have changed your mind about her?"

"It was always a fantasy Nell, as you well know. I always knew that there could be nothing serious between us."

Hurryup the horse trotted gently up the slight hill.

"You are silent. That's strange," said Guy.

"You led me to believe…"

"Ah no, Nell. You led yourself there. I am, it's true, fond of the

Lady Adela. Were she the daughter of the village bailiff, I would no doubt make a play for her but, she is not. And I certainly did not kill her fiancé in order to make her available."

"And so you want to come to stay with us until the knights leave?"

"I can sleep on your floor. I'll make it seem as if I am at home but I'll come to you late, in the dark and during the day, I'll not be alone. Tom will be with me. He's worked in the forge before. It will be good to have his company. He has no building work to do at present."

Nell looked serious, "You don't think that you will be endangering him too?"

"They won't want witnesses to their barbarities, Nell."

"Then I will let you know that I too will look out for you. I'll not have them throwing their weight around. I can see everyone who goes out of the manor gates, from the house."

Guy did not ridicule her for her offer of help. He knew she meant it. "Thank you. That's kind."

The journey home took longer than the journey to the town for poor Hurryup had to pull the lead in the back of the cart as well as the two seated people. At last they saw the village nestled in the fold of the down by the River Kennett and made their way to the forge.

Guy offloaded the metal and then went into the house for something to eat. There was not enough light left in the day to begin the beating of the lead to the thin plate which he would use to mould to the inside of the coffin, but he noticed that the wood worker had delivered it, for it stood against the inner wall of the forge. He did not believe the knights' story about two coffins. There was no money for a second one.

He decided instead to take the lion to the church door and attach it to the surface. It wouldn't take him long.

The lion attached, he stood back to admire his handiwork and stepped onto the toes of Emma Masters.

"Oh, I'm so sorry." Then he looked round. "Oh... it's you again!"

Emma rubbed her foot. "You are a clumsy oaf. However did I

think I might be in love with you?" she grimaced.

"I cannot imagine," said Guy, collecting together his tools.

She sat on the coffin bench, cradling her foot. "That idiot Tom came to talk to me today."

"Did he now?"

"He wants me to say that the account of me seeing you change into a hare is a bag of lies."

"Does he?"

"He says that I do not know what danger I have put you in."

Guy turned to her.

"But, of course, you do." Guy grimaced. "You know exactly what trouble you've caused. You knew that your nasty tale would put me in bad odour with the knights of Courtenay."

"What if I tell you that it wasn't me who told the tale?"

"What?"

"That it wasn't me, I say..."

"You threatened to..."

"I did and thought better of it when I reached home." Emma pulled a blameless expression, "So... I'd look to your innocent little Lady Adela, if I were you."

"You heard her at the feast. She pleaded for my innocence."

"Ah, but you heard her father question her and of course she had to say that there was nothing between you."

"There is nothing between us."

"But in an unguarded moment I did hear her say to her maidservant that she had asked you to 'do something' about her lover. And she thinks that you did. All for love of her."

"Emma... do not speak another word. Both of us could be in great danger if this becomes common knowledge."

Emma Masters flounced again around the porch. "Of course I could promise never to speak a word of it. Not about the fact that the lady asked you to make her fiancé fall from his horse. And of course, I could keep silent about what I saw that morning."

Guy was wary, "And if you made this promise, what would you need in return?"

Emma stood still and looked towards him with an upturned face. "I would want you to go down on your knees..."

"Yes?"

"And ask me to marry you."

"Marry you?"

"Am I so terrible then?"

"You are a terrible, and wicked girl, Emma Masters. And a selfish liar," said a voice.

Emma swivelled on her heel. "Ah... it's Mistress Too-good-to-be-Truman. The harlot of Kennett."

Before Emma knew what was happening, Nell slapped her hard across the face.

"Someone has to bring you to heel, Mistress Masters. For your father will not do it."

Emma had her hand to her reddened cheek. "So it's true... it's really true... you two are lovers."

Neither Nell nor Guy denied it.

"Guy, I need you..." cried Nell.

Emma scoffed. She mimicked scornfully. "Guy, I need you!"

"Guy please... I do need you. It's Father, he's collapsed and I cannot move nor rouse him. Please... will you come... Come now?"

CHAPTER NINE ~ MASTER TRUMAN

Leaving his tools in the porch, Guy followed Nell in the fading light, to the cottage opposite the church, taking long strides until at the cottage garth, he overtook her.

He pushed open the door and scanned the main room.

"He's in the hall!"

Guy threw open the inner door and saw Master Truman on the floor jammed between a heavy bench and a trestle. He lifted the bench aside as if it had been made of parchment and pulled the bailiff from under the table where he had slid. Then carefully he picked up the old man and took him to his bed next to the wall.

Nell went to work looking her father over for wounds, or lumps and bumps for she was certain that he had banged his head as he fell, but there was nothing. She covered him with his blankets.

"What happened, Nell?"

The man was a pasty grey, his lips were tinged with blue but he was breathing—just.

"Get him some water," said Guy, lifting Master Truman by the shoulders and propping him up on his knee.

Nell disappeared for a moment but was back soon with a beaker of water.

"What happened?" repeated Guy.

"I was by the fire and I heard him fall. He just made a huge moan and fell. I ran in and I couldn't make him speak to me and he was such a weight for me to move, so I ran for you. I knew you were at the church. I saw you go into the porch."

Nell put the cup to her father's lips, "Father, please... take a sip."

The bailiff remained inert.

"He is still breathing. There is hope, Nell. Run for Mother Little. She'll know what to do."

This woman was a noted cunning woman and healer in the village. Nell said nothing further and Guy heard the door bang and silence drop over the cottage like a blanket. He began to talk to Master Truman though he was unsure if he could hear him.

"Now then, Master Truman, this is no good. We need for you to open your eyes and see who is with you. It's Guy the blacksmith. We don't want any more frights for dear Nell. You've put her in a real taking, poor girl. She's gone for some help so you just rest and we'll wait quietly..."

The bailiff moaned but did not open his eyes.

"Well, that's good, you can hear me and can answer me. If you can hear me, John," he used the bailiff's first name which he rarely did, "squeeze my hand."

There was no answering squeeze.

"Perhaps you can open your eyes?"

The eyes did not open.

"Well then, you just rest and I'll stay here and keep you company until Nell returns."

Guy did not know how long it took Nell to find the cunning woman and to fetch her back to the cottage though it was fully dark by the time they both came through the door.

"Mother Little, it's good to see you."

The woman was tiny but she took the bailiff from Guy's hands as if she were possessed of the strength of ten men and laid him down to examine him. Guy backed off, giving some privacy to Nell and the village wisewoman.

He heard nothing of what was said, for he wandered into the next room where an untouched supper had been laid out on the trestle by Nell, for Master Truman and herself.

Before he knew it, he had begun to pray for the curmudgeonly old bailiff, asking the saints to intervene and beg God to restore the man to perfect health. He wasn't hopeful. It seemed to Guy that John Truman already had one foot in the next world.

Parnell left her father's side at last.

"Thank you Guy. Thank you for your help. There are not many people close by whom I could ask who would help Father."

"Talking of close by, do you think we should go and ask the priest to come?"

Parnell's eyes filled with tears, "Do you think you could take that task upon yourself Guy? I don't want to leave Father."

Guy Ferrier jumped up.

"I am on my way."

*****

Father Fabian came quickly and ministered to the stricken bailiff. At least should he lose his life his soul would be fit to enter the gates of Heaven and no wicked demon could whisk it away to Hell.

"I will stay and pray for him, Mistress," said the solemn priest, "if it is what you would wish."

"That is kind, Father Fabian."

Guy could not bear to leave. For a while he sat in the corner under a blanket, watching the slight rise and fall of John Truman's breath and after a while he nodded, his head heavy on his chest.

When he woke, the priest and wise woman had gone and Nell and he were alone with her father.

"He is dying isn't he?" said Nell in a choking voice. "He has been unwell for a while and I have chivvied him along but he has been dying slowly, hasn't he?"

Guy leapt up from his place against the wall and folding his blanket said, "He may yet recover."

"Look at him, Guy. He has lost weight over the past few weeks. His face is slumped and as white as a chalk pit. His lips are blue. He has no energy and has found it hard to walk about the manor these past few days."

"He kept the worst from us to save us dismay, I think."

"All the years I have cared for him, after my mother died, he has been ill with one thing or another. I have not really taken much notice because most of it has been... well... I don't like to say, if not untrue then exaggerated; he has cried wolf so many times."

"He wanted your attention, that's all."

"He has thought himself ill; worked himself into a sickness but it has all been in his imagination. And now when he really is ill, I have not believed him and I have jollied him along... and not cared for him in the way I should. Oh, how can I ever forgive myself?"

Guy took Parnell's shoulders in his grasp and she laid her head upon his breast and cried bitterly. Guy kissed the crown of Parnell's head, "You have nothing for which to forgive yourself. You have been a perfect daughter."

The blacksmith's mind was racing ahead in time. What if the bailiff *was* to die? As Truman had himself said, Parnell would then be homeless, for the property in which they lived belonged to the Lord Lillebon. He would wish to install the new bailiff there as soon as it was feasible. There was nowhere else she could go. She had no family; no other house. Her friends did not have the room for her, for they were all young married women with small houses themselves or unmarried women living with parents.

Guy wondered if the Lord Lillebon might take Nell into the manor, find her a role there but it was unlikely, since Nell was a free woman and he had no obvious role for her. He was sure that the Lady Adela would take against that idea and he could not imagine the Lady

Lillebon thinking it a good idea, either.

"What did Mother Little say, Nell?"

Mistress Truman wiped her eyes with the back of her hand. "She said that it was his heart. The humours are displaced and there is a lack of something which is causing his heart to fail. She said that all things and events were in God's perfect plan, and nothing happened by chance."

Guy nodded.

"She said that the heart has the function of feeding the whole body with spirit. And that Father's spirit is weakening and..."

"She sounds more like a doctor than a wise woman."

"She has studied these things more than most. She's not a young woman. She's had many years of experience."

"Yes, I'm sure."

They stood together, Guy with his arms around Nell; neither of them realising how close they were.

"What did she say we should do?"

"He needs rest. And prayer and she has left a small jug of something to give him but I cannot get him to swallow it. We can do nothing but wait for him to wake."

Guy hugged Parnell to him. "Can we get him to the priory in Marlborough do you think?" he asked.

Parnell's brow creased, "It's a long way to travel for a sick man."

"They have a hospice there and are used to looking after people... people... who..."

"Who are at the end of their lives?" supplied Nell with a raised eyebrow.

"I did not like to say it."

"I think Father would rather die in his bed here. And I doubt I would be allowed to see him often if he were to go to the priory. It's a long way to go."

"No, I suppose not." Guy relinquished his hold on Nell. "Then we must look after him ourselves."

"You and I?"

"Yes... the two of us."

"But Guy, you are nothing to him."

"I am a friend. I have known him all my life. And my parents before me."

"Yes... but..."

"I cannot let you carry the burden, Nell... not alone."

"I am sure some of the goodwives in the village will help me."

Nell saw Guy's downcast expression.

"Ah no... I am not rejecting you... Guy... I am really grateful and happy that you are willing to help, but I cannot press upon you too hard. It isn't fair. You have your work to do. I cannot rely on you..."

"But that's just it, you can rely on me."

"I know. I know. Oh... I am not finding the right words." She ran her shaking hand across her forehead. "I am tired and frantic with worry and..." She fell down onto the nearest stool and began to cry in earnest.

Guy went down on his knees.

"What if... what if we were to marry? No, hear me out, Nell. Then I would be his son-in-law and I would have the right to look to him as a member of the family."

"Oh Guy!" Smiling through her tears, Parnell took Guy's head between her two hands, "You are the most generous, kind hearted man I know. But you cannot marry me just so that you can look after my dying father."

Into their exchange came a weak voice, "Nell."

Parnell flew to the bedside and fell onto her knees. "Oh, Father, you are awake."

"Nell..." The old man coughed and struggled for breath.

"Nell... Do not refuse him."

"But Father..."

"No! Listen to me. He will marry you. It is the best... the best thing that may happen... believe me..."

"Father, I have no wish to marry."

"What you wish, girl and what is best for you, are two different things." He took an enormous breath. "Guy!"

"Yes, sir."

"Marry her, and not just so you may look after me. I do not think you'll need to... There is no doubt I am dying."

"Oh, Father, hush," said Nell, snivelling. "You are not going to die."

"I am going to die and die soon. And I would see you safe in your own home with a good man who cares for you."

"I do not..."

"Will you listen to me, you wilful girl."

Nell stopped snivelling.

"Your mother and I were married at twenty. We liked each other, of course we did, but our love grew as the years passed. By the time she died, I loved her beyond measure. Beyond all understanding. I cannot tell you how it happened but it did. And it will be the same for you. Marry Guy, you silly girl."

The long speech had tired him and now he lay, his forehead beaded with sweat, trying to draw in breath as if something heavy were pressing down upon his ribcage. Nell gazed up at Guy.

Guy took her hands. "Nell, you know that you will have no home if your father dies. I can offer you my home. Everything in it, everything I own. My money, everything. I will look after you and care for you, if you will have me."

Nell gazed down at the face of her father, his eyes now closed and his expression one of peace.

"I will..." she said.

John Truman gave an almost silent sigh as he thought he heard his difficulties melt away. It seemed to Nell that at that moment, his spirit passed from his body and he grew slack jawed and relaxed.

"I will... think about it," Nell was saying.

She took in the open mouthed appearance of her father's face, knew that he had gone and threw herself onto his corpse crying as she had never cried before.

*****

Guy was not a sentimental person but his eyes filled with tears as he watched Nell weeping over the body of her father.

He sat silently in the corner remembering the man who, as he'd said, he'd known all his life. He recalled the day his mother died and how stalwart a friend John Truman had been to his father; a man with three daughters and a wife resting in the churchyard and only a young son living. Into his memory came the day his father was buried and how John had taken the eighteen year old blacksmith, Guy, under his wing and had guided him through everyday things until he could make his own way.

So many memories.

He chuckled inwardly as he recalled the Christmas John had almost fallen down the well in the garth of Guy's house, a little too intoxicated after the twelfth night celebrations. Now there would be no further twelfth nights for him.

Guy rested his head in his hands. John Truman had always been there to turn to. Now he was no longer there, what was Guy going to do about the three knights from Berkshire who wished to kill him?

He could no longer shelter in the Truman house and under the power of the bailiff of East Kennett's wings. Suddenly he felt ungrateful and selfish. What was that to the problem Nell faced?

What was Nell going to do?

He stood and eased his shoulders. "Nell, we must ask Alfred to make a coffin. We cannot have your father going into the ground in his shroud. He was a man of influence and power in the village. His funeral must reflect that."

Parnell struggled up from her knees.

"Tomorrow, Guy."

"Yes, tomorrow," he said. "Are you certain you want to stay here tonight; want to be alone? Is there nowhere you can go…?" Guy covered Nell's father's body with the blanket.

"It's very late. I have no wish to knock up one of the neighbours to tell them that my father lies dead in his house… and…"

This speech set up further tears and before he knew it and in two bounds across the floor, Guy was wrapping his arms around her again. "Now, now then… you cry all you want. If you want to stay here, then I will stay with you?"

"We have no other bed for you, Guy," said Nell. "Father lies on his bed and I have mine… in there."

"Ack no, it doesn't matter. I can sleep on the floor."

"If you're sure?"

After a while, Guy convinced Nell that he would be fine on the floor with some blankets and Guy was persuaded that Nell would be alright in her own bed in the tiny partitioned room off the hall.

The wind continued to howl around the cottage. The rain battered the roof but it was a good house with a well-made covering of thatch and they both lay on their respective beds talking quietly until Nell, exhausted and grief-stricken, fell asleep. Guy was left in silence except for the awful November weather beating down on the little village of East Kennett.

Despite his best efforts, he was unable to get comfortable and his mind was churning like the storm outside. He sat up. Had the words he'd spoken about Nell amounted to a promise to Master Truman to marry his daughter? He was not quite sure.

'Nell has promised to think about it,' he said to himself. "It is not yet over and done with," he spoke aloud.

He scrambled up from his makeshift bed and dressed solely in his shirt and braies, tiptoed to the small wooden partition behind which Nell slept.

He stood staring down at her. Her hair unbraided and tangled on the pillow where she had tossed and turned in anguish before falling asleep in utter exhaustion. In the darkness he traced the contours of her face and neck; imagined her laughing eyes. Not those reddened and puffy which he'd seen but an hour ago. He saw her as a young girl, barefoot, chivvying the geese along the road with a stick. He remembered the Christmases they had spent in this house, singing the special songs—some of which Guy had composed.

He laughed.

And despite himself, he began to hum the tune to one of them. The words he had heard Father Francis speak one day when the priest had been looking at his Bible. The good father had told him that it was a hymn sung at Lauds at the Feast of the Transfiguration in August and that they were very ancient.

"*O nata lux de lumine...*" Father Francis had translated the words from the Latin for him.

'*O Light born of Light, Jesus redeemer of the world. With loving kindness grant us this reprieve: receive our prayers and praises. Thou, who once deigned to be clothed in flesh, set our souls free from sin and fear: gather us all, O Lord we beg, to be members of thy blessed body.*'

He did not realise that he had been singing under his breath, the tune he'd composed for these beautiful words.

And as he'd sung, he had been staring down at Nell.

She opened her eyes.

"Oh Guy that was beautiful," she whispered, "a beautiful song for the passing of my father."

"I cannot sleep," he said.

Nell pulled back the blankets which covered her. "Then you shall sing us both to sleep."

Guy backed away. "No... I..."

"Why not? Remember... I am the harlot of Kennett, am I not?"

She opened her arms to him.

"And what can possibly happen? We are almost fully clothed," she smiled.

Guy smiled with her and climbed into the bed beside her.

*****

At last the storm blew itself out and everything went deathly quiet. Nell slept beside Guy, his arms folded around her. The bed was only designed for one small occupant and Guy was hanging from the edge with no covers. He did not sleep. His mind turned over and over with the predicament he was in and suddenly he had resolved it. He decided to appeal to the Lord Lillebon in the morning. Surely he could and would protect him from the wrath of the Courtenay mob?

Nell shifted in her sleep and Guy was almost tipped from the mattress.

He rolled over and out onto his knees. Letting her go, he tucked the blankets back around her.

The pain in his ribs returned and now he also had an arm which was numb with the weight of Nell's body. He stood and flexed his fists raising them above his head.

What was the time?

No owls were hooting. Might there be stars or a moon to give him an approximate hour of the night?

He opened the cottage door silently and padded out into the garth on bare feet. The grass was wet with the rain but it had stopped.

He looked up at the sky where a pale moon was now hanging upside down over the church roof. The plough, that reliable star formation, was directly above him. He knew that meant it was the middle of the night, about three hours past midnight.

Once again he threw his arms over his head and stretched, groaning with the cracking of his muscles. He moved his arms in a semi-circle above his head to test his damaged rib. It pinched and he swore loudly, "By Satan's powers!"

He'd been bunched up in the bed with Nell for hours, not wanting to move in case he disturbed her and now he stretched his whole body revelling in the flexing and relaxing of the muscles. He jogged in a circle then ran on the spot and felt much better.

Once more he stood and stared up at the moon.

A song popped into his head. It was not the first time a song had been formed in his mind in the middle of the night.

"Ah, Mistress Moon!" he cried and then began to sing.

"Oh, mother moon so high in the sky,

Tell me where my true love lies.

Put into her mind a picture of me.

Make her dream of me.

Make your precious white light

Embrace her, like my arms.

See into my heart and know that I am true.

Mother moon, tell her I wait for her..."

Guy stopped singing.

His eyes had spotted a darker shadow in the already dark shadows of the gatehouse to the manor. He narrowed his eyes. The gate was partly open. A figure stood in the little space made by the personnel door in the main gate.

He watched for a while but could not ascertain who it was; however he knew they had seen and heard him and that they were not friendly.

He was almost resolved to go over to the man, for man he believed it to be, when the figure flitted, like a moth, into the courtyard of the manor house and melted away, the door closing silently.

Someone else was obviously awake and unable to sleep this night. Someone else had come out to stare at the moon over the church roof. Guy shivered. It was quite cold out here and his feet were frozen.

He padded back to his makeshift bed in the kitchen and tried to make himself comfortable.

This time he did sleep though his sleep was filled with odd dreams.

First, he found himself out in the garth again, looking at the moon but this time it was full and red gold as it often was in autumn. He heard a whirring of wings and looked back, up to the roof of Master Truman's cottage. A huge angel with a massive wingspan was hovering over the house and the whole place was bathed in a golden light. He had to shield his eyes from its glare. Then the scene changed and Guy was beating out the lead in his forge, singing as the hammer rose and fell. There was a certain steadfastness in this work and he felt a glow of satisfaction as he beat the panels thinner. He realised at that moment that he was happy at this work. Then the story changed yet again and he was by a grave in the churchyard. A body was being lowered into the pit. It was oddly wrapped around with thin strips of lead, like a metal winding sheet and as the body hit the bottom of the grave the covering to the face slipped.

He realised the body was his own.

*****

He awoke to a screech and garbled conversation coming from the hall. He couldn't make out what was happening. It was now quite light. Sunshine was peeping through the shutters.

He could hear Parnell's voice calling over and over upon God's mercy as she sobbed. But in between the sobs, he realised she was laughing. Was she still hysterical from the night before? Guy thought that she had exhausted all her tears and had calmed before they slept together. This was odd. Nell was not a weak, sentimental woman. This morning he was convinced she should be calm and accepting.

He rose and drew on his cotte not bothering to buckle a belt over it and barefooted once more he made for the hall door.

A man's voice was quietly speaking with Parnell. Should he enter? It might be the priest again and Nell might wish to be alone with God's representative and her father's body.

He put his ear to the wood. No! It couldn't be!

Guy burst into the room and stood, his arms dangling to his sides in utter shock.

"Hello, my lad," said Master Truman, buzzing as heartily as a hive of bees. "I feel so much better today!"

CHAPTER TEN ~ INTERROGATION

"Necromancy?"

"Yes, my lord."

"So not content with sorcery you tell me we now have necromancy, too?"

"Yes, my lord."

Sir Walter Lillebon shook his head, "I don't believe it."

"My lord, I saw it with my own eyes. Heard it with my own ears."

"My blacksmith, Guy Ferrier, caused my bailiff, John Truman, to come back from the dead?"

Sir Thomas Courtenay gave a small bow of the head. "My lord, speak to your priest. He will tell you that Master Truman was at death's door. He administered extreme unction. The woman Mother.. .whatever her name is... she will tell you that Truman had but hours to live when she last saw him. No one makes such a recovery without... infernal interference."

The Lord of East Kennett's Manor paced around his hall. "Whilst I am very glad to hear that my bailiff is not waiting to be laid in the earth just yet, I can't have such... unholy... practices... here at... go un-investigated."

"My lord..." Sir Thomas interrupted. "Ask his daughter. Put her to the test. She dare not lie. Not before the Bible. She saw him dead... dead for a few hours and this morning... "

"As bright as a May morning, my Lord Walter," said Lady Lillebon. "Walking about the village and into church as if he'd acquired a new soul... which of course..." She did not like to carry on. The expression on her husband's face was menacing. She rarely saw this side of him and when she did, she knew to keep quiet.

Walter Lillebon sat down heavily. "Tell me again what you saw, Sir Thomas."

The man ranged himself in front of Lord Lillebon and planted his feet. "It is said that the bailiff died before the midnight hour; his body lay in the house and his daughter and her lover..."

"Ferrier?"

"Yes, the woman and the blacksmith, were abed. I went to use the privy late on and took a turn around the courtyard, when I heard singing. That is when I saw Ferrier out of the house and in the garden of the bailiff's cottage. Firstly he stretched his hands to the moon and cried out, "By Satan's powers!""

"Dastardly," muttered Lady Lillebon.

"Then he made some passes with his hands, no doubt secret symbols designed to invoke the Dark One."

"You saw no... no... sign of..."

"No, my lord. But he made a circle, withershynnes, and danced inside it for a while. Then he began his infernal incantations."

"Incantations? Good Lord!"

"He called upon his mistress the moon. I was not able to hear the rest and I was, as you can imagine, quite perturbed by it all and withdrew to the safety of the manor."

Many present crossed themselves to be on the safe side.

"And you tell me that this was all enacted in the bailiff's garden and at the same hour as this was taking place, the man Truman was restored to life?"

"Yes, my lord."

"How do you know, eh? How... eh?"

Thomas licked his lips. "This morning early, I sent my servant to spy through the shutters. I know it was not exactly... but... he will tell you what he saw."

"And that was?"

"Master Truman rising from his deathbed whilst his daughter yelled and cried and cavorted..."

"Cavorted, you say?"

"Danced about in her shift, my lord. No doubt giving thanks to the Dark Lord."

"And where was my blacksmith at this time?"

"In the same house, sir, giving praise no doubt, to his infernal lord and master."

Walter Lillebon chewed his lip. "We will have them all here. All of them. Now. We shall get to the bottom of this."

"There must be some innocent explanation for it all," said Adela Lillebon suddenly, who had been standing behind her father's chair.

He grasped the arms of that chair and swivelled to look at her with a stare which froze her blood. "You mistress, will have nothing to say on this matter. You will leave the hall and go to your rooms."

"But Father..."

"I'll not have it Adela. If there is something foul here I'll not have it. I pray to God you are not involved."

"No, of course I am not involved," said Adela bravely. She threw a nasty glance at Sir Thomas. "I do not believe it's anything horrible, that's all."

"Go! I will speak to you later!"

Adela Lillebon took in a breath to cry out, thought better of it, turned and fled the hall.

Henri Courtenay gave his cousin Thomas a black look. "My lord. We must let the blacksmith explain. It would be unfair to take just the one man's word for it."

He knew his cousin Thomas for a liar. He didn't entirely trust him.

"I am a fair man, Sir Henri. I will listen," said Walter Lillebon. "Go fetch them all. I will wait."

*****

Guy had been sitting in the hall with John Truman and Parnell. Truman had eaten porridge and drunk ale and although pale, was listening to Guy and Nell explain what they had experienced that night.

"You were dead, Father. You were."

"I felt dead, I must admit. But now... well... I feel like a new man."

"What happened?" said Guy, totally perplexed.

"God decided that he didn't want me just yet, after all," said Truman flippantly.

"You were not breathing, you had such a deathly pallor that we thought..."

"Your lips were blue, Father. And as Guy said you were so deathly pale. We could not find your life's beat."

"Well... here I am as live as a frolicking frog!"

"I don't think that's quite true, Father. You still look pale to me."

"Best you rest today, sir," said Guy. "I don't think it will do you any harm to do nothing much today. Your body has certainly had a bit of a shock."

"Nonsense. I have work to do. And I must go to church to give thanks..."

"No, Father, please..." began Parnell but John Truman wouldn't listen.

A little later he went into the church to give thanks for his miraculous recovery and that was when some village folk had seen him. The story was all over the manor in no time. And that is where Sir Thomas had learned that the man had... died.

Eventually Guy made his way to his forge. His mind was in complete denial. How could this have happened? Parnell and Guy—both of them—had believed her father dead. The priest and Mother

Little had not expected him to survive the night.

Guy laid out his tools and rekindled his forge fire. Had they all been so wrong? All of them? Was the man in some sort of sleeping state where breathing could not be detected? Was this even possible?

He began to fashion the promised lining for the coffin, all the while pondering on the meaning of life and the manner of death and the fact that death was so very close to them all; all the time.

This brought back his problem—the Courtenays.

He was busy flattening the lead when Tom arrived at the forge.

"Well you're a dark horse!" was the first thing he said.

"A what?"

"A secretive soul, Guy Ferrier."

"Why's that?"

"I saw you coming out of Master Truman's cottage this morning. Been there all night had you?"

"You do not know the half of it, Tom," said Guy.

Tom laughed in a rather suggestive way, "So, when are we to have the banns read, eh?"

"I beg your pardon?"

"You and Parnell."

"Parnell... Ah."

"Come on. I'm only your oldest and best friend. I think I ought to know first."

"I haven't been keeping anything from you, Tom."

"Oh no... of course you haven't. I thought you said that Nell didn't want to marry."

"She doesn't but... things have... oh sit down and I'll explain."

*****

Guy was just nearing the end of his tale when a figure arrived at the forge door.

His heart took a leap.

It was Sir Henri Courtenay.

"Ferrier. A word."

Guy bowed low and his rib twinged.

"Sir Henri, what might I do for you?"

"The Lord Lillebon wants to see you... immediately."

"Oh?"

"And a word of warning. My cousin Thomas…"

"Yes?"

"I'll tell you now. He is poisoning the ear of your lord with some fantastic tale about necromancy. Be warned. He might be my cousin but… he's not trustworthy. Just so you're prepared."

Guy took a swift look at Tom.

"Thank you, sir."

The man nodded peremptorily and stepped back inviting Guy to accompany him.

Guy covered his fire and closed the forge doors.

"I am ready."

*****

They were all there. Master Bailiff, looking pale and drawn again. Parnell, her arm through his. The priest and Mother Little and glowering at them all; Sir Thomas Courtenay, his hand on the pommel of his sword.

Above them on the dais was Lord Walter Lillebon clasping and unclasping his hands; his Lady beside him with a face like gargoyle; brows drawn down and lips pursed.

The steward took Guy down the hall and presented him to the lord.

"The blacksmith, Ferrier, my lord."

"Of course it's him, you foolish man!" said Walter. "I can see that!"

Steward Masters sniffed his displeasure and, his nose in the air, retired to the back of the room.

142

Guy bowed. "My Lord Lillebon. You sent for me."

"Aye, I did. I've heard a tale from Sir Thomas Courtenay and I've already heard what Master Truman has to say upon the matter. Goodwoman Little and Father Fabian have spoken. What's your story, Ferrier?"

"Story, my lord...? I'm afraid I don't understand..." Guy looked genuinely puzzled.

"Tell him, Courtenay," said the lord.

Sir Thomas stepped forward. "In the blackest hour of the night, Master Blacksmith, I saw you in the garden of the bailiff of this manor..."

"This is quite true. I was there."

It was obvious that the knight had expected a denial for he was a little taken aback.

"And I saw you appealing to your heathen goddess and calling up the devil." He pointed angrily at Guy, "You sir, were casting spells in order to draw back the soul of the dead bailiff into his body. And you succeeded, against the laws of God, for here he is, hale and hearty."

"Oh, I wouldn't go so far as to say that," said John Truman. "I'm still quite poorly, you know." Nell squeezed his arm.

Guy's face creased into a huge grin. "Casting spells...?" He threw back his head and laughed. "And what form did these 'spells' take, Sir Thomas?"

For the first time, the knight seemed a little uncertain. "I didn't hear the whole of it but I did hear you call upon the devil, 'By Satan's powers,' you cried. And then you began to sing... I heard, 'Oh Mistress Moon!' "

Again Guy laughed and turned to the dais, "Sir Thomas heard me cursing, my lord... that in itself is, I'm sorry to say, reprehensible and I will no doubt do penance for it when I next make confession. Indeed I did cry out. I was in pain, for as you probably know, I have sustained an injury to my ribs and it still gives me much sorrow."

Walter Lillebon narrowed his eyes. "No... no I didn't know this."

"It's true my Lord, if you will forgive me," said John Truman. "He broke a rib or two a while ago." Nell and a few others nodded.

"And the recitation which the good knight heard was merely me making up one of my songs. You know, my lord, how these things come to me. And in order to remember them, I must sing them to fix them in my head." And he began to sing the song which he'd composed the night before.

'Oh mother moon so high in the sky,

Tell me where my love lies.

Put into her mind a picture of me...."

"Yes... yes..." said the Lord Lillebon bad temperedly, "we don't need to hear the whole thing."

Courtenay carried on, "But my lord... his dancing... *withershynnes,* his waving, his gesticulations!"

"Has no man ever stretched till his sinews cracked? Has no man here ever found himself yawning and stretching like a cat when he's been cooped up half the night?"

"Cooped up man?" said Lillebon.

"In a bed too small for him." Ah. Guy wished he had not spoken those words.

Master Truman let go of his daughter's arm. "Cooped up in which bed?" he said.

Parnell sighed, "Mine, Father. Guy was giving me comfort, for we all thought you dead, did we not."

"Comfort?" said Bailiff Truman, his face for a change showing some colour. "That's what they are calling it nowadays are they?"

"If I might... speak?" Guy stepped forward. "There was nothing immoral or wicked in what Parnell and I have done."

Lord Lillebon's eyebrow rose and a slight smile escaped the corner of his mouth.

"Disgusting!" said his wife.

"Hush... we shall hear the blacksmith speak."

Guy reached behind him and took hold of Parnell's arm. "We have for some time been plighted, my lord. We have declared our intentions to each other—that we shall become man and wife but have yet to speak vows in the church porch before witnesses." Guy hoped this would diffuse the situation and he desperately hoped that Nell would not argue with him.

Aid came from an unlooked for source.

"My lord, if I might speak a humble word?" The priest, Father Fabian, now stepped forward.

"I have known about this for some time and have no doubt that Master Guy and Mistress Parnell would, in the fullness of time, have come to me to arrange a marriage. Indeed yes. And very soon."

There was a silence in which they all heard the lowing of the cattle in the north pasture barn.

Guy recovered his poise. Well! He had not expected the priest to come to their rescue.

"This is so, my lord. Parnell and I are ready to exchange vows at the church porch. We just needed time to organise it and to speak to Master Truman. As you know, your bailiff is not a well man, as has been shown by what happened to him last night and Nell leaving him to become my wife and living in the forge house, must needs take some planning."

'Good Lord,' said Guy to himself, 'this is like extemporising a new song... so many lines to think of.'

The Lord Lillebon rubbed the side of his nose in some perturbation, "A marriage you say?"

"Yes my lord," said Guy and Nell together. And Guy was relieved that Nell had taken his story and run with it.

"And of course, when we had eventually organised ourselves, we would have come to you and asked for your blessing."

"You are both freemen, you don't need my say so," said the lord.

"No, but we'd still like to have your blessing, sir," said Guy nodding reverently.

"Oh. Right... yes..." Walter stood and cleared his throat.

"Let it be known that I give my blessing to Guy Ferrier and Parnell Truman on the announcement of their forthcoming marriage."

"At last!" said Truman. "They've been blowing hot and cold for months now." He took hold of his daughter's arm again. "At last!" and he gave her a smacking kiss on the cheek.

They all heard the stamp of a foot and a frustrated "Argh!" as the steward's daughter, red faced and angry, stormed out of the hall.

"What's the matter with her?" asked a bemused Lord Lillebon.

No one answered him but the knight Thomas Courtenay looked round the people assembled. "I know what I saw. I know what I heard. The blacksmith is evil and should be punished."

John Truman mumbled under his breath, "Punished for bringing me back to life? I don't think so…"

Parnell shook her father's arm, "Shhh."

Henri Courtenay followed his cousin from the hall. "I will speak to him, my lord," he said. And the outer door banged.

*****

Guy took Parnell by the arm and steered her away from the rest of the party.

"I am sorry Nell," he whispered. "It was the only thing I could think of."

"The only way out of a difficult situation?"

"If you are still determined to remain single then we shall leave it a while and…"

"And then I will forever be a scarlet woman, who ensnared the village blacksmith and dumped him when he declared in front of everyone how we'd slept together?"

"That's all we did. Sleep. Though if truth were known, I didn't sleep much."

Nell chuckled. "No. You were out in the garden calling up devils!"

"You'd better be playing the fool, Parnell Truman, for I couldn't possibly marry a woman who thought her future husband was a necromancer."

"Of course not, you silly goose."

The mention of goose made Guy's brain fall back to the work lying yet to be finished in his forge.

He dropped her arm as they approached her cottage. "I have the coffin lining to make. Shall I see you later?"

"Come for supper tonight."

He nodded and planted a kiss on her cheek.

Would this be how it was when they were married? Him rushing off to his work and she staying behind to plan supper, do the household chores and see to her ageing father living alone in a different house? The places would be reversed. It would take some getting used to.

As he approached his forge he saw the figure of a man in a dark brown cotte furtively hiding by the doors. His guts lurched. Courtenay!

But no, it was the priest Father Fabian.

"Ah… Master Ferrier…"

"Thank you Father, for your help today. You have no idea how much easier you made it to…"

"Oh, but I do," he smiled.

"Come in and I'll kindle the fire. We should be warm at least."

The priest watched Guy bustle about the forge. "I am very glad that you and Mistress Truman have decided to marry at last."

"We have been skirting around the edge of it for a long time."

"I can see why Mistress Parnell would not wish to leave her father. He is a very sick man, as we have seen."

Guy made a moue. "It will be difficult. But I've no doubt Nell will manage two men perfectly well."

"And two homes."

Guy laid out his lead. "I must begin my task, Sir Priest, if it is to be done in time for the body to be taken to Thatcham."

"Ah yes. I understand. I come to thank you for the very fine work you have done on the door of the church. I have now had an opportunity to gaze upon it at leisure. It's very fine."

"It is my pleasure. And my contribution to the glory of God's house."

Guy pressed down the lever of his bellows and the flames shot upward with a whoosh. The priest jumped. "I am come to ask you... if... er... if you might execute another task in the church?"

"Another? What would that be?"

"The bell housing. Much of it is wood and that was renewed, I hear, last year in the time of Father Francis, but some of the workings are metal and are in need of a little tender care."

"Ah, yes."

"I have a terrible feeling when I pull upon the rope, the whole thing is going to land upon my head," he chuckled nervously.

"I will look at it and see what must be done."

"Thank you." The handsome face screwed itself into a grinning smile.

"But I must also have the word of the Lord Lillebon to execute such a task. It's a different matter using up small pieces of iron for the patterns on the door than large and costly pieces of metal for the bell frame," said Guy.

"Ah yes, I suppose it is."

The priest thought for a moment whilst Guy held his breath and his hammer ready to strike. "Then I will speak to him... forthwith."

"Let me know when you have done that, Father Fabian," said Guy and he struck the lead with a dull clang.

*****

He spent the whole day on the lining of the coffin. As the sun was about to dip down over the trees towards Avebury, Guy took the last piece of his decoration for the church door, slung his bag over his shoulder and walked the short distance to the building.

He stood with his hands on his hips for a long while, staring at the door's surface with its story of the flood.

At the very top were Noah and his wife. Their dog lurked in the curlicues towards the hinges and on the other side, a sheep and three comical chickens followed each other in a line. A goat appeared in the next curlicue pursued by a mean looking wolf, its jaws open and its teeth sharp. The oliphant sat above the lock of the door and marching across the surface with its foliate decoration were, in line, a pig, a horse and a cow.

By the bottom hinge were the little birds and the tree. Guy chuckled as he looked at the last few animals for they were all of them eating the leaves of the tree; a badger, a fox and a rather large mouse which dominated a sad looking donkey. At the hinge end stood a strange creature with a hump on its back. Guy had no idea what that was supposed to represent. The large eared hare which Guy had made, sat underneath them, looking up, seeing everything above him.

The blacksmith took the last piece, the owl, in his hands and placed it in the very last curlicue by the lowest hinge. He was about to knock in the pins when he heard a furtive whispering.

"I can't... I can't do it. You know that!" A man's voice.

"Why not?" A girl's voice.

"It's all very well us lying together at my house and taking whatever opportunity we can to..."

"You are telling me you don't care?"

"I do care, of course I care but you must know that anything more would be impossible."

"And why is it impossible?"

"Oh, you silly woman, you know it well. The church now forbids clergy to be married. I could no sooner be your husband than... than I could fly from the roof of my church."

"So, you admit to me... you lied."

"I never promised marriage. Never! I wish I could, but I can't."

"Please... please..." The girl's voice took on a whining, pleading tone. "If we went away from here we could start again. No one would know us."

"And I could not be a priest. You could not be a priest's wife."

"There is something else we might do, I'm sure."

"You have not thought it through. You haven't. It has to stop now."

"Fabian... no... you are my only chance."

"I have been a foolish man. Led by Satan into temptation. My lusts will be the end of me, I fear. I am going to... yes... I am going to..."

"Confess your sins? Oh, you wicked man!" said the voice. "Oh no! You cannot. No! I will deny it all!"

"No, Emma. I would not implicate you. I promise... if you will keep quiet... Then there is a chance we..."

"I've heard the rumours. You and your lusts!"

"Did you really think you were the only one? At first ... and then..."

"Ah yes..." hissed the woman, "I have heard the rumours! It's true after all. The Widow Poulter, isn't it? That unrepentant trull!"

"It was her... until I met you... and then, as I love Jesus my Redeemer, once I had met you, you were the only one." Father Fabian sighed loudly. "I am going away. I am going to leave this church and ask the Bishop for another."

"Please Fabian... please. I love you. I can't live without you. You can't leave me."

"Ha! You can't live without me now. Now that you know your wonderful Guy Ferrier is to be married to Mistress Parnell."

"Oh him... Oh come now, you know I never really wanted him. I just enjoyed baiting him. He's such a dullard."

"That's not what I heard."

"You cannot think that I would be content to take a village blacksmith to husband when I can have the second son of a nobleman."

Guy's eyebrows rose into his hair, he said to himself, 'Ah, our proud and disdainful priest does have a noble background! Well, well...'

"You will no doubt make your marriage to your tedious

Marlborough artisan and be happy about it."

Emma stamped her foot. "I will not! I only want you."

Guy had heard enough. He began to hum loudly and allowed his tune to reverberate around the stone porch. Then he began to sing as he knocked the few pins into the figure of the owl.

"The Owl, the owl is the Queen of the Fowl,

Her eyes are large and her ears hear all.

At night she flies, you hear her howl.

She hears your words through the cottage wall..."

If that didn't make the two of them shudder, then nothing would.

There was silence in the nave of the church.

Then Guy heard a door bang—the north door or Devil's door, so called because this is the opening through which the Devil was said to leave the church at baptisms—Emma Masters had gone.

Slowly the south door opened a crack.

"Ah... Father Fabian," said Guy. "I was here to put the last animal on the door. Here, see." He pointed to his work. "What do you think?"

"Ah yes... an owl," said the priest in a small nervy voice. "Excellent."

"And since you want me to look at the bell housing, I thought I could do that too before it became too dark to see?"

"Ah yes... please do… erm... come into the church." The man was jittery and nervous. The blacksmith was convinced that he knew that Guy had overheard what had been said. He knocked in the last pins quickly.

Guy grinned and once more hoisting his bag on his shoulder, he nonchalantly ducked under the door lintel.

The bell was housed in a small squat tower and the rope fell down through thirty feet or so to its base at the western end. In order to check the structure of the bell housing, Guy would have to scale a ladder which was secured rather imperfectly to the southern wall of the tower.

Hooking his bag over his shoulder, he began his ascent, looking up now and again at the ancient stonework of the original masons.

All around the bell was a narrow platform which allowed work to be performed on the mechanism and its medium sized bell.

Guy looked down. He noticed Father Fabian's hands on the bottom of the ladder. He was clasping the uprights with a white knuckled grip. His face gradually looked up at Guy under his eye lids. That look took on a devilish glare in the failing light.

And Fabian began to shake the ladder with all his might.

CHAPTER ELEVEN ~ THE HANGING

"Guy... Guy are you in there?" Nell had heard the hum of conversation and had been sure that the priest and Guy were in the church together.

Her voice echoed up the nave and into the tower where Guy was hanging onto the ladder for his life.

He dropped his bag of tools with a great clatter.

"Oh..." Parnell came round the inner corner of the tower. "I'm sorry, did I startle you both?"

Father Fabian stepped back, his face as white as the plaster covering the walls of his church.

"You did, Mistress Truman." The priest crossed himself and closed his eyes.

He looked up at the blacksmith and cleared his throat. "Come down Master Ferrier, it's too dark to achieve what we wanted now anyway."

Guy swallowed. What had just happened? Had he mistaken it? Had the priest been trying to make him fall from the ladder or did he imagine it?

Gradually and shakily he stepped down and retrieved his tool bag.

"I'll return then tomorrow, shall I?"

"Yes... yes..." Father Fabian wiped his forehead and Guy noticed he swallowed several times.

"I must go to prepare for vespers."

"Best you don't ring the bell for the services... just in case," said Guy in a voice loaded with meaning.

Father Fabian backed away. "I am sorry... so sorry... the Devil's work."

Parnell swore she heard him say as he fled into the nave, "So close... so close to damnation. God forgive me... so close."

*****

"I am a humble blacksmith, Nell, wanting a quiet life and people are wishing me dead at every turn! I can't understand it."

"No Guy... surely not. Why would he?"

Guy sat down on his one good stool. He felt beset all around. Everything was moving too fast for him. He was no longer in control of his life.

"Because when I was in the porch finishing the door, I overheard the good father and... and Emma Masters plotting together. You know how it echoes in there. Fabian was admitting to an illicit relationship with her and told her that he was no longer prepared to carry on with it. She, as you can imagine, was having none of it and tried to coerce him into leaving the village and running away with her."

Nell's open mouthed face wore a similar expression to the painting of Eve on the church wall showing when God banished her from Eden. She simply couldn't believe it.

"No! Emma Masters?" she said after a while..."When everyone was talking about Father Fabian and the Widow Poulter?"

"Oh yes... the man admits to that too."

Parnell slipped down to her knees in front of Guy. "Good Lord. And this man has been willing to hear our confessions, has been preaching to us... An unclean priest!"

"He's been playing the holy priest, when all along... If word got out he'd be severely disciplined by his bishop."

"I told you he wouldn't last till Christmas," said Nell. She took hold of Guy's hand. "You really think he was trying to kill you?"

"To rid himself of one who knows his sordid secret?"

"Is it really possible? You're sure? You're really sure?"

"It all happened so fast and he let go of the ladder when he heard you approach. He seemed genuinely repentant to me. It was a momentary lapse, I think."

"But if I hadn't called out when I did…?"

Guy rubbed his hands over his face, "I don't know. I really can't say."

"Would he have continued to try to dislodge you?"

"Perhaps the moment of his realisation of guilt and your appearance were one and the same and he wouldn't have continued with…"

"His plan?"

"We can't call it a plan. It was definitely a spur of the moment thing." Guy was shaking his head over and over. "I simply can't say, though. I don't know. To be truthful, I am now beginning to doubt the whole episode."

They had lit no candle upon arriving at Guy's house and it now lay in darkness. They stared at each other's pale face for a little while trying to take it all in.

Then Nell said.

"Well there's one thing for sure."

"Hmm?"

"We are not going to vespers tonight."

*****

Once the shock had worn off, Nell told Guy why she had been looking for him.

"Father has been very tired today. The euphoria of this morning soon faded and he's back to being tired and breathless. I was trying to find you to tell you that a celebratory supper was cancelled."

"You must return to him, Nell."

"But you can't be left alone. What if the good father returns? What if his regret at what he tried to do changes to determination to dispose of you after all?"

"Ah no... Now I'll be prepared. You go home."

"Come back with me."

"You go and tend to your father. He needs you."

Mistress Truman was not easy to dissuade but eventually, she nodded and left him with, "I will return in a little while with some hot food."

Her chickens had been laying well and she was going to make her father a herb omelette. It was no trouble, she said, to make him something too.

Guy yawned and watched her disappear into the darkness, down the road and into the bailiff's cottage. He hadn't realised how tired he was. He locked and bolted the door, closed all the shutters and lay down to rest for a short while before Nell was to return with his supper.

He didn't know how much later it was when he awoke with a start. Had he been dreaming? He'd heard a shattering sound. The shattering and splintering of wood.

He sat up on his bed and stretched his ears. There it came again.

Another sound, a metallic banging, reached his house. Fumbling around in the dark, he pushed on his boots, took up his quarterstaff and made for the exit leading to his forge.

He smelled smoke as soon as he opened the door. A terrible feeling began behind his breastbone. Fire! The most feared thing. Forges were particularly prone to catching fire—that much was inescapable—but Guy was meticulous in looking after his forge; he never left a spark unsuppressed; never left the fire burning nor an ember unquenched. He'd never in all his years had a significantly dangerous fire at the forge.

He burst through the workshop door to find his roof alight and both front doors wide open. He knew he'd secured them that night and he also knew that they'd been forced.

The building was not large but there were many dark patches where a man might hide.

Guy hefted his quarterstaff.

"Come out you coward and show yourself!"

There was no answer. He decided to step further in and douse the flames now engulfing the roof by the door. Luckily he had filled his trough from the river only yesterday and it was full. Dropping his staff, he grabbed a bucket, ladled and threw it on the flames. There was a loud hissing and a plume of steam.

No one came to help him. The forge was on the edge of the village and unless he called for help, none would be forthcoming.

Again he dipped his bucket; once more he threw it at the flames. Sparks which were falling ready to engulf other combustible items in the building needed to be beaten out. Guy took up his besom and desperately tried to kill the little flames here and there before they grew and overwhelmed his forge. His breath came in short, sharp gasps as he laboured with his not-quite-mended ribs.

His mouth a rictus of pain and anguish, he beat with his bare hands at some of the little flames dropping onto his woodpile and then decided to tip it out and allow the rolling of the logs to do the work. He reached for his apron of leather and used it to beat the flames from the door posts and roof struts where he could reach.

More water from his trough was employed to douse the rest and gradually the fire was under control.

Guy was tired, hot and out of breath.

He staggered out into the night and looked up and down the road. No sign of the perpetrators.

He turned his back on the grassy area just before his forge; the area which led down to the river Kennett.

Suddenly, springing from the shadows of the small bushes across from his workplace, three men came bounding for him. He'd let go of his quarterstaff when he'd grabbed the bucket of water and so now he was unarmed, except for the knife at his waist. He had no time to draw it, for a rope came over his head, around his torso and was tightened, pinning his arms.

He was yanked backwards and stumbled.

"For the love of God!"

Then he heard a devilish laugh. In the dark it seemed to come from everywhere.

"One way to get you out of your home, you bastard!" said a voice. "Threaten your precious forge."

Into the light of a lantern held by a man in a blue cotte, came Sir Thomas Courtenay.

"And so now we have you."

"Finish me off now and you'll never house your cousin in his protective coffin," yelled Guy. "You'll be taking a decomposing and dripping corpse to Thatcham with you!"

"That will never do, Blacksmith."

Someone kicked him in the back and Guy fell on his knees. "It's not finished, I tell you."

"We've seen it...' said another voice. "It's nearly complete. We shall see it done tonight and then..."

"You will be food for the kites, come tomorrow," finished Sir Thomas, laying his arm across his cousin's shoulder.

"Up, now!"

Guy was wrenched upwards by the rope and dragged into the forge.

"We have seen just how close you are to finishing it," said one man.

"Complete it... now!" concluded Sir Thomas Courtenay.

"How can I, trussed up like a pig?"

"Maurice... undo it but keep a wary eye on him."

The rope was removed but Guy heard a sword being slid from a scabbard, as Sir Maurice pointed it at him.

Guy ran his hands through his hair. He could not seal the coffin. If he did he was sealing his own fate. He somehow had to elude his captors.

He reached for a lamp to light his work. 'Make everything as slow as you can Guy, in the hope someone will come and aid you,' he said to himself. But he wasn't hopeful.

"Careful now, we don't want accidents, do we?" said Sir Thomas sarcastically. The other two chuckled.

"I cannot work in the dark."

"Piers, light a candle or two."

"Yes, Tom."

Guy reached for his pliers.

"Steady now… everything where we can see it, please. Some of the tools in here could be used as a weapon, as I am sure you realise, Blacksmith."

Slowly Guy drew a piece of the beaten lead towards him. "I must build up the fire and heat the metal to seal the edges of the lead," he said.

"Then do it slowly." Thomas perched his backside on the tree trunk upon which Adela had sat that first day.

Thomas took the turves from his fire and fed it with twigs. The flames flickered and danced, throwing shadows over the forge walls.

A tawny owl hooted on the willow tree by the river.

Guy waited until the flames were a little higher and sturdier and then pulled on the bellows.

Woosh! The sound made the youngest man jump.

"Oh for Heaven's sake, Maurice…" said Sir Thomas, like a pedagogue. "Are you really such a ninny?"

Guy allowed the flames to grow. He added the charcoal.

"Now we wait," said Guy. "For the heat to build."

"The longer we wait, the further away your death lies, you

think? We have time... you do not. Once your task is done, so are you Blacksmith."

Guy glared at the man and pulled once more on his lever. The air exited the large bellows with a great rush and the flames leapt up above and beyond the usual level. The shock of it gave him a small window of time.

Guy made a dash for the door, pulling down some iron bars which he'd lodged against the wall, to impede pursuit by the nearest man, the one called Piers.

"Argh!" He went down in a flailing of arms as the bars of iron rolled under his feet.

Guy vaulted his anvil and made for the door.

Sir Thomas was there with a drawn sword.

Guy barged into him with all his might, knocking him sideways, just as a length of wood came crashing down on his skull.

The world went topsy turvy for a moment and then Guy was falling backwards, his vision taking in the roof beams of the forge.

He heard. "Not in the fire! Dammit. We still need him!"

And he watched as an arm came out to snatch him and two dark shapes closed in from the side of his vision like a curtain.

He fell into darkness.

*****

Parnell was cutting chunks of meat from a baked ham.

"You eat your supper Father and I will take some sustenance to Guy."

"Don't be long now!"

"No, I won't. You make sure you drink water with your food and take it slowly. No more coughing, now."

"Oh, all right!"

Nell wrapped some meat, bread and cheese in a cloth, tying the corners and then put them into her basket. She took a platter and scooped out the omelette she had made onto it, carefully covering it with a thin cloth and finished the basket with a flask of ale.

"And make sure you say grace before you eat and give thanks afterwards. The day you've had, you need God's favour," said Nell.

Master Truman tossed his head and made a wordless mouthing of some words just to annoy his daughter, "Nah... nah... ha."

She left him chuckling to himself.

Taking a lantern from a shelf by the door, she settled the basket on her arm and turned for Guy's cottage a matter of two hundred steps away.

She'd passed Tom's house and reached the trees by Guy's house when she realised that the forge doors were open. She could see, despite the dark, the shape of three horses tied to the bushes behind the house. Nell crept forward and put down her basket in the darker shadow of the trees.

There was light in the forge and voices, though she could not hear Guy speaking. She heard,

"Bring him round!"

"How...?"

"Water, you cretin!"

"Yes, Tom."

There was a splashing sound and coughing.

Nell turned on her heel and on light feet tripped back to her house.

She almost fell in the door. "Quick Father, rouse the village... anyone, men... with weapons."

"Well, that didn't take long."

"Listen to me, Guy is in danger. Those black hearted Courtenay cousins have him. Quick! We need to help. I think they are going to kill him!"

"What?"

"Out... out... quickly, go and fetch Steward Masters. Anyone. Tom... Anyone. And get someone to run to the manor to explain what's happening."

"Where are you going?"

Parnell had reached for a bow and some arrows propped up in the corner of the room. "I'm going back. If I can delay them… until you can come with more people…"

"Daughter… do you know what you're doing?"

"Of course I know what I'm doing. My affianced is in trouble. I'm going to help!"

"No, I mean…"

"Oh, Father, stop wittering. Go! I can use a bow, as well you know. Now go!"

Master Truman reached for his boots.

"No time… go in your feet! GO!"

And Nell rushed back out through the door.

*****

It wasn't until she was halfway to the forge that she realised she had just sent her very poorly father out in the dark and cold, into the cruel night vapours to execute a task perhaps more swiftly than he was able. Under her breath she whispered. "No Father, do not run… please just take your time. Sweet Jesus, look after him"

She slung the thick linen quiver across her shoulder and took out an arrow.

Would she be willing to kill a man to save Guy?

Would she be willing to attack a knight of the realm, to prevent Guy from coming to harm?

She pushed that question to the back of her mind.

Creeping up to the folded door she listened carefully. Now she could hear the sounds of Guy working his metal.

The three men were talking quietly together .

There was a hiss as metal was quenched in the trough, and Guy once more heated a crucible to white hot and poured the resultant liquid lead onto the join. Nell peered through the crack in the door.

Now Guy was working the lead in the wooden coffin with his back to her.

"It's not a work of art, blacksmith," said Sir Thomas. "You don't have to labour over it; to make it pretty... unlike your animals for the church door."

Guy turned and gave him an evil look. Nell could see he had a bloody bruise on his forehead.

"No one is going to see it. Unless our dear cousin Guiscard is able to see it... from the inside."

The one called Maurice crossed himself. "Tom please... that's..."

"What? You frightened that his ghost will come and exact revenge for not coffining him correctly?"

"No, but…"

Tom leaned in close to his young relative. "More likely he'll haunt us for not obtaining justice for his murder."

He straightened. "You finished yet, Ferrier?"

"It will suffice."

"Good. Leave it there. We'll collect it in the morning."

He prodded Guy with his sword tip. "Now... move... out."

Guy put up his hands to show that he was complying with the man's instructions and made for the door. The rope was retrieved by the youngest cousin and they all stood in the middle of the road.

Sir Thomas was looking up at the moon which was waxing and shone quite brightly that night.

"Fetch the horses, Piers."

One man ran off. Guy wondered if he might be able to successfully tackle the knight but the rope dropping once more over his torso and tightening and a knife pointing at his throat put paid to that idea.

He was dragged out further into the open and onto the grassy area in front of his forge.

He looked up at the moon. "Please, Mistress Moon, help me." But he knew that help was not forthcoming from that sphere. His mind, usually calm and fertile, was suddenly dull and panicked.

The horses were retrieved and they came docilely clopping around the corner of the main house onto the grass.

Guy's mind was quickly sifting through ideas but without knowing exactly what they planned, he could come up with no counter ideas.

He thought he heard a scuffling sound up by the forge but no, it was nothing. Just a small nocturnal animal fleeing the noisy men.

Should he call out? He filled his lungs as best he could... "Tom. Tom Kennett!"

That earned him a buffet on the head which made his ears ring.

"Stuff his mouth up," said Sir Thomas. "Calling out; asking his infernal master for help; reciting a spell... We can't have any of that!"

A dirty rag was retrieved from the forge and shoved into his mouth.

Slowly they waded through the wet grasses and came to the large willow tree, one branch of which leaned out over the water, with another sturdy branch arching over the field.

"Bring Falcon. He's the fastest and toughest."

A beautiful roan horse was brought up, tossing his head. He wanted his nice warm stable. He did not want to be out here with these foolish men in the cold. Did they not know that this time of night was for eating and rest?

Sir Thomas bellowed, "Over that branch, Piers."

The end of the rope was thrown over the willow branch.

"It'll break Tom," said Maurice. "Sure as Mother Mary is as pure as..."

"Hush your mouth, you fool!"

Maurice quickly looked down at his feet and the other man, Piers, chuckled to himself, "Not man enough for it eh, Maurice?"

"Of course I am." He squared his puny shoulders.

"You're sweating like a felon at a trial."

"I'm not."

"Oh, be quiet," yelled Sir Thomas, impervious to the echo of his voice which resounded down the river valley. "Let's get it done then we can go to bed, satisfied."

He took the rope end from the man called Piers and secured it to the saddle of the horse called Falcon.

"Right." The man spread his feet and took hold of the belt at his waist.

"I, Sir Thomas Courtenay of Thatcham in the county of Berkshire, do swear before… before these men here present." He looked up, "And the moon above us, that this man Guy Ferrier, blacksmith of this God forsaken place of East Kennett, is guilty of the crime of sorcery. He did cause my beloved cousin Guiscard Courtenay to fall from his horse, by making the semblance of a running hare."

Guy shook his head and mumbled into his gag.

"And we find you guilty of that crime for which you shall hang by the neck ... until you are dead." He stepped forward, loosened the rope and moved it around Guy's neck. Guy tried to resist but Sir Thomas punched him in the face.

Guy tried to knee him in the groin but he was too late. The man danced away with a chuckle. Guy then tried a kick but for the same reason he made no contact. That earned him a buffet to the side of the head with the butt of Sir Thomas' knife.

"Who wants to get the horse going?"

Suddenly the other two were not so brave.

"Oh for God's sake... he's only a blacksmith." And Thomas slapped the horse Falcon hard on the rump. The crack rolled around the river valley as the horse set off along the wet grass like a fox startled from his hole and came up short when he was at the limit of the rope. But he kept running, heaving on it.

Guy's body was hoisted into the air.

"Jesus!" he cried into his gag before the rope bit into him and he began to throttle.

He scrabbled at the rope with his finger ends but it was too tight. He simply succeeded in bloodying them and breaking his nails.

Guy tried to look up at the tree on high.

In the moonlight he could just see that the branch was not too far above him. Perhaps he could stretch up—his hands were free—and reach it so that the rope didn't bite. Then he might pull his legs up and scale the tree.

Desperately he reached up. He found the rope and pulled on it, hoisting himself so that the noose was not so tight.

"Damn, we should have bound his hands," yelled Sir Thomas, leaping forward.

Guy pulled harder, feeling his breath constricting in his chest, his head pounding as the blood congested there. But he managed to make some headway in loosening the rope. His arms ached enormously and his throat burned.

Then Sir Thomas Courtenay grabbed and pulled on his legs. "Oh, no you don't!" he said.

The rope tightened further.

*****

From her hiding place by the forge doors, Parnell saw the knights lead Guy across the road.

She saw the horses arrive.

"What on earth were horses doing there? The men were not even a furlong or so from the manor. Why did they need to ride here? Ah yes… they were knights. They'd never walk anywhere when they could ride. Damn their arrogance.

Parnell peered into the darkness lit only by the moon.

'I need to be closer,' she said to herself. 'I can see very little at this distance.'

She scurried silently along the bank of bushes until she was almost at the riverbank but behind the men.

Their voices were muted and garbled. Then she heard Guy cry out. "Tom, Tom Kennett!" He was instantly silenced.

One man ran past her; she held her breath. He had scurried into the forge and soon returned. He hadn't seen her though he had passed her by only a couple of feet. In his hand he held some rags.

There was more muttering and then she heard Sir Thomas yell, "Oh, be quiet."

His outburst was like a crack of thunder in the stillness of the night.

"I, Sir Thomas Courtenay…"

Nell inched forward.

"And we find you guilty of that crime for which you shall hang by the neck… until you are dead."

Nell stiffened. They were going to hang him! Over her dead body!

She rose carefully, keeping the men in her sight. One horse had been brought forward. Were they going to seat Guy and then drive the horse from under him so that he dropped? She'd heard that was what they sometimes did with felons.

If that was the case, Guy would very likely break his neck.

She decided to wait and see what they did. But not too long.

No, they didn't seat the blacksmith but they did put the noose around his neck.

Nell stiffened herself and drew an arrow from her quiver. She nocked it.

She would not shoot until she knew exactly what the knights planned.

The Courtenay cousins were so taken up by their own actions they did not see Nell behind them with her arrow aimed at them.

Three of them… there were three of them and she was but one. Soon help would come and she perhaps would not need to loose her arrow after all.

She listened for the sound of anyone approaching.

No one. All was silent save for the snuffling of the horses, the rushing of the river and the murmuring of the men.

The horse snuffled and she saw it bolt across the grass.

She heard Guy cry out a muffled, "Jesus!" and watched as his bulk was hoisted up in the air.

"Let him down!" she cried out instantly. "Let him down now or I swear I will kill you all."

As a body, the men turned. The knight, Sir Thomas had hold of Guy's legs and was pulling him down to throttle him.

"Ah… the redoubtable Mistress Truman," he said.

Nell let go her arrow. It sped across the grass and embedded itself in the tree very close to where Sir Thomas stood.

Very close.

The man let go of Guy's legs but Guy continued to throttle.

"I said let him down."

Thomas calmly waved a hand in her direction, "Get her Piers."

Piers was undecided.

In that moment of indecision, Nell had another arrow in her bow and yet again it landed inches from the now startled Sir Piers Courtenay.

Maurice shrieked.

"Oh, c'mon, boys," said Sir Thomas. "She's a girl. And if she was able, she would not have missed and we'd be spiked full of arrows by now."

"I don't know, Tom," said Maurice, with a quavering voice.

Nell shrieked as loudly as she could, "The next arrow will pierce one of you. Be assured of that. Which one is it to be?"

She steadied her aim. "Get him down… NOW!"

No one moved.

Nell drew back her arm…

"For the love of God, Tom!" shouted Maurice.

Piers made a feint towards her. The arrow released and it hit him in his foot.

"Argh!" he screamed and fell into the wet grass.

"Now you are two…" she said. "Let him down."

Sir Thomas moved slowly towards Guy. "Oh dear, I fear we are too late."

He turned back to her, "So sorry!"

In another breath, Nell had one more arrow in her bow. Could she do it? In the dark... in the moonlight... She knew she was good but... this...?

She fixed her eye on the rope, held her breath and released.

The arrow flew straight and true and in an eye-blink had severed the rope strands of the noose. The weight pulled the strands apart and Guy fell to the ground in a heap.

Sir Thomas made to jump forward and lay hands on her but yet another arrow was loaded and pointed at him before he could draw breath.

"You want to put your speculation to the test, Sir Knight? Please do. It will give me great pleasure to spit you."

The man Piers on the ground clutching his injured foot cried out. "God in his Heaven Tom, leave it be!"

"Come... I cannot let a chit like her defeat me." Sir Thomas moved closer. "She would not pin me. She has not the courage."

Nell drew back her bow. Sir Maurice was running across the grass making his escape into the darkness, shouting, "Damn you, Thomas Courtenay."

Nell let the arrow fly. It landed with a thud in Sir Thomas's upper right arm.

He bowled over with a shriek.

"Now who has courage, you white arsed coward?"

The one called Piers gritted his teeth. "Please mistress, the arrow, pull it out. please." He pointed to his foot, whimpering.

But Nell was running towards Guy who was motionless on the ground

"Guy, Guy," She laid her bow carefully against the tree but kept it close and another arrow in it just in case.

"Guy... Oh Guy."

Out of the corner of her eye, she saw Sir Thomas stand shakily, holding his wounded arm.

"Where was the help she'd asked for? Where was Tom, the steward, the lord's men?"

She took Guy's head on her knee. "Guy please, speak to me…"

She pulled the noose and shirt away from his neck. There lit by the moonlight was a livid bruise, red and angry. She stroked his neck.

"Oh no… No, Guy!"

"Mistress?"

Through her blurry tears she saw another man moving towards her.

She reached for her bow.

"No, no you'll not need it. It's Henri."

"You too are a Courtenay," she spat. Not convinced she drew the bowstring back.

"I promise you. I may be a Courtenay but I am from a different mould." He smiled gently. "I'm sorry. Am I too late?"

Parnell sobbed. "I'm not sure."

"May I?" said Henri Courtenay gesturing towards Guy who lay still on the grass.

He went down on his knees, stretched out Guy's large frame and listened for the life beat at Guy's chest. Then he put his ear to Guy's mouth.

"He lives."

Nell gave a small whimper.

"Henri!" shouted Sir Thomas. "What do you think you're doing?"

"I am clearing up after you, you brainless imbecile," answered Sir Henri with venom in his voice. "Go back to the manor. And take Piers with you."

The two men stared at each other for a heartbeat.

"I said, go!"

It seemed that Sir Henri had some authority over the other Courtenays.

"Allow me."

Even though he staggered with Guy's weight, Sir Henri got poor

Guy into his house and onto his bed.

"Do you have any sal amoniac?"

Nell looked puzzled.

"*Salis armoniaci*. Smelling salts?"

"No… no…"

The man looked around the room. "Then there's nothing for it."

He took out his knife…

Parnell gasped.

"No, no… Do not fear." Sir Henri lifted a lock of his hair and snipped it off.

Then he went to the covered fire and removed a turf. Reaching for a piece of kindling from the pile by the door, he thrust the end into the red embers.

Nell watched, curious.

He touched the glowing end of the twig to his hair and with a rapid movement made for Guy on the bed and held it under his nose.

Guy took in a huge breath and coughed. The awful smell was indescribable.

Sir Henri burned his fingers and sucked on them. "Works every time," he smiled.

"Oh Guy!" said Parnell. "Are you all right?"

Guy tried to speak but found he could not.

"Leave it a while. Take drink. Rest. Salve that rope burn," said the capable Sir Henri.

Guy closed his eyes and mouthed, 'thank you.'

"Ah no… It's not me you should be thanking. It's this good lady here. She is the heroine of the day."

Guy shuddered as his memory caught up with him, "What..?"

"You were hanged but have come back to us, Guy," said Parnell.

She rose to her feet and curtsied.

"There's no need for that," said Sir Henri, smiling.

Guy's eyes were closing; he was so tired. His throat was sore and he was thirsty but not enough to stay awake. Even if he'd tried, his eyes would not obey the dictate to stay open.

"Thank you, sir. Thank you. Did my father manage to get to the manor and rouse you?" asked Parnell.

"Your father? He is the bailiff is he not?"

"The same. Truman the bailiff, sir. I sent him as soon as I knew what was afoot and asked him to rouse the manor and call for Tom, who is Guy's friend."

"No, mistress, I'm sorry. I did not see your father. I was looking for those idiots who went out of the manor late. It took me a while to work out where they'd gone. Then when I realised, and that they'd taken horses, I knew it was serious. Thomas had been drinking all afternoon and had been working his way up through irritated and angry into furious. I knew the imbecile would do something. I had no idea it would be this…." His arm gestured to Guy on his back on the bed. "Tend him Mistress Truman. I will report to the Lord Lillebon."

He turned to walk to the door.

"My father, sir… You have not seen him?"

"No, mistress."

Then, out of breath, in through the door bowled Tom Kennett, Guy's friend.

"Nell… Oh Nell! Here you are!"

"Tom! Have you seen Father? I sent him to you. The Courtenay's have tried to hang Guy."

Tom's eyes flicked to Henri and he tugged his forelock, "Sir."

"No. Not this Courtenay… He has been very helpful," said Nell.

She stepped a pace nearer to Tom. "Have you seen Father? Did he tell you we needed help? Why didn't you come?"

Tom's face took on a sorrowful expression, "Oh Nell… Nell. I'm sorry."

"He's alive Tom… Guy's alive."

"Thanks to this brave young lady and her remarkable bow skills," said Henri with a smile.

"No… Nell…"

Tom came towards Parnell with his arms outstretched. "Your father got to our house. He never got to the manor."

"He told you…"

"He told me that you thought something was afoot with Guy. At the forge. I had no idea…"

"What do you mean?"

"He didn't know why you needed us. But you did, he said. He said he couldn't remember."

"Couldn't remember… but I told him that…"

"Oh Nell, I am so terribly sorry."

Sir Henri stepped forward. "What do you mean Tom? Spit it out."

"He got to our house and… he told us you needed us… But he didn't know where and then…"

"Then?"

"He staggered and clutched his chest."

"NO!"

"He was so out of breath and his chest was heaving…"

"Oh, Tom!"

"Nell, oh Nell… I don't know how to say this but…"

'"No!"

"Nell, your father—he is dead."

*****

Nell staggered as if someone had struck her.

"Dead?"

"He just fell down dead at my feet."

Nell's eyes ceased to see. In her mind's eye she saw her father as she'd left him, mouthing placatory words at her. She'd told him to go out into the night, in his bare feet, to hurry. To fetch help.

"Oh my God! It's all my fault."

Nell's knees gave way and she slipped downwards.

Sir Henri, who was closest, put out his arms to catch her before she hit the floor. He succeeded in clasping her to his bosom.

"Now... now... shall we sit you down?"

He wrapped his arms around her.

At that moment, Guy struggled awake and with a jerk came fully into consciousness.

He turned his head to see Sir Henri Courtenay embracing his wife to be.

"Oh God!" he said and closed his eyes.

CHAPTER TWELVE
THE CHURCH TOWER

It seemed to Parnell that she had already cried all her sorrows. She felt numbed but strangely no tears sprang into her eyes. There was no horrible feeling along her breast bone. No heart pounding. No awful constriction of the throat as there had been on the first occasion of her father's 'death'. However, her legs would not hold her up and Sir Henri Courtenay lifted her as if she'd been made of straw and swiftly sat her on a stool. Luckily it had its back to the wall and she could lean and not be afraid of falling off. It was the only intact stool in Guy's house, she remembered, since the devastation by the knights.

Henri turned to Tom. "You are absolutely sure, Master…?"

"Kennett, sir. Tom Kennett. And yes, though please, go and make yourself certain that the news I bring is true. My wife Alys is with Master Truman's body. Our house is next along, by the trees."

Henri simply nodded and was gone.

Parnell stared at the wall, "Has he really gone, Tom? My father?"

"I… I think so, Nell."

"My father… dear Guy… what is happening in our little village Tom?"

"I don't know. Perhaps we are cursed?"

Nell gave him a look of incredulity.

Then they remained silent until Sir Henri returned. He stood in the open doorway, leaning at the door post.

"Mistress Truman, I am so sorry. Your father is indeed dead."

He came into the house and knelt before her, taking her hands in his own, chafing them.

"I am so very, very sorry."

Nell's eyes at last filled with tears, though she did not sob.

"We must get him to his own house for tonight and tomorrow we must take him to the church," said Nell.

"It can be done."

Henri stood up.

"If you are able, can you tell me in your own words what happened tonight? I only saw the very latest events." He smiled rather wryly, "Your amazingly accurate arrow strike and the behaviour of my three... and I am ashamed to say it, reprehensible Courtenay cousins."

Nell wiped her eyes. And began her tale.

"Ah... the reason you received no immediate aid is clear now, isn't it?"

"My father did not reach the manor, he suffered a malfunction of his memory before he could summon aid."

"I told you Nell, when he came into the house he was distracted and distressed. And he died before he could... tell us anything further," said Tom sadly.

Guy, lying on his bed by the wall, moaned, rose and lifted himself from the covers. Swinging his legs over the edge of the bed he clutched his head and massaged the back of his neck.

"What...?" he whispered.

The next few moments were taken up with Nell explaining to him how she had been coming to the forge and how she had prevented the Courtenays from hanging him.

Sir Henri took over the tale.

"Mistress Nell is a remarkable woman, Master Ferrier. You owe her your life."

"And thanks must go to you too sir, for coming when you did," said Nell with a weak smile at the knight.

"It was not me who severed the rope with an arrow, mistress."

"I was unsure if I could do it... but what was there to lose?"

Tom chuckled, despite himself, "Nell has always been the best bowman amongst us, sir."

Guy watched them all through a hazy fug. His eyes seemed to be misty and not quite focussing properly. No doubt an effect of the almost-hanging.

He managed to croak, "Thank you, Sir Henri."

He tried to rise but was very unsteady.

Nell was immediately by his side.

"No, Guy, you must rest. Do not attempt to move." Her strong hand sat him down again.

She seated herself on the bed beside him.

"I have some... some bad news, Guy."

"Bad news? Is this the third thing today, then? They say bad things come in threes." His voice was very weak and breathy.

Tom poured him some ale and Guy took it gratefully.

"Is that you, Tom Kennett?"

"Aye, it's me, Guy."

"I cannot see you perfectly."

"Guy," Nell licked her lips. "Tonight, when I saw you being attacked by those... men..." She looked up at Sir Henri and received a small nod of encouragement. "I ran back home to get Father to go out and summon help."

"Oh?"

"He went out into the night and sadly, when he got to Tom's house, he fell down... and died..."

Guy mouthed her last word.

"My father is dead..." And now she began to weep in earnest.

Guy lifted her head to his shoulder and despite all his aches and pains, he squeezed her tightly to him.

"Oh my poor darling," he said.

*****

Master John Truman lay on a bier before the altar of the church at East Kennett. Four black candles burned one at each corner. The whiteness of the altar cloth, in the darkness of the church, made the eyes immediately draw to the body under its decorated pall and the window space above it, shining with the morning light.

Guy nodded to the open coffined corpse as he stood alone in the nave.

"I am sorry old friend that I had to be the cause of your demise. If I could, I would take back time and speak to you one last time." He bowed his head. "Go with God... rest easily," he sighed. "As I promised, I will take care of Parnell."

A few more moments of reflection and Guy turned to the west end to leave.

There, standing in a shaft of sunlight was Adela Lillebon, her mouse of a maid standing a little way off. "I heard what happened."

"My Lady Lillebon." Guy bowed.

"I am sorry they had to be so..." she searched for a word. "Angry."

Guy watched her carefully as she walked down the nave. Today she wore the palest blue. It set off her blonde hair to perfection. He experienced a shiver of delight upon seeing her.

"If I could have stopped them, I would have... I would have done anything to stop them... But I did not know."

"No need, my lady. There is no need for you to say anything."

"They have gone. The two Courtenays. Henri and my father sent them packing. Two of them were wounded."

"I know that someone has taken the coffin and presumably Sir Guiscard."

"There is no need for them to return here."

He was now close enough to see the tears which made her eyes shine so brightly.

"I am sorry," she said. 'Sorry I brought you so close to death."

"No… No mistress. It was not your fault."

"I knew it was wrong but…"

"No… No."

"I was cross… and I said things…"

Guy thought that she was somehow asking for forgiveness.

"If you believe that is the case then, it is forgiven… freely."

His heart gave a huge lurch as she smiled at him. "Master Ferrier. You are a good man."

She took in a shuddering breath.

"I see you have completed the figures for the door."

He nodded. "I have."

"They are quite simply superb. I hope they will be there for many years to come, though I will not be here to see them"

"You are going home to Milton Lillebon?"

"My father thinks it best, with all that has happened, that I am… removed… from East Kennett."

"Oh."

"I will not return."

Guy's throat constricted. "I am very sorry to hear it, my lady… Might you not visit… now and again…?"

"I am to be married. I go to live in Berkshire."

"Oh."

"My father seems to think that it is a good idea, now that my original husband to be, is no more, that I marry into the Courtenays even so."

"Oh?"

"Sir Henri has offered for me and my father has accepted. He is Guiscard's heir it seems. I am to be passed on like best bed hangings or an old iron pot!"

"Or a jewel of inestimable value, my lady."

She blinked, then and stepped closer.

Her maidservant Marjorie, cleared her throat.

"I know, I know what my father has instructed," said Adela to the girl in the shadows. "But you can go. I will meet you outside."

"But my lady…"

"Go!"

The south door banged and then there was silence.

"I will be married before Christmas. I am to be gone today."

"So soon? I am sorry to hear it."

One step closer. Guy's heart began to pound.

"Will you do something for me…?"

"Oh mistress, every time you ask me this… there's trouble."

Her laugh rose up to the nave roof.

"No. It should not cost you. In any way."

"What do you want me to do?"

She laid a hand on his arm and pulled.

"I want you to kiss me."

"My lady… I can't do that!"

"Please, Guy. I will never see you again and… and… I do love you so. Please, just this once."

She came closer. His head came down and their lips met. It was an innocent kiss with no fervour and lasted but a heartbeat.

It was a moment he would never forget his entire life. The sweetness of it.

They drew apart. "Oh Adela. I should not say it but I do love you too."

She laid a finger to his lips.

"Be happy in your marriage to Mistress Truman. As I shall try to be happy in mine to Sir Henri."

"He is a good man."

"Yes. Yes he is. Though he is not as good as you." She stepped away. "Goodbye Guy. God be with you."

"And with you, my lady."

The south door banged once more.

Despite his sadness, and the aching of his heart, he chuckled to himself, 'No wonder the decorations will not stay on that door... the treatment it gets!'

*****

After a while, Guy made his way out into the church porch. It was a beautiful December morning; cold but there had been no frost. He looked back at his door. At Adela's door. He would always think of it as Adela's door.

He swore the creature with the hump to his back winked at him, 'I must find out somehow what that animal is called.'

Thinking thus, the face of Emma Masters came into his mind. No doubt she'd know. Mistress Know-all, but he was not going to ask her. He would be very happy if he never saw her again. She was a woman whom he hoped would disappear from East Kennett forever and marry elsewhere.

Guy walked as jauntily as he could, back to his forge where he took out his tools and began to fashion the blade of a spade for Master Plimmon.

People came and went along the road in front of his forge, some of them calling out a greeting. Some of them, stopping for a moment to inquire after his health.

Word had got around. He was a man to be celebrated. A man who almost hanged. Who'd almost died. His reputation as a magical blacksmith began to reforge itself.

Along with his spade, Guy began to fashion a new song. One about a man who was hanged but who came back to life. He sang the last verse.

'He married his sweetheart...
His bright little bird
And was happy forever,
Or so I have heard.'

Was this true? Was he about to marry his sweetheart? His thoughts of marriage brought the priest Father Fabian back into his mind.

Oh God! What did he think was going to happen?

This was the man who was going to marry Parnell and himself. Did they want to be married by a man who had professed a vow of celibacy but who had lustfully worked his way through many of his parishioners. What would that mean to them when the man was, for want of a better word, unclean, forsworn?

Besides that, could Guy trust the man? Did he really try to injure him that day?

He turned that thought aside. What would be, would be.

Around midday and after his dinner of ham and a boiled egg, Guy heard the hooves of many horses come trooping down the lane and the rattle of wheels. The Lillebons were leaving for their Christmas quarters at their manor of Milton.

"Ah Guy!" shouted his lord when he caught sight of him through the forge doors. "I know I said that we'd have you sing for us at Christmas but we've decided to spend the season at Milton instead."

Guy bowed. "That is alright, my Lord. I shall be here when you return and maybe at Easter I can sing for you?"

"Good man. Good man." Walter Lillebon scratched his face with a rasping sound. "You quite recovered?"

"I have a sore throat…" Guy stroked the red weal around his neck.

"Perhaps it's best you don't sing then," chuckled the affable lord.

"Indeed My Lord, but apart from that and a few bruises, I am quite recovered."

The Lord Lillebon did not seem inclined to speak about what had happened in the night.

"Good, well… I will see you and your good lady when I return."

Guy bowed again.

The man waved his retinue on and the covered coach in which Adela, Lady Lillebon and some of the female servants travelled, trundled past. Guy caught sight of Adela's pale face through the barred window.

Suddenly it ground to a halt in front of the forge door.

"Ah, I nearly forgot," Sir Walter turned in his saddle and spoke loudly, "Father Fabian has asked me to give permission for a new bell housing for the church. Might you do that Guy? Fashion the metal frame?"

"Yes, my lord. Of course."

"Have the expenses sent to my steward. He will be here at Christmas."

"Yes, sir."

All the while Guy was looking at Adela through the carriage window.

His heart swelled and was so huge it almost projected into his mouth. She smiled at him sweetly.

And then they were gone.

He went back to his spade.

*****

The day wore on. Parnell came to him as the light was fading in the sky.

"The Lord Lillebon has gone to Milton," she said.

"Yes, I saw him."

"He has given me grace to stay in the house until we can organise…"

"Until he appoints a new bailiff?"

"Ah… no. Until we are married."

"That was kind of him."

"Yes."

Parnell came into the forge and perched on the tree trunk where Adela had once sat. "There is no need for us to marry here. We could go to Avebury or St. Nicholas' at Fyfield."

"I have been thinking about it. Do we really want that forsworn priest to marry us Nell? What might that mean for us?"

"That we are married, but not married properly?"

"With less... sanctity?"

"Oh, I doubt it. God sees into our hearts, Guy. If we are sincere, then does it matter which priest marries us? And a church marriage is only a gloss."

"Let us bury your dear father and we'll turn our minds to mourning and after this to marriage, eh?"

Nell's mouth turned up at the corner in what passed for a smile "You are so... practical, Guy. So organised."

"A blacksmith must be so, my love."

Parnell turned to leave and then realising he had spoken a word she'd never heard him say to her before, she spun around."

"Guy?"

"Yes, Nell?"

"Am I really your love?"

He put down his tools and wiped his hands on his apron.

"You must never ever forget it."

He drew her to him; the sparrow to the heron; leaned down and kissed her with great feeling.

"Oh!" She became flustered. "Oh... that was nice."

Guy chuckled, "Then you'll be wanting another?"

Parnell snuggled up to him.

"Yes please," she said.

*****

Christmas came upon them quickly. The weather was dank and miserable. Fogs and cold mizzle had marred the season of Advent but it didn't stop the village mummers from going door to door.

Guy played his usual part though his voice had not quite yet achieved its former volume or brightness.

"Room, give us room, to play and to sing,
I'll rhyme you a rhyme and sing you a thing.

If you don't believe the words I say,

Here comes Saint George. Who'll clear him the way?"

The mummers had eventually collected on the road by the old bailiff's house, opposite the manor gates and in front of the church lych gate.

"Here comes St. George," cried Tom Kennett.

"Master of this motley crew.

I've come to sing for all of you.

If you don't believe these words I say,

Enter the doctor and he'll clear the way."

The three men paraded round with wooden weapons over their shoulders.

The 'doctor' now spoke up.

"I've conquered in 'Viz-es, I've conquered in Thame,"...

Devizes and Thame were two places the 'doctor' had visited for he was the manor's marshal, who looked to the horses and the most widely travelled man of them all. He usually lived at Milton but at this time of year, and for the twelve days Christmas, he had leave from his master to stay in East Kennett to visit his elderly mother.

"And I'll be back to old Ireland,

To conquer again!"

No, Master Marshall had never been to Ireland but he knew the King had, and that made it all the better.

Now a fourth man joined them. This was young Plimmon, the Plough.

"Here comes I, the bold Green Knight

Willing to the death for to fight

I say, Master Doctor, you lie, sir

Take out your sword and try, sir."

They began to fight,

"Ah 'tis a sorry thing," cried Guy in his character of the lord of the revels, "To see such men their swords to swing.

Put up. Put up. A beast draws near,

We need you both to fight and jeer."

A huge roar now went up and folk chuckled as a capering monster now came into the ring.

Master Dorman, the manor gatekeeper, waved his tendril-like arms, covered in leather strips, and growled like a boar. The women present giggled and affected to be frightened, drawing back from him as he circled the audience.

Guy, watching, caught sight of the priest, Father Fabian, his arms folded, standing just inside the church gate. He had preached against unnatural and pagan practices in his last sermon. No doubt he was there to see just how heathen the mummer's troupe was, for this was his first Christmas at Kennett.

'Perhaps his last,' thought Guy.

The priest shook his head and tutted but despite himself, he chuckled along with all the rest.

Once the playing was over and folk were standing about chatting, fortified by spiced cider provided by the manor kitchen, the priest made his way around them. He was offered a mug of cider and took it.

"I've never seen an entertainment quite like it," said the priest to Mistress Truman who was on the fringes of the crowd.

"It's been performed in the village since I was a child. In fact, since my grandfather was a child," she said.

"I suppose there is no real harm in it."

"None at all, sir priest," said Parnell. "It's all about the triumph of good over evil. Saint George over the wicked Devil. I would have thought you would approve of that."

Father Fabian gave her a mock bow. "How can I not, Mistress Truman?"

Parnell was feeling very warm. If truth were known, she was a little tipsy and so it was the cider speaking when she said,

"Father Fabian. The Devil is all around us and God protects us from his evil, am I right?"

"This is why, my child, we pray... in our paternoster, "Lead us not into temptation but deliver us from evil…"

"Like the day I found you in the tower with Guy up the ladder. Was the Devil trying to lead you into temptation then? I thought I heard you say 'the Devil's work. So close to damnation. God forgive me. So close.' What was that about, Father?"

The priest's face turned pale. He mouthed a silent oath, swore softly and then turned and walked away with rapid steps.

"What was that, Parnell?" said Guy as he joined her, having woven his way through the crowd.

"Oh, dear." Nell hiccoughed, "I have had too much of Mistress Palmer's cider. I can never hold my tongue when I have had her cider."

Guy looked serious, "What did you say to him?"

"I simply asked him if he thought the mummer's play was the Devil's work and asked him why he said what he said when he tried to push you from that ladder." She smiled inanely.

"Oh, Nell!"

"He didn't like it."

Guy wiped his hand across his brow. "I wasn't going to mention it. I was going to let him think that we had believed him innocent of any wrongdoing. I was hoping he'd think you hadn't heard him correctly."

"I'm sorry Guy…'"

"Well, it's done now." Guy took hold of Nell and wrapped his arm around her. "I think you need to go home and sleep. Come let me take you there."

His arm around her shoulder, Guy towed Nell up the slight slope and into her house.

The afternoon was moving on and there were to be no more outings for the mummer's play for the day. The next time it would be performed would be at twelfth night.

Guy laid Nell on her bed, took off her shoes and covered her with a blanket. "You sleep now," he said. "I will call in later and we shall have supper together."

Leaving the house of the bailiff, Guy caught sight of Father Fabian scurrying into his church.

He followed. Truly, he did not know why, but he felt that there was some unfinished business between them and since Nell had now brought it to the surface, it would be best to air it.

Standing at the open outer door, Guy stared at the decorated porch door for a long time. He smiled at his handiwork. The oliphant, the hare, the goose. It brought back memories of Adela. He thought he saw her leaning on the door and speaking about the animals on her father's parchment. No. Upon coming closer he realised it was but a figment of his imagination. She was now in Milton, a few miles away but it might as well have been the moon. Soon she would be in Thatcham. He did not know exactly how many miles away that was, but to him, that was, without doubt, as far as the moon.

He pushed open the door.

Father Fabian was on his knees at the altar, his hands clasped in front of him, his eyes closed, his head down.

The man turned as he heard Guy's footsteps upon the ancient flagstones.

"Ah, Master Ferrier."

"Good afternoon, Father. I hope I'm not disturbing you."

The man struggled up. He was pale and there were beads of sweat upon his forehead.

"Are you quite alright, sir?" asked Guy.

"As right as a mortal sinner can be, Master Ferrier. A sinner who seeks the light of Christ and the forgiveness of the Lord."

"We must all do that, Father."

"Ah but, Guy... I may call you Guy, may I not?"

"Certainly."

"I am a priest, things are... different for me."

"How so?"

The man turned and sat on the lowest altar step, looking up at Guy.

"I will tell you and you may judge me accordingly."

"I would never presume to judge you, Father."

The handsome face smiled; the perfect skin glistened in the failing light of the afternoon.

"No, I think you do not."

The sigh which he uttered made Guy suddenly feel sorry for the man.

"Uniquely among man's occupations, priests may not marry, unlike you as a blacksmith, for example. It is a stipulation of their vocation; nor should they engage in any sexual acts, as proscribed by our moral teaching. Priests live in a world unfamiliar to most men in this world of ours. This is a world—a world in which physical attractions and behaviours are not pursued and celebrated as they are in others, but are forbidden. Most men would not and do not volunteer to live in such a world as this; those who would be priests do exactly that."

"I understand what you are saying." Guy gestured to the step. "May I?"

Father Fabian nodded. Guy genuflected to the altar, crossed himself and then sat.

The priest went on. "In many who take vows, there's a deep seated need to serve their fellow men. Many have an extreme urge to become the centre of parish life. The reasons why a man may be drawn to the priesthood are many and various. There may be a desire to stand aside from others, to be revered, to help his fellow men."

"You do all those things, Father."

Fabian turned his head to look at the blacksmith. His eyes, those dark pools, darker still in the gloom of the chancel, raked Guy's face as if he would see into his soul.

"We are often speaking of love... are we not? The love of Christ, the love of our fellow man..."

"Spiritual love, sir?"

"It is often spoken about, in here." He threw his hand out, gesturing to the walls. "But what we do not speak about is that other love. The love of a man for a woman."

"Except at weddings, Father," smiled Guy.

"Ah yes... at weddings." He chuckled. "It's always about someone else."

Guy did not speak. He thought it best to just listen.

"In your world, Guy, this is usually a happy event, is it not? Love? In the celibate world, it cannot be happy, constrained as it is by the watchful eyes of parishioners and superiors of the church, by public expectation, by..." Here he faltered. "By personal feelings of guilt, and the lack of a clear path to fidelity."

"Sir, if I might ask... If you realise, as you obviously do, that it is not and never can be in your nature to be celibate... then why did you allow yourself to take the vows you did. Why become a priest?"

Again Fabian stared at Guy. "Why did you become a blacksmith, Guy?"

Guy stretched out his legs.

My father was a farrier and his father before him. It was natural that I should learn from my father."

"And when you have children, will you require them, one of them perhaps, to follow into the blacksmithing trade after you?"

Guy stared up at the west window. "Perhaps not. Only if the child wishes it. If metal is in his blood. Perhaps one may become a priest?"

Fabian smiled. "Some of us do not have such a choice. Some of us are..."

"Destined for the church in childhood, because..."

"Our fathers wish it and it is a wish which cannot be gainsaid," added the priest.

A little siffling wind came in through the nearest window and stirred up the dust at their feet.

"You come from a noble family, I believe, sir?"

"I do. A younger son of a family of south Wiltshire."

"Mandeville? Of Sutton Mandeville?"

"I see you know your family histories."

"It was a guess."

"I was a very young man when I entered the priesthood at Gloucester. I was influenced and bullied by turns, it wasn't easy."

"No, I don't suppose it was."

"I thought that I could keep myself in check. I thought that it would not matter too much, if I confessed my sins..."

"And then... you fell in love?"

"Oh Guy, you are the most shrewd of men. Is there nothing that escapes you?"

"You fell in love and... then it became too difficult to ignore."

"It did."

Guy lifted his knees and dangled his arms over them, clasping his hands.

"Why have you led me to this moment of confession, Father?"

Fabian smiled a sad smile. "Because I have wronged you and I must make you aware that I have wronged you and must beg for your forgiveness."

Without an instant's pause Guy answered him, "You have my forgiveness."

"I tried... I might have killed you, Guy... and for that I am so very deeply sorry."

Guy put a hand on the priest's arm. "But you did not."

"No, God led me away from that terrible sin."

"You are forgiven by me. I am sure that if you speak to God, as only you can, he will forgive also."

Father Fabian put his head in his hands. "I pray daily. I pray for forgiveness and for strength."

"You will be answered, of that I am sure. You are not a bad man. Simply, human."

Fabian smiled at him and they both rose from the step.

"This conversation is forgotten, Father," said Guy. "As is anything else I might have heard."

He was half way down the nave when Fabian's voice echoing in the depths of the roof said, "Come to the church on Plough Monday. We shall explore the bell housing together."

Guy turned back and nodded.

*****

"I think we have misjudged Father Fabian," said Guy that evening as he reached for the bread and broke it in two.

Parnell had her elbows on the table and her chin in her hands. "Oh why is that?"

"Are you not going to eat tonight?"

"I will eat a little, in a while."

Guy chortled, "Too much cider does that to you."

Nell pulled a face.

"I had a long conversation with him this afternoon, in the church."

Nell perked up. "Alone... in the church?"

"Yes, we were alone."

"And... what happened?"

"Nothing happened, save that he apologised to me for trying to tip me from that ladder..."

"Oh, so he really did try to injure you?"

"He did. And he explained to me why he was so tempted to do me harm."

"You had overheard him. You knew too much."

Guy chewed. "He is a tormented man, Nell. It was a momentary aberration for which he is sincerely contrite. He is not a bad man, just a weak one."

"He is a lecher, Guy."

"Aye, he has been."

"Has been? Has he suddenly mended his ways?"

Nell reached for a piece of bread. She decided she was hungry after all.

"In a way."

Nell stood and fetched some green cheese from the pot board and smeared some onto her bread.

"He has fallen in love."

At that moment, Nell was about to take a bite but her mouth fell open and she stared at Guy. "Love?"

"Once upon a time, the man was governed merely by his lusts. Now, he saves himself for one woman."

"The Widow Poulter?"

"No. It's not her."

Nell bit into her bread. "No. I don't believe it. He told you all this did he?"

"He told me much of it, the rest I—surmised. I overheard them talking so I think I know…"

"Oh, tell me."

"The man has opened his heart to me, Nell. I cannot betray his trust."

Nell narrowed her eyes, "No! It can't be?"

She put down her bread.

"It truly is! Emma. Emma Masters? That foul tongued, flat chested, shrew of a woman?"

"He doesn't see her as that. And I do believe his affection is returned."

Nell shook her head in disbelief. "No! She's many a time flirted with you and there was that time when she asked you to marry her, wasn't there?"

"She cannot marry her priest. But she can marry to stay in the village to be nearer to him though. I think I was just being used. If she'd married me she would have committed adultery with Father Fabian, I fear. Over and over. She loves him."

Nell coughed as her bread went down the wrong way.

"Guy, she's affianced to a wealthy weaver in town!"

"She doesn't want to leave for Marlborough. She wants to stay here, close to Fabian. And then…"

"What?"

"No. I cannot say. I have already said too much. Nell you must keep quiet about all this. Promise me."

Reluctantly she assured him she would keep quiet

They chewed on in silence.

*****

Plough Monday was the first Monday after the twelve days of Christmas when the village plough, housed in a large barn on the estate, was dragged around the village houses, to bring good luck to all who contributed a small amount to a fund. Those who refused would find their garth ploughed up to mud.

As promised Guy went up into the church tower with Father Fabian; the priest rising up the ladder first to show good will, to look at the metal parts of the bell housing.

There was no doubt that the structure was unstable.

Guy worked on deciding what intervention was necessary and Father Fabian stood by the little window, his arms folded across his chest and they spoke of setting a date for the wedding of Parnell Truman and Guy Ferrier.

"Does Mistress Truman have a preference for a day?"

"January is as good a time as any, nay better, and Nell will not mind the day."

"Then I shall prepare to read the banns."

"Father?"

Guy stood and banged his head upon a wooden strut. They laughed companionably.

"There is just one thing." He rubbed his bruised pate.

"Oh...?"

"Nell is concerned that... oh this is difficult to say."

"Come Guy, we are friends now, are we not?"

Guy began to put his tools back into his bag.

"Nell is worried that your… past indiscretions… will impact upon the sanctity of our marriage. I'm sorry to have to say it but she is not convinced that you are the right man to marry us."

Fabian leaned against the wall.

"In the bible, in the story of David and the wife of Uriah the Hittite, David covets Bathsheba, he commits adultery with her, and he plans and carries out the murder of her husband with all the deceitfulness that such a deed requires. But when Nathan intervenes, David discovers the wickedness of his ways, repents, publishes his guilt and regret for all to see and yet manages to remain on his throne and live virtuously."

Guy shrugged. "So you are saying that your repentance—your owning up—even if only to your confessor, makes you a fit person once more?"

Fabian smiled. "You must come to your own conclusion."

Guy returned the smile warmly. "I will speak to Nell," he said.

*****

January wore on in dull and dank days. Guy was glad of his forge fire and carried on his work until the light failed, as it did early at this time of year.

One afternoon as he was fashioning a shoe for one of the manor plough horses, he heard a commotion at the crossroads where lay Nell's house and the church lych gate.

Poking his head from the forge, he saw a small crowd gathered.

"What on earth?"

He laid down his tools, patted Dobbin on the rump and jogged down the road.

"Stay there, good boy. I'll be back shortly."

Nell was already running up the lane to meet him.

"What's going on?"

"It's Emma, Emma Masters, she's taken leave of her senses."

"Where is she?"

"At the top of the church tower. Oh Guy... I think she means to throw herself off!"

Guy took Nell's upper arms in his strong hands. "Find her father... I'll go and see if I can talk to her."

"Oh, Guy, be careful."

"I'm going to try to find out what's the matter and talk her down before she falls... if indeed that is what she's thinking of doing."

Nell nodded, picked up her skirts and ran into the manor courtyard.

Guy, peering up into the gloomy sky above the church tried to locate any figure standing on the tower. He could see no one.

Up the ladder to the bell room, he went, then onward up above to the roof of the tower.

"Mistress Emma?"

He could hear a faint sobbing and a gentle voice humming words of a placatory nature.

"No, no... There's nothing I can do about it. You know that." The priest, Fabian.

Guy slowly walked out onto the leads. "Father... Emma?"

Emma was sitting with her back to the tower wall. Her face was puffy and red and she had obviously been crying for a long time, for she was almost unable to take in a breath without hiccoughing.

"Emma, my love. See who's here," said Father Fabian.

The girl's eyes focussed. "What help can he be?"

"He is a friend, dearest one; a friend who knows our secret..."

"He knows?"

"I do know Emma and I am very sorry for your... predicament," whispered Guy.

The girl hugged her knees encased as they were in her yellow supertunic.

"But there's nothing he can do," she sniffled.

Father Fabian looked at Guy with a pleading expression. It was clear he had been reasoning with her for some time and had run out of arguments and ideas.

"Come down Emma... come down into the warmth of Nell's house and take a little ale with Nell and me. And we can talk about it."

"Talk about what?"

"About the fact that... you are in love with a priest and are with child by him."

In the ensuing silence, all that could be heard was the hum of the people below who were watching the tower. Then, a jackdaw, alighting a few feet away from the party on the roof, walked along the parapet and made such a squawk, that they all jumped.

The bird stayed looking at them in perplexity. What were they doing on his roof?

"Emma, you know I cannot marry you. If it were possible, I would do so today for I love you, but I cannot. I am so sorry that I have brought you to such a state. It was not my intention..." said Fabian.

"It's always the girl who is punished. It's always the poor girl who has to deal with the situation alone," sobbed Emma.

"I will not escape punishment, Emma, I promise you."

"No... No, perhaps not. But I will bear this child and have him as a reminder, a reminder of you, for the rest of my life. And what a life? Ruin... that's what!"

"Emma!" The manor steward, Emma's father, now yelled up at the church tower. "Emma, what are you doing? Come down here at this instant!"

Emma bounced up from her hiding place behind the parapet.

"Go away! Leave me alone," she shouted down to the ground. "I don't want to see you."

"I'll thank you to speak civilly to your father and to come down here immediately."

"I will not!"

"What in God's name are you doing up there?"

Emma turned back to her paramour.

"I will not live without you. I'll not bear this child alone. I'll not go to Marlborough to marry and forget you. I'll end all this now."

Fabian leapt forward and grabbed hold of her sleeve.

"No, Emma. You must not, it is a mortal sin."

"I don't care."

"Emma, no!"

The girl had leaned over the stones of the parapet. "Stand back. I have no wish to hurt anyone," she yelled down to the onlookers.

"Emma Masters!" cried Guy in the most authoritative voice he could muster. "Listen to me."

She stopped then and Fabian was able to get his arm around her and draw her to himself.

"You need a husband. One who lives in the village. You need a father for your child. You have no wish to leave Kennet, I understand that. You wish to stay near to Fabian. It can all be kept secret. I will marry you, I promise. I will help you... help you both, in your awkward situation." Guy could hardly credit that he'd said the words.

Emma's face creased into a disbelieving smile. "No!"

"Believe me..."

"Guy... no," said Fabian. "You cannot do this. It's not right."

"Emma, promise me that you will come away from the edge and come down with me and I in turn will promise before witnesses to marry you."

The girl laughed. "And what about Mistress Perfect Parnell?"

"I..." Guy had no immediate answer for her.

"Ah no. This is just a ruse to stop me doing what I want to do. You have no more intention of marrying me than... marrying that bird there."

The jackdaw was peering at them with an inquisitive white eye from a distance of a few feet.

"Emma... please," said Fabian. "Let us think about this."

"I have had a lot of time to think about it." She turned once more to the empty air. "I have had enough of thinking."

"Emma. Do as you are told and come down here this instant!" shouted her father.

She looked back sadly at Guy. "Never let it be said that I am not an obedient daughter," she said with a strange skewed smile.

Fabian holding onto her made a firmer grab for her as she tipped herself from the parapet.

And swiftly Guy made a grab for Fabian. But he missed.

The jackdaw rose into the air with an unearthly cackle and safely glided upwards on blue-black wings.

Unlike the bird, both Emma and Father Fabian fell, clutching each other as they disappeared over the edge.

Guy watched as they both plunged to the ground and landed with a dull thwack on the frozen earth beneath.

He looked up quickly, not wishing to see the ruination below and located the jackdaw speeding over the manor roof.

CHAPTER THIRTEEN ~ THE LOVERS

The screams of the onlookers travelled upwards in the cold air, to Guy on his lonely tower. He fell back and, as Emma had done, he backed himself to the wall and sat with his knees up. What was he to do? Could he—should he—tell what had actually happened here on the tower? Emma had been determined to take her own life. Fabian had been determined to stop her. Emma had committed *felo de se*—self murder—but she had taken her lover with her. Was this murder? Quickly Guy rehearsed his story. He could not allow the truth to be known. Emma would be buried as a criminal, for self-murder was a crime as well as a sin. And Fabian? Had he at the last moment made the decision to go with his lover? He was a priest and was absolutely convinced of the sinfulness of the act. No, thought Guy. His death had been an accident. Sadly, he stood and, calming himself with deep breaths, he shakily travelled the ladder back to the ground floor.

Nell was waiting for him in the nave. "Oh Guy! You're alright. I was so worried for you. I had a terrible vision of you falling from the sky, like... they did... and, oh I could not bear it. Oh Guy, I love you so much. I could not bear it." She rushed at him and he opened his arms to take her in an embrace.

"Hush. I am here and I am perfectly alright."

He rested his chin on the crown of her head as they embraced. "Are they?"

"Both dead. Oh, it's awful. Both dead."

After a while when he had said nothing, she pulled away, "What happened?"

"Hush. I will tell you later but first I need to explain something to Steward Masters."

Guy sought out the manor steward who was staring down at the mangled body of his daughter, in absolute disbelief.

He kept saying to himself "What... what?" None of the onlookers answered him.

"Sir... Might I have a word? I was up on the tower. I heard and saw it all. I need to tell you..."

"Yes..." The man cleared his throat, "Yes, Ferrier... what...?

Guy took hold of the manor steward and moved him to the church wall out of the way; out of the vision of the ruined bodies.

"Mistress Emma was so upset. She had told me and also Father Fabian, that she had no wish to go to Marlborough to marry into the wealthy family you had chosen for her. She could not leave you, she said, for without her, who would look to you?"

Masters' eyes narrowed. Guy was not sure if his tale was going to be believed but he ploughed on.

"Father Fabian came to console Emma and explain that it was all for her own good but she was having none of it. Father Fabian was convincing her of the rightness of things..."

"She took her own life, because of that?"

"No... no. I do not think she really had any intention of throwing herself from the tower. Not really. Father Fabian was giving comfort to Emma, praying with her for God's aid in understanding how her life was about to change when... when a jackdaw alighted very close to them both and Emma, startled by the shriek of the wicked bird grabbed Fabian for security, missed her footing and they both fell. Fabian tried to save her."

"You saw all this?"

"I did, sir."

Guy pointed up to the sky, "See... there is the offending bird. See how he cackles and crows. No doubt an evil spirit taking advantage of the moment to try to drag two innocent people to their deaths and claim their souls."

"Oh, my Lord!"

Someone had come with a blanket and it was laid over the two bodies on the ground.

"We must send for the priest at Overton, sir, immediately. We must save their souls."

Guy took hold of the steward's arm and led him a short way away in front of the church porch. "Someone must stay here until he arrives. I can do that. I can, as a blacksmith, cast a few helpful holy spells which will protect their souls. Leave it to me."

Steward Masters was bemused. His face was blank but he thanked Guy and was led away by neighbours and friends.

Guy sat by the church wall and dangled his hands over his knees.

Jesus, what a story! Would it be believed? Guy did not wish any word of the affair between Father Fabian and Emma Masters to leak out. He did not want anyone to know that Emma carried Fabian's child.

He saw Nell waiting for him by the church door and trembling, stood to go to her. "Come, I need some Holy water."

"Why?"

"To protect the bodies until the priest from Overton can get here."

He wrapped his arm around her shoulder. "Come into the church with me."

"Why you, Guy?"

He smiled down at her and pecked her on the cheek.

"Ah... well... the blacksmith is a magical fellow. You know that, for I have often told you so. I can keep the devil's minions from Emma and Fabian with a well formed spell and a little Holy water."

They pushed the door open. The humped creature who had no name winked at the blacksmith once again. He was sure it did.

Guy found what he was looking for in the priest's room and together, Nell and he went to the two bodies by the base of the church tower, now sadly alone together.

"In the name of the Father and the Son and the Holy Ghost, I command you creatures of Satan to depart and to keep your distance from these two innocent souls. They died today, perhaps unshriven and in sin but God will take them to his bosom, for he understands the power of love and says that love is the greatest gift one can bestow upon another. He will rightly judge these two lovers but he will understand their predicament."

He dropped the Holy water over them.

Once more Nell came up to him. She took his hand. "Oh, Guy you are the most amazing man. I'm such a lucky woman to have you!"

"Am I?"

"How could I not see before just how wonderful you are?"

He did not answer her. His mind was suddenly away, over the downs, following a carriage where a young woman with blonde hair was weeping into her hands, more and more earnestly as the miles piled up behind her.

"Father could see it... of course he could. But I did not—not immediately. I have always thought you a wonderful man but love you—no—but now, I know I do love you and I do want to marry you. Now I am so happy."

She beamed up at him.

His eye was following the jackdaw as he wheeled across the sky to join several others who disappeared as tiny black pinpricks, over the hill at the Sanctuary.

"I am glad you are happy," said Guy at last. "Perhaps we can now turn our minds to our wedding. What say you we approach the priest at Overton? It's not far to go, for there will be no priest here immediately."

Nell hugged him to her.
"Whatever you say, Guy."

*****

After a long while there grew a legend. It grew out of a song, they say. No one knew who had composed the song but everyone knew of it.

'All in the leaden month of January
When skies were grey and air was cold
Young William took his lady love
To the church, but not to marry.
Or so it has, for years been told.

"Oh follow me to the tower my love
And we shall climb into God's sight.
For a love as ours is holy as the dove
And we shall rise to Heaven's height."

She took his hand, her lovely priest,
For in that there was no disgrace
And they climbed the steps and faced the east,
And there they did embrace.

And slowly, slowly they did embrace
And slowly, slowly they did kiss
Until they moved to the tower's edge space
Where lay the dread abyss.

A wicked jackdaw with wings so blacked
Rose up with a cry so hard
That the lovers fell as if attacked

Into the sere churchyard.

Oh father, father dig my grave,
Go dig it wide and narrow
For we both died for love today
And we shall be buried tomorrow.

She was buried in the old churchyard,
And William was laid beside her,
Out of her heart grew a wild, wild rose
And out of his, a briar.

They grew and grew in the old churchyard,
Till they could grow no higher
At the end they formed a true lover's knot
And the rose grew 'round the briar.'

The church was haunted by the ghosts of a priest and his lover. On a dark night in winter, the two of them could be seen embracing on the top of the church tower and after a short time they could be seen to plunge soundlessly to the earth. Their mangled bodies remain at the base of the tower but their spirits rise and hand in hand they float over the ground to be lost in the mists which grow thick around the river bank. Gradually their poor bodies disappeared into nothing.

No one knew how this story had grown up.

No one knew if it was true.

But it might have been.

After all there were two people in the decorations on the church door. Perhaps they were not Noah and his wife, after all.

CHAPTER FOURTEEN
THE BEAST FROM THE EAST
FEBRUARY 2018

Snow flurries were making driving difficult, but the little van ploughed on along the lengthy and straight road from Devizes to Beckhampton. It was always like this here in bad weather, as there was little cover and no windbreaks and the tempest roared over the downs like a demented dragon.

The driver cursed. Would he ever get home?

He switched on the car radio and began humming the tune playing. He knew it well, of course. It was the folk song, 'Barbara Allen' and it wasn't long before he was singing the sad lyrics in his deep bass voice, along with the group on the radio.

He turned into the roundabout at Beckhampton and slid around the lane. Good job there was no other vehicle on the road.

Past the mound of Silbury Hill covered in a dusting of snow which was rapidly becoming a white icing, he turned into the narrow road to East Kennet. Carefully he negotiated the bends and the small bridge over the river. Just a mile now before he could rest in his cottage at West Overton, sit beside his Rayburn with a hot cuppa and toast his cold toes.

The road turned towards the Old Forge, the B&B on the right hand side; almost the first building in East Kennet and the first close by the road.

The van slipped sideways to avoid a grey horse at the side of the road.

"Jesus!" said Guy to himself. "That was a near miss."

Parking up, Guy looked round, his windscreen wipers going backwards and forwards, clearing the soft snow efficiently.

"What the devil?"

There didn't seem to be anyone with the horse but then, a dark shape rose up from the bank by the carpark.

"Oh, that was quick!" said a voice.

"I beg your pardon," said Guy, winding down the window.

"I've only just left a message on your answerphone."

"What?" Guy took out his phone. There was no message. He had another business carphone and that hadn't rung since he had been in Devizes over an hour ago.

"Er... you sure it was me you rang?"

"Oliver's Mobile Farrier... oh..." said the girl looking at the lettering upon Guy's van. "Oh... it's not you."

"No. I'm Guy Webb—Master Farrier. Mobile farrier."

"Oh..." The girl looked rather embarrassed.

"What's the matter? Has he cast a shoe?"

She took her lip in her teeth. "I think so."

"Well now I'm here. Would you like me to look at your beast?"

"Beast?" The girl's pale face under her navy coloured hood trimmed with fake fur, wore a perplexed expression. "Oh yes... horse. Thank you."

She came and took the reins which had been looped over the fence, in her hand.

"He went lame up the hill. I'd been walking the Ridgeway with him before it snowed really badly and I must admit I got a bit lost."

"You got lost... on the Ridgeway?"

"I turned the wrong way. I should have crossed the road and gone on the bridleway down the hill but I missed it. It was hard to see with the snow flurries. It was almost a blizzard."

Guy was looking at the horse's hoof.

"He has cast a shoe."

"Yes, I thought that was it. He's not used to this sort of flinty, stony ground."

"You're not local then?"

"No, I come from Milton Lillebourne"

Guy's brow furrowed. "That's a way off. Have you ridden all the way?"

"Ah, no. I'm staying with my cousin in the manor house at Overton."

"Ah, that's where I live," he said gleefully. He took off his glove and offered his hand.

"Guy Webb, as I said. Crooked Cottage, Overton."

The girl took his hand and they shook. It was a workman's hand; hard, blackened and sturdy.

"Adela, Adela Lilbourne. My father farms out at Milton. The Manor Farm."

"Big red brick building. I know of it but I've never been there."

They looked at each other through the snow.

"Look... this is rather impossible. What say we go into the manor here..? I know the people well and they won't mind. I can shoe your horse for you there and we can get out of the cold. It's not good for him to travel too far on metalled roads without a shoe. Pity I don't have my horsebox."

She cocked her head. "Do I know you…? I seem to think that... no, it's foolish. You've never shod horses at Milton, you say."

"Oh, I have, in the village but just not at the manor."

"Ah, perhaps I've seen you about."

Guy wanted to say, "If I'd seen you, I'd certainly remember." But he kept quiet.

"The manor is a few yards further on. Walk up to the gate and I'll follow in my van."

*****

It took a short time for Guy to heat up his portable forge and fit a shoe to Adela's horse.

"What's his name?"

"You'll laugh."

"No, I won't. You'd be surprised at some of the silly names people give their horses.

"Charlemagne. Charles, for short."

"Now, that's a good and noble name," said Guy with a smile.

"Yes... I have a great interest in history, you see, early history and so..."

"It seems apt. He suits his name... being a grey."

"I think so."

"How long are you staying at your cousin's?"

"Oh, I'm here for my cousin's birthday. She's twenty one and she's having a big party. My cousin Eleanor would have been out with me today but she's sprained her ankle and is laid up. Right before her birthday too!"

"Ah yes... I know Nell," said Guy. "You wouldn't have been lost if she'd been with you."

The girl laughed, embarrassed. "No. I am a bit of a dunce when it comes to directions."

Guy took payment with his card machine, eventually getting a signal by waving it about madly.

"This is the worst place for a blasted signal," he laughed. "Loads of places I visit don't have a signal. I wonder some days why I bother with this card machine. Signals on mobiles are pretty useless here too."

Adela laughed. "Well, I could have paid you on the internet at home. That might be easier."

"It might. Here—have a card—just in case you need me again." He handed her a business card. "I have a website."

Guy began to pack up his things.

"Erm… I wonder. If when you've stabled your… Charles… might you like to go for a drink. The Bell in Overton isn't bad at all."

Adela smiled sweetly at him.

"That would be lovely," she said with a shy smile.

*****

The pub was invitingly warm and Guy and Adela sat by the log fire until they thawed and Adela's cheeks became pink. Charlemagne had been returned to his stable at Overton Manor none the worse for his trip along the snowy Ridgeway.

"When will you go home to Milton Lilbourne?" asked Guy.

"Well, Ellie's party is at the weekend and I thought I'd stay until Monday. At least I have Monday off from work."

"Oh…?" Guy took a swig of his Guinness. "What do you do then?"

"I work for a solicitor in Devizes, or I did until recently."

"You say until recently? What about now?"

Adela tossed her shoulder length blonde hair, "Well, I have a new job but I don't start it until March 5th. I'm having a bit of time off."

"Everyone needs that now and again," he smiled.

"I have to say, I hated working for that firm and I was glad to get away."

Guy leaned back in his seat and stretched his legs to the fire, "So you have been travelling the countryside with your grey, Charlemagne, and getting lost on the Ridgeway."

"Now you're being unkind," laughed Adela.

"Not at all. So what are you doing with yourself when you aren't visiting your cousin or getting lost?"

"You are being…"

"No… really, sorry. I'm just pulling your leg!"

"Well, again… you'll laugh."

"No, hand on heart. I won't laugh."

"Well… I like visiting churches. I really like church architecture and I heard from my cousin that the church at East Kennet has an amazing door."

"Does it?" Guy suddenly felt as if a cold wind had been driven up his back. He looked over his shoulder but, no, the outer door of the pub had not been opened.

"It's full of little figures of people and animals and I thought I'd go and have a look. Take some photos for Facebook. I belong to a few pages about church architecture, you see."

"That's really interesting."

"What do you do when you're not shoeing horses?"

"Oh... I like to play around on my guitar. Make up little songs. I'm not very good though."

"I'd like to hear you. You have a wonderful speaking voice so I bet you have a great singing voice."

"Now who's pulling legs?"

Guy's mind pictured the little church at East Kennet. He'd never even been into the churchyard. To be honest when he'd had cause to go up the little stub of a road called Church Lane which led to the building, he'd suddenly become very uncomfortable and had to turn around. Inexplicable really.

"Well... if you'd like to go tomorrow and you don't mind me tagging along? I'd like to have a look too."

Adela sipped her white wine. "I don't see why not."

*****

Guy picked up Adela in his van the next morning and they travelled the mile from Overton to East Kennet.

Adela shivered as she got out of the car. It was still very cold and even her furry hood didn't seem to keep her warm.

She looked around. "Who lives there, where we were yesterday?" She pointed.

"East Kennet Manor as was, now Manor Farm...? Well, a retired clergyman has it now."

"A clergyman? Such a large house?"

"Ah yes... he was something high up in the cathedral at Salisbury before he retired. It was in his family I believe. His son mostly runs the farm now. Fabian Matthews."

"Ah, I see."

Adela looked at the white gates which were attached to impressive stone plinths and a strange feeling came over her. Why should she be feeling a sense of dread? She gave a quick sidelong look at Guy and then she jammed her hands into her pockets.

"Come on then."

Side by side they walked up the narrow path to the church porch. The outer door had a lattice of wood and Guy pushed it with a stuttering sound.

A musty, damp smell invaded his nose and he sniffed momentarily.

"Well here it is."

Adela was reluctant to enter the porch for some unaccountable reason. She grew incredibly sad and the feeling of dread increased. But as she actually entered the building the feeling subsided to be replaced by a sense of happiness and love. To cover her embarrassment she said, "Of course, this isn't the original church. This one was built over the old one, as they often were. The old one was mentioned in Domesday..." She watched as Guy's face creased in humour.

"You really take this church stuff seriously don't you?"

"I do. It's a serious hobby, if you like."

"So if this isn't the original church, how old is the door with its figures?"

"It seems that the old door was added to the new church. The book I read said it was very old but that the figures dated from the thirteenth century."

"Wow... so old!"

Guy stood back and peered into the gloom where the door lay. As his eyes became accustomed to the dimness, he could see the metal workings of the decorations.

And suddenly, the oddest feeling came over him. He didn't know where he was.

*****

He sat back quickly on the stone ledge which ran down each side of the porch.

For a tiny moment, his eyes grew misty and he saw before him a girl with long blonde hair in a plait held back by a silver band. She was incredibly beautiful with bright blue eyes and skin as soft as silk. She smiled at him and came nearer. Her clothes were odd to Guy's eyes. She wore a long shapeless violet coloured wool dress cinched at the waist with a narrow blue leather belt which dangled down to her knees.

Guy blinked. This was not Adela. She wore blue jeans and her navy jacket with the fur hood.

He closed his eyes.

"Adela?"

Quickly she sat beside him. "Are you alright, Guy?"

"Didn't you see her?" he asked breathlessly.

"See who?"

"The girl... she looked a little like you but she was wearing a long dress."

Adela looked round quickly. "There's no one else here, Guy."

There was a terrible rushing sound in his ears and his heart began to pound rapidly. He leaned forward and put his head over his knees.

"You look very hot and bothered," said Adela. "Are you alright?"

"I think I have just seen a ghost," he chuckled.

He knew that Adela wanted to laugh at him but she didn't dare. "A ghost?"

"There is a legend about this church—that it's haunted," he said.

"Oh? And you believe it?"

"I think I have to now. I think I have just seen her."

Adela looked out of the porch door at the winter sunshine flooding the graveyard. The aconites were bright pinpricks of yellow in the muted greens and browns of the snowy churchyard. The clumps of snowdrops nodded their heads in the slight breeze. You couldn't find somewhere less like a place which might be haunted, she thought.

"Have you... ever... seen anything like it... before?" she asked, a little hesitantly.

"No... never. But I swear it's what I saw."

He took a deep breath to clear his head. "Right. Let's look at this door."

If he thought he'd felt strange a moment before, he felt worse when his eyes raked the ancient door.

A voice inside his head said...'The oliphant.'

He looked over his shoulder quickly. Adela was correct, there was no one else there. But someone had spoken to him.

His eye travelled from the door ring up to the top of the wood and slowly down to the base, where sat what looked like the remains of a metal hare with its nose pointing to the sky. One ear was missing.

Several pieces of the decorations overall were missing but it was almost possible to see what the door had been like with all the decorations intact.

"I... I... I've seen this door before," he said shakily.

"But you said you'd never been here before."

"No, no. I haven't."

"Perhaps you've read about it or seen photos?"

Guy stared at the little animals.

"No. It's not that. I know them. I actually know them. I have held them in my hands. They're my creation. I made them," he said almost to himself.

Adela stood up and went to sit on the other ledge opposite to look at him carefully. What a strange man he was.

"Made them?"

Guy lifted his hands into his view. "These hands have held them. They've made them, I swear it."

"But…"

"Truly—I know it—absolutely. How I know it, I—can't say."

"Alright…" drawled Adela, looking at him oddly, "I believe you."

"No you don't. And I don't blame you. But…"

Guy stood and faced the door. He pointed.

"This was known as the oliphant—what we'd call an elephant. We didn't really know what an elephant looked like back at the time these door decorations were made. The blacksmith—I think that must have been me—had to guess what it looked like from descriptions. And the camel—the creature with a hump. I know what it is now. But then, I didn't know."

"Guy, you're frightening me. It's like you're speaking about another world; in another tense and time. What do you mean?"

"I'm sorry. I don't mean to frighten you. I don't know what I'm saying." He rubbed his temples.

"The dog and the pig, the goose… I recognise them. I made them all."

"But you've never been here before. How can you have made them?"

"I don't know. I just know I did. I remember holding them in my hands. I remember the forge where I made them… it's just down the road."

"Oh Guy, now you really are worrying me."

"No really. It is. That's where you tethered your horse yesterday; in front of the forge—where we met."

"But it was a B&B."

"Yes, it's called The Old Forge. My ancestors owned it before it was sold and became a private building. My grandfather Webb still worked there. I remember it."

"But the building isn't that old," said Adela.

"No, it's been built upon over and over, in the centuries—like this church—but it's been a forge for ever. And I remember being in it. For the first time in my life, I remember working there." Guy scratched his head. "Come on... I'll show you." He grabbed Adela by the hand and towed her down the church path.

The poor girl followed even though she was rather unsettled by this strange young man with his talk of memories.

They walked rapidly down the road, dodging one or two fast cars on the rat run between the main A4 road and the villages further into the downs. Eventually they stood before the forge building; the B&B which lay right on the road.

In Guy's mind's eye the present building, with its two wings and central door, wavered in a fog and the forge he thought he remembered, eventually came into his vision as clear as day.

"There is a double door... almost always open. On the left hand side is a stall for an animal... a small horse and outside there is a cart." He was now in full flow and Adela watched him fascinated.

"The fire was there and the chimney, there. " He pointed. "With the huge bellows and... some trunks of trees placed here and there around the anvil... where... Oh my God!"

"What?"

"Where the girl I saw in the church porch is sitting." He turned to her with an eye glinting with excitement.

"Adela... Adela..."

She noticed he'd gone very pale under his outdoor tan.

"What?"

"It's you."

"Oh don't be ridiculous."

"I'm sorry... I'm just saying what I see. There's a girl just like you sitting on one of the tree trunks and she is wearing a red coloured dress to the floor."

"I never wear dresses," said Adela, a little irritated, "if I can help it."

"But then... then... in those days, you would have had no choice would you?"

Now there was disbelief in her voice, "And when was then?"

Guy swallowed. "I'm no expert but if the door was made in the thirteenth century then... it must have been then."

Adela backed off and began to walk back to the van.

"That would make me 800 years old. I'm only twenty four for Heaven's sake!"

"And I'm thirty... but..."

Adela started to run. Did she need to get away from this nutcase?

Guy followed. She ran past the van and into the church this time, pushing open the inner door with its lovely decorations and entering the dusty nave.

"Where are you going?"

"There must be a guide book. I want to read it."

For two pounds they managed to purchase a guide book, dropping the coins into a box in the wall, and sitting at the back of the nave they thumbed through it. Past adverts for gardeners and plumbers, sponsors for missionary work and other things, they found at last, the page which explained the patterns on the door.

Guy closed his eyes as Adela scanned the text.

"No, don't tell me. Now I tell you truthfully I have never seen this book before but I'll tell you what I know. How I know it I just can't say. It depicts Noah's flood. Noah and his wife are at the top with their dog and then other animals parade on down the surface. An elephant and a camel and a goose and..."

Adela looked at him sidelong.

"The door shows Noah and his wife and many of the animals which were stowed away in the ark. It was made in the twelfth century and remade in the thirteenth when many of the animals were added," she read.

"Yes—by me."

"You're a farrier—not a blacksmith," said Adela with a sharp note to her voice.

"No, but in those days, blacksmiths were both."

She opened her mouth to say something but thought better of it and continued to read.

"The old door was saved from destruction at the Reformation by being removed to the Manor where it was rediscovered in the 19th century and replaced. In 1863 the church was rebuilt, endowed by the Matthews family of East Kennett Manor. The new church was constructed with chequered stonework and knapped flint and incorporated a nave with north tower and spire, a south porch and a chancel. The work was carried out by Gane and Co. of Trowbridge."

"The Matthews are still in the village now."

"So I was right, this church didn't exist in the thirteenth century. This one is Victorian."

"But another did," said Guy. "Can't you feel it?"

Adela laid aside the guidebook and walked up the nave.

"Well... feel it... no, but I can imagine it."

She turned at the chancel arch and looked down the short nave.

"Then imagine," said Guy.

Adela closed her eyes as Guy chanted,

"It was small, narrow and filled with paintings. Here... " He gestured. "Over the chancel arch is a naively painted Garden of Eden with Adam and Eve either side of a tree with pink blossoms and red apples. The north and south walls are painted with Biblical Kings, Saul, Solomon and David, with their fashionable clothes of the day and huge crowns. And here and there are painted interesting patterns of spots and wavy lines dotted with the faces of little coloured devils."

Adela opened her eyes. She turned back to the altar where to her amazement stood a priest in full regalia with his back to her.

The altar was a simple block of stone. Gone was the modern wide chancel arch with its large stained glass window behind. Gone was the green and gold altar frontal with the beautiful figures painted on the reredo. Gone were the wooden pews and the marble tombs. In their place was a bare stone cell with three steps up to the altar.

"Excuse me," said Adela to the priest. "Sorry to interrupt you but might you be able to tell us a little about the…"

The figure wavered in front of her, like a distant scene does in hot weather and then disappeared.

She staggered in surprise and Guy was suddenly there to hold her up.

"You alright?"

"I… don't know."

"What did you see?"

"A priest at the altar. With dark hair and… Oh this is ridiculous. It's the power of suggestion."

Guy sighed and sat down in one of the nearer pews. "I don't understand any of this… any more than you do… but I just know I have been here before, a very long time ago. And so have you, I think."

Adela was reading the list of priests printed at the back of the guide book. "Father Francis Longspele, Father Fabian …."

"Mandeville…"

She looked up slowly.

"Yes." She snapped the booklet shut. "Look… If this is some kind of cheap trick to get me to…?"

"Adela, I wouldn't do that. I promise. Truly. I'm not like that."

She stared at his face. His honest, open, somewhat beguiling face.

"I promise you that I am not telling you lies nor have I rehearsed all this nor ever been here before. Not in this body anyway."

They continued to stare at each other.

"God, I need a drink!" said Guy eventually.

*****

Back at the local, the Bell, Guy sat with his pint of Guinness and Adela with her glass of dry white wine.

She couldn't get the image from her mind, the priest with his collar length dark hair and long robes; the simple church with its bare altar.

What had she seen? What had Guy seen?

And why?

Guy stared into his untouched pint as the head frothed in the glass. Before she'd known it, Adela had downed her first glass of wine.

"What we need is someone who knows the local history," said Guy at last. "Someone who knows the distant past of the place."

"How are we going to find that?"

"My friend Tom Kennett is a librarian at the Devizes museum. Well actually he's an antiquarian, he'll know where to look."

"Devizes? That's miles away."

"No it's not. We could go there this afternoon."

"I have to be back for Ellie's party."

"We can do that."

Guy looked at her empty glass. "Another?"

"Not without lunch."

He laughed. "OK. Lunch it is and then Devizes."

*****

"We really don't have a lot of information about the earliest times at East Kennett, Guy," said Tom when introductions had been made. "We know more about the prehistoric era than we do about the early Mediaeval."

He flipped over the page of a catalogue. "Most of the records start in the fifteenth century."

"There's a list of vicars at the back of the guidebook," said Adela. "That might help us. And the three which are listed for the early thirteenth century are, Francis Longspele, Fabian Mandeville and Thomas of Lockeridge."

"Ah, they come from a manuscript written about fifty years after the events."

"Events? What events…?"

"Well it's only a legend but it says that Fabian Mandeville got a girl of the village pregnant and she threw herself from the church tower, the old church of course—not the one that's there now."

"Who wrote this manuscript? The record?"

"Oh, it's a man called..." Tom fetched up a screen on his computer. "Adam. Adam Ferrier. Priest."

"Ferrier... That name indicates the man had been a blacksmith. Or the son of one maybe. Taking the family name but not practising himself." Guy swallowed an uncomfortable feeling. "What's the date of it?"

"It's..." He squinted at the screen. "1243, I believe."

"Right... Yes... That makes sense."

"It does?" asked Adela.

"I'll explain in a moment," said Guy. "So I presume this is the origin of the legend that the church and graveyard is haunted?"

"Ah, now that..." Tom scrolled down his pages. "That isn't recorded until the fourteenth century. In 1301. That's the first written record. But of course..."

"Oral records will have predated this," said Guy smiling.

"Precisely."

"Thanks Tom. It's not much but it helps."

Tom grinned. "Pleased to be useful. What's all the interest suddenly?"

Guy grinned back. "Adela wants to know more about her ancestors. They were lords of the manor in the 13th century."

"Ah... the Lillebons?"

"Yes..." said Adela a little self-consciously, "I'm a Lillebourne."

Tom smiled sweetly. "Nice to meet someone with such a long pedigree," he said.

"How did you meet him?" asked Adela when they were back in the van.

"Oh..." Guy chuckled. "We were both on a course. I wanted to learn all about building with wattle and daub and there was a course at the museum. We both enrolled. Tom Kennett has an interest in

Mediaeval building, you see."

"Oh." She sat thinking for a moment watching Guy tapping the steering wheel.

"You were going to tell me about the written record."

"Ah yes…" He shifted to look at her. "Now this is going to sound very odd, unlikely, crazy even. But, if the blacksmith who forged the door decorations was me and I was a young man in the early 1200s, then Adam might have been my son. Not a blacksmith but a priest—not impossible, I suppose."

"And he will have known the story from his father and written it down."

"Possibly. Because I probably won't have been able to write. And he would be able to write, as a priest. He'd be educated."

Guy searched Adela's lovely face. She wore no makeup… she was naturally beautiful without it. And her hair… her hair was like spun gold, wavy and falling in waves around her oval face. His heart gave a lurch.

Adela stared back. She saw a handsome young man with dark curly hair, and with laughter lines creasing the corners of his brown eyes. Yes, there was no doubt he had a sense of humour. But there was also a sense of seriousness with him. She realised that she rather liked him.

"I have a party to go to… I'd better get back."

Guy cleared his throat. "Ah yes, of course…"

"Erm… I'm sure Ellie wouldn't mind if you came too."

"Are you inviting me to accompany you to a party?"

"Well, yes. If you'd like to."

"Are you sure you trust me? I'm this mad man who sees things… remember?"

"Well, if you're mad, then so am I," said Adela. "I saw things too."

*****

"Nice to see you, Guy," said Nell. "I haven't seen you around and about for ages."

Guy squirmed. "No, I've been really busy."

"And you met my cousin. How amazing."

"Yes... we, erm... bumped into each other when it was snowing. Her horse..."

"Yes. I know, Addy told me."

There was an uncomfortable silence.

"Well... get yourself a drink and we'll catch up later."

Adela watched her cousin in her tight red dress, cross the floor of the manor ballroom like an actress in a B movie.

"I notice her ankle is mended."

"Hmmm. She was always the dressy one," said Adela.

"But you are the prettier one," said Guy without really engaging his brain.

"Oh..." said Adela under her breath.

Guy seemed to follow Ellie with his eyes narrowed. It wasn't an admiring look.

"How do you know my cousin?"

"Oh, Nell's older sister Emma and I were at the same school when we were small. Until she left for her fancy private one in Marlborough. And when she came back from university, Emma introduced us, and Nell and I went out together for a while."

"Oh."

"It wasn't a good idea."

"She never said."

"She wouldn't. We didn't really get on. She's a bit..."

"Bossy?"

Guy laughed. "A bit too full of herself for me."

They found a table on the edge of the dance floor and sat close together. Not really having any interest in the music, the food or the dancing they just sat and watched for a while.

Adela wore a pale blue patterned tunic with sharp navy trousers and Guy thought she outshone all the other women in the room with their short skirts and skimpy tops or clinging dresses all shiny with sequins.

Very quickly their conversation came round to what they'd learned that day.

The music got louder as more people arrived and filled the dance floor.

They couldn't hear each other speak.

Adela took hold of Guy's hand and steered him to the door. "They have a conservatory. It'll be quieter in there. We can talk."

"The music's not really to my liking anyway," he yelled.

"Mine neither."

"Oh?"

"I like Classical music," said Adela.

"And I like folk but I'm not adverse to a bit of Mozart," smiled Guy.

"This modern stuff... it's all... noise." Adela's voice carried on but her mind was off elsewhere.

Suddenly she'd stopped. Into her head had popped a song—a tune—how odd. Where had it come from? Where had she heard it? How had she learned it?

They reached the quiet of the conservatory.

"Guy..."

"Yes?"

"You talked about the oliphant?"

"I did... it's an..."

"Elephant, I know. It's odd but I have remembered a really old song about an elephant. I have absolutely no idea how I know it, but all I know is, it's really old."

She began to sing very quietly and shyly in an extremely odd language. Guy recognised the sound of it immediately. He was able to translate it in his head.

"I am grey but I am not a cloud,

I have two tails and I'm not a cat,

I have big ears but I'm not a hare.

I am huge, stand tall and proud,

I am grand but I am not fat,

Approach me if you dare.'

Guy's heart raced as Adela began the second verse.

'My roar is louder than the lion,

My feet are harder than the iron,"...

Guy joined in. How did he know this language?

"My horns are sharper than the sword,

I once was human, a mighty lord,

Strong and wise, but I changed my form,

As necromancers can perform.

Beware the oliphant's fearsome brawn

Lest he bring you down."

They realised that their faces were very close together. Her breath was tickling his cheek.

Guy leaned in a little. They touched noses. And they kissed. It was a quick kiss, innocent and sweet and Guy suddenly remembered another like it.

"Oh my God," he said. "I... I wrote that song."

*****

"Well, well, well. If it isn't our friendly neighbourhood farrier... and who is this lovely lady, Guy?"

"Hiya Fabian," said Guy, pulling away. "Adela Lillbourne, meet my friend Fabian Matthews who farms at Manor Farm in East Kennet."

"I am very pleased to meet you." He took Adela's hand and put his lips to her knuckles. Fabian always was a charmer and old fashioned to boot.

Guy was certain he felt Adela shiver.

"Well... where did our local farrier find you?"

"She's cousin to Nell... lives out at Milton Lilbourne."

"Ah, so this is Nell's esteemed guest?"

"No please," said Adela. "I'm just plain Addy."

"Well, I am doubly pleased to meet you Addy," said Fabian. "Any friend of Guy's and Nell's is a friend of mine."

He squeezed himself in by Adela.

"Of course, I've met your father once or twice. Farming meetings and such."

"Oh, have you?" said Adela with uncertainty. "Well my father does get about a bit."

Fabian laughed. "Well of course he does. He's a very important man."

Adela laughed nervously and threw a quick look at Guy.

"I'm sure he'd laugh if he heard himself described as 'important'," she said. "Guy, shall we go back to the...?"

"Justice of the Peace, Member of Parliament... and High Sheriff of the County..."

"Only once. And only for a short while."

"And lord of hundreds of acres of prime agricultural land."

Adela grimaced and stood up quickly. "Guy, I think I'd like to get another drink..."

"But you haven't finished that one yet."

"It's always good to have one in reserve with the clamour at the bar."

Fabian stood and nodded to Adela. "Have a good time, Guy. See you later, my lady."

*****

"Why didn't you tell me your father was Lord Lilbourne?"

Adela grimaced. "I didn't want to say. When people know who my father is and then they know who I am, they usually get the wrong idea."

"Oh? What idea?"

"You know... pots of money... stuck up... privately educated..." She tailed off as she saw his face resolving itself into a grin.

"Rubbish."

"I am simply Addy Lilbourne. I might have a title but... I never use it... it means nothing to me."

"Then it'll mean nothing to me either."

"I don't think that's the same with your friend Fabian."

Guy scoffed. "He's not really a friend. I know him that's all. I know his brother Henri better. He's a doctor in Marlborough. Fabian's ok. He's just a bit well—you know—up himself. Henri and he are like chalk and cheese. Henri's really great."

They were now standing on a terrace of flagstones outside a pair of French windows, open to the night air because of the heat from the dance floor. The night was chilly and neither of them was wearing a coat or jacket. Guy put his arm round Adela's shoulders.

"Warmer?"

"Definitely," she lied.

"So what would your father think about you going out with a humble farrier? Would his lordship throw a terrible fit?"

Adela laughed. "I doubt it very much. My mother was a local primary school teacher—he wouldn't have a leg to stand on."

"Well then, Lady Adela... can I ask you, would you like to come out to dinner with me in the week?"

Adela smiled sweetly. "I'd love to but I'm expected at home tomorrow."

"Well then, I will just have to come and fetch you," said Guy. "From your home, in Milton."

CHAPTER FIFTEEN
PAST LIVES. THIS LIFE

Guy spoke to Addy on his phone. "It's a smart place so it'll be posh dress code. Is that ok?"

"Of course. That would be lovely. I can dress up when I have to, you know. I'll even wear a dress."

"When you said you never did…?"

Guy had secured them a table for dinner at a well-known expensive restaurant in Marlborough.

When Adela saw him in his suit and tie, her heart skipped a beat. He looked incredibly handsome. Gone were the jeans, rugby shirt and well-used Barbour and the way he looked at her in her black cocktail dress, with her hair piled on her head and secured with a diamante comb, she knew he thought much the same—that she looked beautiful.

However, it seemed a little odd getting into his van in such attire.

"Do you only have this old van thing?" she asked.

"I'll have you know that Dolly is the best vehicle a farrier could ever want."

"Dolly?" she giggled. "You call it Dolly?"

"Dolly! I have had her since she was two."

"And now she's what…?"

"Eleven."

"My father always says if you look after a vehicle it will give you a lifetime of service."

"And he's quite right."

"Sometimes I call her Hurryup... but that's just when I'm late for an appointment."

Adela looked at him strangely.

The manor house door closed slowly as Adela's father, Lord Lilbourne disappeared back into the brightness of the manor's hall light after waving them off.

"Are you sure he's alright with you coming out with me?"

"Of course he is and besides... he can't stop me. I'm over twenty one."

He chuckled and started his van, "Off we go then."

It wasn't long before their conversation turned to the church at East Kennett.

"So, what can we do to find out more about the people of the village all that long time ago?" said Adela.

"It's so far back, it's hard to know."

"I'm not sure if my family have any documents which might help."

"It's worth a look."

"I do know that the Lilbourne family owned much more land in the Mediaeval era than it does now. Maybe I could find a map or something. I'll have a look through the papers we have."

"Perhaps your father will help."

"But I don't think we can tell him exactly what we think... why we want to know, can we?"

"Well no... that would be foolish. It'd better stay a secret," said Guy. "Let's face it, we don't understand it. How could he be expected to do so?"

A corner table, candlelight, soft music and Guy and Adela began to truly relax in each other's company for the first time since they'd met. As they ate their wonderful dinner, they mulled over what they knew.

"Guy, tell me... and tell me truly, what do you think has happened?"

"I can only say what has happened to me. That I am suddenly certain about a thirteenth century place I have known about, but not truly explored, all my adult life—in this life—this time frame. There might be a perfectly innocent explanation for it all but for the life of me, I can't fathom it."

She reached for his hand, "What do we know?"

"Nothing for certain but that we both of us, saw the church in its thirteenth century form, that we understand the door with its little figures, that we know a song in a language we have never spoken in our lives..."

"And that for some reason we seem to be thrown together."

"Well, yes. That too. We have been, as you say, thrown together." His eyes strayed over her left shoulder. "Oh no..."

"Oh no, what?"

"Just act normally. I hope he hasn't seen us."

"Who?" Adela was about to turn around, but Guy squeezed her hand.

"Just someone I know. Someone I don't like. Someone I'd rather not see. Don't look."

"Who?"

"A man by the name of Wishart Courtenay."

Adela went very pale. "No..." she whispered.

"Don't worry. He's very busy with his latest conquest. He hasn't seen me. Just keep your back to him and I'll hide behind you... we are almost ready to leave anyway."

Adela stood up abruptly and grabbed her bag..."I must go to the ladies."

"Wha...?"

"I won't be long," and she fled.

*****

Guy waited a long time for Adela to return. Eventually he went to the waiter's station.

"Excuse me, I am worried about my friend. She went into the ladies' a long time ago and she hasn't come out."

The maître D gave him a strange look. "I'll ask one of the female staff to go and look, sir." He stared down his nose at him.

Guy returned to his table and eventually asked for the bill.

One of the waitresses came up and performed the transaction with a card machine. "Your lady friend is waiting out by your car, sir," she said. "She asked me to tell you that she just had to leave."

Guy threw on his coat and rushed out into the night air.

"Adela... Addy... are you alright?"

Adela's pale face rose up to his in the meagre light as he unlocked the van.

"Oh, I'm so sorry, Guy. So sorry..."

He noticed she'd been crying and was shivering in her thin dress and coat.

"Quickly get in the car and I'll put the heating on full blast."

Once she'd settled, he put his arm around her shoulder. "Now what's up? You're shivering."

"You must think me very ungrateful. It was such a lovely place and a wonderful meal and... I had a super time really..."

"But? There's a but coming, isn't there?"

She giggled. "But... when you said that the man Courtenay was there..."

"Wishart Courtenay... yes... I know him. I've had dealings with him and his firm. Thieving bastard... Oh forgive me..."

"No, no. I agree with you. You see... I know him too."

Suddenly Guy remembered Adela saying that she had worked for a firm of solicitors in Devizes.

"Courtenays—you worked for Courtenays of Devizes?"

"I did. For two years. And Wishart made my life a misery."

"He's why you left?"

She nodded a little nervously. "Like you say, he's a bastard.

Wandering hands... a bully and he's a liar... and a cheat... I can't tell you what he's tried."

"He cheated me out of money. Not much. But once I'd realised... well... I called him out."

"Oh do that and he'll be very unpleasant."

"And he's been... unpleasant to you too?"

"Oh Guy, let's not talk about it. It was such a lovely evening, thank you and I don't want him to spoil it."

He stroked her cheek in the light from the overhead lamps in the car park.

"Then we shan't speak of Guiscard again."

Adela took in a little surprised breath and Guy's heart skipped a beat. He had intended to kiss her tenderly but his slip of the tongue had prevented it.

"What did you call him?" she asked.

"Guiscard... I called him Guiscard. I don't know why..."

"But that's right isn't it? That's him."

"What?"

"Oh Guy, that's why he makes me feel the way he does. He's always revolted me. It's Guiscard."

Guy closed his eyes and memories flooded back.

Both of them, sitting in the car in the cold with the heating blasting onto them said together, "Because we knew him then, didn't we?"

*****

"Will the church be open at this time of night?" asked Adela as they bowled along the dark lanes.

"I think they lock it in the evening. Most churches do now with all the vandalism."

"Ah yes."

"Why?"

"I want to go back there. I want to see what else I remember."

"Are you sure?" asked Guy. "It seems to me it might be quite painful for us both. But especially for you."

"I need to know. It's the not knowing which is hard to live with."

"Alright then. At the weekend. Yes? Now I must get you home before your father thinks I have abducted you."

Adela laughed. "Would that be so terrible?"

"I'm sure your father would think so. I can see the newspaper headlines now. 'Daughter of Peer of the Realm abducted by local farrier!' "

They drove out onto the dark roads.

"Do you think that I was the daughter of a Peer of the Realm and you were a blacksmith—back then?"

"I don't know but it might be true. History repeating itself."

"I'll go poking around tomorrow and see what I can come up with from my father's muniment room."

"His what?"

"The room where he keeps all the old documents and books."

"And shall we meet again at the weekend?"

"Of course we shall," smiled Adela pecking him on the cheek. "And thank you."

*****

On Saturday they sat in the church of All Saints East Kennet, side by side in one of the pews at the back and carefully spread out a piece of ancient yellowed parchment between them.

"This was all I could find. Father says it's probably twelfth century, though he's not so sure, because the language of the annotation is thirteenth. Dad says that the language changed a little bit, but he knows very little about it."

"Can we read it?"

"Well, I can't, that's for sure."

"No. I can't make it out either."

"There are rather a lot of holes and bits missing."

"But we can see what it shows."

"The door with all its animals," said Adela.

They gazed at it in the poor light of a miserable January day. They knew they'd both seen it before.

A voice broke in over their reverie.

"What are you two doing all clandestinely hunkered down in a pew then?"

Guy looked up quickly. "Ah Thomas… Hiya."

It was the local vicar who sat down near them, informally throwing his leg over the end of the pew and swishing his scarf around his neck. He looked most uncomfortable.

"And who is this delightful young lady?"

"This is my friend Adela, Thomas, Adela Lilbourne, and Adela, this is the vicar of this parish—an Overton man born and bred, Vicar Tom."

"Four churches to be precise… have to spread ourselves around these days." He offered his hand.

"Overton, Fyfield, East Kennet and Preshute…" said Guy with a chuckle in his voice, "Never quite know where he's going to be. He's a hard man to pin down."

"Oooh Guy, you naughty man!" said Tom with a ribald laugh. "Well, today… I'm here." He sat up and wriggled up the pew. "Anything I can help you with?" He craned his neck and looked over at the parchment which they held in a hand each.

Adela let go.

"Just a little riddle…"

"Oh now I love those!" said Thomas, in a very camp voice. "Can't resist a riddle. Do tell."

"We have a parchment here which belongs to Adela's father, Lord Lilbourne. It shows the church door and all the figures on it. But we can't fathom the writing."

Thomas took out his glasses, "Let's have a butcher's then."

He ran his eye along the parchment, "Oh this is very old isn't it?"

"We think it might be eight hundred years old. We promised on our lives to take great care of it and return to dad it in one piece tonight," said Addy.

"Oh, this is amazing."

"Tom, can you read it?" asked Guy.

"Well, I can have a go. It's Latin of course and quite a good clerkly hand."

"Thomas comes from an old family who have connections with Thame is it?"

"Thatcham, dear boy."

"Ah yes... that's right isn't it? The Mandevilles of Thatcham."

"Thomas Bartlett Mandeville—lot of good a name like that does you! And I read Classics at Uni. before I went into the church."

Thomas peered at the manuscript, "Gotta bit of light?"

"I have my mobile," said Addy fiddling in her pocket and switching on the torch.

"Now, what does this say? Well, this is a list of all the animals on the door of the church here. All the Latin names. Except one bit here which is in English—smythe."

"Which no doubt is the equivalent of smith?" said Guy.

"It basically says a man, a smythe made all these figures to the glory of God and to... I think it says expiate a sin?"

"A sin?" said Adela in a tremulous voice. "A sin like adultery or... murder?"

"Ah maybe, but in those days it was probably just something like vanity or gluttony. Things have loosened up a bit in eight hundred years. Thank goodness."

Guy looked up at the rafters, "Or maybe... lust?"

"Oh dear boy... trust you to come up with that one." He tapped Guy gently on the breast.

The vicar jumped up and gave the parchment back to Adela.

"Thank you for letting me look at it. I have to rush. I'm due at the vicarage in forty minutes, for choir practice. But before that I have to talk about a wedding."

"The choir doesn't practice here?" asked Addy.

"Ah no, bless you, sweetheart. We might in the summer but at the moment it's far too cold."

He did up his navy duffle coat as if to illustrate the coldness of the place.

"I forgot my music. Toodle pip."

And he ran off into the vestry.

Guy and Adela looked at each other and tried not to smile.

"Yes. It's just as you think. He's as gay as a bunch of parrots but he's a very popular vicar and really loved hereabouts."

"I think he's lovely."

Thomas Mandeville tripped out of the vestry and out of the main door with a, "Don't freeze yourselves together now. It's probably warmer in the churchyard! But don't get up to any hanky-panky!"

They chuckled as they rolled the parchment again carefully. The door banged. The automatic door closer was broken. Again. Addy moved out into the nave.

As the noise of the door reverberated around the church, Guy's vision shifted and he saw a different scene than the one he'd been looking at with his modern eyes. Suddenly, there was the old church as it had been in the thirteenth century. There was a figure in a cloak looking up into the chancel, her blonde hair free and held only by a silver filet.

She smiled at him. It was definitely Adela.

He stood and moved out into the nave to face her.

The modern world faded and all was total silence.

One step closer. Guy's heart began to pound.

"Will you do something for me?" he heard her say.

He had answered before his modern brain knew that he would reply, "Oh mistress, every time you ask me this... there's trouble."

Her laugh rose up to the nave roof. "No. It should not cost you. In any way."

"What do you want me to do?"

She laid a hand on his arm and pulled, "I want you to kiss me."

"My lady... I can't do that."

"Please Guy. I will never see you again and... I do love you so. Please, just this once."

She came closer. His head came down and their lips met. It was an innocent kiss with no fervour and lasted but a heartbeat. But it was lovely.

They drew apart. "Oh Adela, I should not say this, but I love you still."

All that had gone before suddenly came flooding back to them both. All those people who had been around them then and were still around them, came crowding in like figures in a fast moving pantomime—Thomas, Henri, Nell, Emma, Guiscard—all of them revolving around them and then falling away.

They stood close with their heads together for quite some time until the world intruded once more. A car horn sounded.

"Oh... I am so sorry," said Guy. "I didn't mean to..."

"No but I did. It was I that kissed you."

"Yes...." Guy grinned, "Yes you did, didn't you?"

Adela grinned back.

"Mind if I do it again?"

"Oh no... Please be my guest."

This time the kiss was long and really meant something to them both; they were reluctant to let go.

"They couldn't be together, could they?" said Adela at last, with her chin on his shoulder. "Back then."

"No, no they couldn't. It was not permitted."

"But they can now—we can now."

Guy crushed her to his chest. "Yes indeed we can... if your father doesn't mind."

"My father has no say—this time, Guy Ferrier," smiled Addy.

"Mistress Lillebon, will you marry me? If you don't think that two days' acquaintance is too short a time."

Adela chuckled with glee, "Oh come, Master Ferrier—it's eight hundred years really."

"Then you will marry me?"

"Only if your friend Thomas Mandeville will marry us. He would be wonderful!"

*****

They wandered out into the churchyard hand in hand and found themselves idling around the graves just looking at the snowdrops and aconites which peppered the ground.

"I know this isn't the same church. But do you have a feeling that things out here haven't changed so much?" asked Guy.

"Well there are dozens more graves of course and they didn't have headstones in the thirteenth century."

"Ah no. But I just have a feeling that... you remember Emma and Fabian?"

"No. I remember the priest was called Fabian and that my father had a steward who had a daughter called Emma. Is that who you mean?"

"I do. They were lovers, did you know?"

"No. I don't think so. I didn't know."

"You'd already gone to Milton when the thing happened."

"I heard... oooh let me think, try to remember what I know. They fell off the church tower?"

"I was there. In my other life, I was there on the church tower. It was an accident but surely it was for the best because Emma was pregnant with Fabian's child. What an unholy mess!"

"Well it would certainly have been in the thirteenth century, like us they could never have been together."

"No, it was impossible then."

A voice hailed them from the gate.

They clasped hands even more firmly.

"Hey Guy! Nice to see you again. And... Adela isn't it? Either of you seen Emma about?" Fabian came bounding up the church path in his pink corduroy trousers and hacking jacket.

Addy and Guy exchanged glances.

"Emma? Nell's sister?"

"I thought I'd said meet her by the gate but she's not there."

"Oh really?"

"We have a meeting with the vicar."

"Thomas? Oh we saw him go to the vicarage a little while ago," said Addy.

"Oh right. I expect she's met him and gone in with him," said Fabian. "It's such a cold day. Not a day for hanging around is it?"

"Gone... in....?" said Adela, mystified.

"We are talking to Vicar Tom about getting married, me and Emma. Emma and I." Fabian beamed. "We are keeping it a bit quiet as yet. So hush, hush."

"Well, well. That's great," said Guy squeezing Adela's hand. "We are very glad about that... Aren't we Addy?"

She beamed up at him. "Oh yes.... indeed we are. Congratulations."

It was on the tip of their tongues to add that they too were going to marry but a glance between them made them keep silent.

"We hope you'll be very happy," said Guy.

As Fabian jogged down the path, waving at them, their eyes travelled up the old church tower to a mischievous jackdaw who was perched on the parapet cawing for all he was worth, his breath blowing smokily in the cold air..

They watched as he flew down and started to peck at the earth at the base of the tower.

There, bare of leaves and of course with no flowers in this season, climbing up the masonry, was a rambling rose and twining in amongst it was a briar with wicked sharp thorns.

Guy began to sing in his mellow bass voice, as they walked down the church path, hand in hand.

"She was buried in the old churchyard,
And William was laid beside her,
Out of her heart grew a wild, wild rose
And out of his, a briar.

They grew and grew in the old churchyard,
Till they could grow no higher
At the end they formed a true lover's knot
And the rose grew round the briar."

FIN

GLOSSARY

Amerced - Arrested/ charged with a crime and fined.

Bailiff - The man who is employed by the lord to manage his farms and lands. His managerial duties can include collecting rent, taxes and supervising both farm operations and labourers.

Besom - A brush.

Brantle - An alternative form of the French bransles, a type of dance.

Breechclout - Nappy. Diaper.

Buttermilk - A fermented dairy drink. Traditionally, it was the liquid left behind after churning butter out of cream.

Chancel - The part of a church near the altar, reserved for the clergy and choir, and typically separated from the nave by steps or a screen.

Clunch - Soft limestone capable of being easily worked.

Coffin bench - The stone ledge often seen running along the side of a porch of a church.

Compline - The final church service of the day.

Cotte - A long sleeved shift or tunic. A coat worn by men and women.

Cry wolf - To keep saying that there is a problem when there is not, with the result that people do not believe you when there really is a problem.

Dais - A part of the floor at the end of a Mediaeval hall, raised a step above the rest of the room.

Curmudgeonly - Grumpy.

Dalmatic - A long, wide-sleeved tunic, which serves as a liturgical vestment in Catholic churches.

Dowry - An amount of property or money brought by a bride to her husband on their marriage.

Espoused - Of a woman engaged to be married.

Felo de se - Suicide

Freeman - A person who is not a slave or serf.

Fulcrum - The point against which a lever is placed to get a purchase, or on which it turns or is supported.

Gaskin - Part of the hind leg of a horse.

Gurning - Pulling a grotesque face.

Heartsease - Pansies. A term of endearment.

Humours - Four substances in the body known as humours - blood, phlegm, black bile and yellow bile - were thought to control the health and temperament of every individual.

Kirtle - Dress.

Lauds - Morning prayers usually chanted at daybreak.

Libra - The seventh astrological sign in the zodiac. Libra is Latin for scales. It spans 180°–210° celestial longitude. The Sun transits this sign on average between September 23 and October 23.

Mesnie - The armed part of a lord's entourage.

Michaelmas - A Christian festival observed on 29 September. Michaelmas has been one of the four quarter days of the financial, judicial, and academic year.

Mummers - Group of (usually men) actors who go about the village and perform folklore plays based on George and the Dragon.

Muniment room - Place where papers and books are kept at a manor.

Necromancy - The practice of magic involving communication with the dead – either by summoning their spirits as apparitions, visions or raising them bodily.

Nocked - A bowstring put into an arrow.

Palfrey - A type of horse that was highly valued as a riding horse in the Middle Ages. It was a lighter-weight horse, usually a smooth gaited one that could amble, suitable for riding over long distances.

Pall - A cloth which covers the dead when waiting for burial.

Pattens - Overshoes for bad weather usually of wood.

Pedagogue - Teacher.

Plighted - Engaged.

Plough Monday - The traditional start of the English agricultural year. Generally the first Monday after Twelfth Night, 6 January. A plough was hauled from house to house in a procession and they collected money for the poor and for the church.

Quarterstaff - Also short staff or simply staff is a traditional mediaeval pole weapon.

Rayburn - a type of stove.

Reredo - An ornamental screen covering the wall at the back of an altar.

Rushlight - A type of candle or miniature torch formed by soaking the dried pith of the rush plant in fat or grease.

Sal Amoniac - A preparation of a rare naturally occurring mineral composed of ammonium chloride which smells terrible and is used to bring folk round from a faint.

Steward - A servant who supervised both the lord's estate and his household.

Supertunic - Overdress.

A taking - Slang for upset.

Terce - Is a fixed time of prayer of the Divine Office in the Christian liturgy. It consists mainly of psalms and is said at 9 a.m.

Twelfth Night - The last day of Christmas when there was a celebration and the giving of gifts in mediaeval times.

Unguent - A soft greasy or viscous substance used as ointment or for lubrication.

Vespers - A sunset evening prayer service in the Catholic church.

Wayland the Smith - Was a smith who was enslaved by a king. Wayland takes revenge by killing the king's sons and then escapes by crafting a winged cloak and flying away.

Withershynnes - In a direction contrary to the sun's course, considered as unlucky; anticlockwise.

Winding sheet - A sheet in which a corpse is wrapped for burial; a shroud.

AUTHOR'S NOTE

You always fall in love with the most unexpected person at the most unexpected moment and sometimes for the most unexpected reason.
(Anonymous)

This novel grew out of my Savernake series, murder mysteries of the 13th century. If you know the area you'll find that the descriptions of the villages around are accurate but places may not always be exactly where I've placed them.

The forge really exists and is, as I say in the book, now a B&B run by my good friends Leslie and Laura. I stay there often.

Their website is here: https://theoldforge-avebury.co.uk/

Thanks go to Leslie for the information about the history of East Kennett village and the church, used in the book.

The church doesn't have a door like I describe in this tale so don't go looking for it! It's pure fiction. But the church was and is as I describe in the 13th and 21st centuries. Now, at the date of writing, it doesn't seem to have its lovely reredo.

I have used some of the names for my characters which are to be found in local manuscripts. However the names of who owns what in the village in the 21st century, have been largely changed.

Blacksmiths were considered magical men in the mediaeval era; revered and yet feared. Anyone who could turn a piece of bog metal into a usable item like a spade or a sword was bound to be magical!

The hare was the animal folklore of magic and shapeshifting. Even today we have a fascination with this reclusive animal bordering on the reverent.

The name of this book comes from a piece of music by George Frederick Handel. A legend attaches to these musical variations; that Handel heard a blacksmith one day, whistling a tune. When he returned home he wrote a series of musical variations upon the theme and it had become known as The Harmonious Blacksmith. The tune is the first song Guy Ferrier composes in the book. You'll be able to sing the words he composed to Handel's tune if you know it.

I never intended for this book to end in the 21st century but somehow... it took over. It seemed right and proper for Adela and Guy and Fabian and Emma to at last be destined to be together happily in one life.

And Thomas Courtenay in the thirteenth century is an unpleasant character as is his cousin Guiscard. However his 21st century counterpart is a thoroughly nice man. Wishart, though... hasn't learned any lessons!

Susanna M. Newstead January 2021

ABOUT THE AUTHOR

Susanna has known the area around Marlborough all her life. After a period at the University of Wales studying Speech Therapy, she returned to Wiltshire where she soaked up the abundant history of the area, particularly that of the 12th and 13th centuries, and began to write about it in her twenties. She now lives in Northamptonshire with her husband and a small wire haired fox terrier called Tabor. Forty years of writing Mediaeval murder mysteries and now we have number three in the romance series. Susanna hopes to return fairly soon to her beloved Wiltshire downs where she will continue to write the Savernake series, her romances and her Medieval fantasy series set in the area around Marlborough, Wiltshire.

ALSO BY SUSANNA M. NEWSTEAD

Please visit her website for further information
https://susannamnewstead.co.uk/